TOM
And His
HyperSonic Spaceplane

BY

Victor Appleton II

Published in The United States of America

©opyright 2020 by the author of this book (Victor Appleton II - pseud. of Thomas Hudson). The book author retains sole copyright to his or her contributions to this book.

This book is a work of fan fiction. It is not claimed to be part of any previously published adventures of the main characters. It has been self-published and is not intended to supplant any authored works attributed to the pseudononomous author or to claim the rights of any legitimate publishing entity.

While some of the technology such as the Aerospike rocket engines is real, it is the author's interpretation of descriptions of it that might be more fantasy than reality. In no manner was any intent made to describe proprietary technology.

The cover's main image is a composite of several images taken from various Internet sources. Without attribution of copyrights, I am using them without any intent to subvert anyone's copyright.

THE NEW TOM SWIFT INVENTION SERIES

Tom Swift and His HyperSonic Spaceplane

By Victor Appleton II

Tom Swift and his father have been the creative forces behind a number of successful aircraft over the years. When the younger man comes to his father with the idea to revitalize and greatly upscale one of his first airplanes—something he'd called his nuclear hyperplane, a misnomer as there was nothing nuclear about it—it intrigues the older inventor.

"If you can make it commercial in some manner, then you have your funding."

It is a challenge Tom takes up and throws himself into. This is a welcome "stay at home" project his wife approves of. That is, until Tom's life is endangered.

To top it off, at least two foreign entities see this as a potential spy plane and begin to try to ensure it never flies.

Tom is challenged to make the spaceplane work and head on into the very wild and often not-so-blue yonder.

This time around, the first man to break the speed of sound, Chuck Yeager, is the dedicatee. But it wasn't a one-man project by any stretch. It took hundreds or even thousands of men and women working to build the X-1 rocket plane and then another hundred or more to get it into the air. Plus, it was not a first time thing. All of that conceived before the end of World War II and built in 1945, and he and the X-1 exceeded 1,000 miles per hour in 1948. And, yes I know, this was not the first time a jet or plane had broken the sound barrier, but it was the first time in level flight and with the altitude ability the X-1 had. Here's to you, General, and your *Galmorous Glennis*!

Oh, and congratulations on beating another odds. General Yeager, at this writing in 2019, is 96 years old.

As the one-man test plane took to the sky, Bud prepared to fire up the hypersonic engines, but something was keeping them from working and the jet began to drop toward the ground. **CHAPTER 8**

TABLE OF CONTENTS

CHAPTER		PAGE
1	Back on The Path to Boredom	9
2	Remember When…?	19
3	Mystery Jet	29
4	Rockets Aren't Always the Solution	39
5	A Lot to Do For a Civilian Aircraft!	49
6	Encountering an Old Friend	55
7	The *Demonstrator*	65
8	Up in the Air, Mr. Birdman!	75
9	Harlan is Discouraged	85
10	Good Test Flight; Bad Landing	95
11	Even More Testing is Warranted	105
12	The Enemy Encounter	115
13	Taking a Gander At…	125
14	*Super Queen* Proves Her Mettle	135
15	Black Beauty	145
16	BiCoastal Run…	155
17	Back Home to More Troubles	165
18	Planning The Dangerous Journey	173
19	Bad People Ferreted Out	181
20	Tom Swift and His HyperSonic Spaceplane	191

AUTHOR'S NOTE

Okay. First off, twenty-nine as a number is not a real, "Hurray! I did it! I'm *nearly* thirty!" celebratory figure. Think of when you turned 29. Not nearly the same as that 30th birthday, was it? Nobody endlessly kidding you about finally joining the geriatric brigade or telling you it's time to stop celebrating because the next one is the start of the big downhill slide. Or, receiving a Care package from a younger sister with Geritol, Vitamin D supplements and a tube of ointment best left undescribed where it is to be rubbed. And, why?

Or, was that just me?

Anyway, I am happy to have arrived at this number because I had this title in mind even before I had those for books 28 and 27. Huh? I'll try to explain.

After 26, and Tom's Neptune trip, I knew I needed to solve the recovery of the miniature space submarine Tom and crew lost in the Mariana Trench. Obviously it needed to be more than that, and I hope you have already read that. Following that came a little piece that had been scudding across my synapses for about a year, and although I wanted to get to this one I felt it prudent to wait until I had the idea/title for the follow-on book, to be number 30 in this series it has been my pleasure and honor to write over these ten or so years.

And so, with only a vague thought of anything other than the title, and how this story ends, I began writing. Imagine my surprise when it tumbled out of my fingers, at least the first 14 chapters, in just three weeks. Then, imagine my dismay as I stared at my words and could not figure out how to get to that ending for over a full month. A word here, a spelling mistake there, but not a substantial amount of typing.

Golly, does that mean I'm "losing it?" Well, if it does I can be happy with the accomplishment of **THIRTY BOOKS** in one series, and all the other collections I've hammered together in between novels.

(Plus, I already have numbers 31 and 32 planned and plotted!)

Copies of all of this author's works may be found at:

http://www.lulu.com/spotlight/tedwardfoxatyahoodotcom

My Tom Swift novels and collections are available on Amazon.com in paperbound and Kindle editions. BarnesAndNoble.com sells Nook ebook editions of many of these same works.

Tom Swift and His HyperSonic Spaceplane

FOREWORD

In that my metaphorical father—another, and the first, Victor Appleton—was a conglomeration, I have been constantly surprised that, for purposes of this particular series, I am just the one entity. I have not, it turns out, also written children's books about an elderly yet adventurous rabbit gentleman, endless mysteries aimed at 10-14 year olds, books about some spoiled children always harping on their Daddy to take them some place or another, or many others, AND a series about a reporter, Larry Dexter, that were aimed at older teens and young adults that were more personally satisfying to that author.

Sorry, Howard, but you were prolific but too prone to pseudonyms.

So, take me or leave me, I am just one man and one of a few who were induced by a love of these characters and a desire to remain out of my wife's hair that I took up the writing "call" as we hit retirement age. Believe me it was for the love of it, not for money.

The characters have aged with mostly grace, and I believe are a little more true to life than the very first Tom Swift characters were more than a century ago—certainly less racist—and even better than the son of *that* Tom and his main associates.

Over the years our "young" inventor has become a man with a wife and three children and, as mentioned near the end of book 28, he might have decided to slow down the pace of his life. Obviously, he's attempted that before only to be dragged back into some dangerous adventure or another, but Tom, like many heroes, perseveres and answers the "call to action."

Will there be a lot more Tom Swift Invention Series books? Likely. I now want to top the 33 of the original Tom Jr. series by at least 1 or maybe 2.

We shall see what comes to pass.

Victor Appleton II

CHAPTER 1 /
BACK ON THE PATH TO BOREDOM

TOM SWIFT, the thirty year old inventor and number two man in his family's companies—including Swift Enterprises, the older Construction Company, the Swift MotorCar Company (all located in Shopton, New York) along with the Citadel nuclear facility in New Mexico, and a number of others—sat slumped in his chair in the office he and his father, Damon Swift, shared on most days.

He was starting to wonder why he wasn't sitting in one of the very comfortable leather chairs just seven feet away in the conference area of the enormous room.

Tom and a crew of twenty men had returned from a mission to give a big shove to a lone planet that had wandered into the solar system several months earlier. That planet, named with a small dash of irony, Wanderer, had successfully been veered from a course that would have taken it into a position months later where it likely would have impacted either Jupiter or Saturn which would be in the proverbial wrong place at that particular wrong time.

And, while the inventor was enjoying his time at home with his wife, Bashalli, and their three children, during his work hours he was feeling the tug of boredom on his brain.

He was about to launch himself up to take a walk around the building cluster at Enterprises set in the north-middle of the four-mile-square complex, when his best friend for half his life—now his brother-in-law—Bud Barclay opened the door and peeked inside. The dark-haired man turned to speak to someone outside the office.

"It's okay, Trent. He's alive and awake. I'll tiptoe in like a little mouse."

This having been stated in a rather loud voice made Tom chuckle. He got up but not with any urgency.

"Hello, flyboy. Thanks for the quiet entrance. What's up?"

Bud walked to the conference area and took a seat. He patted the chair next to his and looked at Tom expectantly.

Tom obliged him by coming over and taking the indicated seat. "Okay, what's up now that I'm over here?"

"Well, as you and I have discussed, and as Sandy—remember your sister? Well, as she and I have discussed, we are starting the long and winding road toward an eventual adoption."

Tom nodded. He well knew his sister and Bud had been trying to have a baby for about as many years as they had been married. A few months longer, if he knew his sister.

"Sure. How is that going?"

Bud shrugged. "I guess it is going well. Jackson Rimmer up in Legal helped us with the first round of paperwork, but now we have to wait. It could be a year or more before we hear anything and Sandy is starting to worry we might have put something down that is wrong." He sighed. "Jackson told us to not get our hopes up for something right away, but Sandy is... well. She's *Sandy*."

It was true. Sandy Swift-Barclay had been a determined teen holding her parents to the stream of, "You can do/get/be that once you turn sixteen," promises. These included makeup, her driving license, her pilot's license, and most important to her, dating the boy she though of as "her hunk," Bud Barclay. They had been together ever since, and with her being just a year younger than Bud and her brother, that meant they had been a pair for nearly fourteen years.

It was also true that the blond had matured over the years. Gone were the days of her stomping and pouting when she did not get her way (up until about the age of eight). She also had become more diligent in her approach to working for a living. Where once her coming from a rich family had made her feel as if she did not need to work, now she approached her job with vigor and determination to succeed.

Like Bud, she was a pilot in the stable of about a dozen at Enterprises. But, where he was of of the main test pilots, she was a *Demonstrator* pilot frequently introducing reluctant spouses—mostly wives—to how safe and fun flying could be in a Swift aircraft. Her first love was the *Pigeon Special*, a two-person propeller plane that had been a tremendous seller for about nine years. When that was discontinued, she immediately took to the *Racing Pigeon*—a four-seater—and the larger and much faster *Pigeon Commander* and excelled in her little sideline.

Normally she worked in the Communications Department at Enterprises working for one of the longest-running employees in the Swift organization, George Dilling.

Tom looked at his friend. "I know Sandy can be a little, as you said, *Sandy*, but we both know how much she's wanted to be a mom. I think having our mother gave her the idea and a very good example to follow. Just hold her hand, and hold her, every day and reassure her that it will work out."

Bud grinned. "Right. So, now for the real reason I came over... how about we take a reasonably short flight over to that little airport we did the resurfacing job on in Rhode Island? Quonset? You might recall another little something happening about that time." He looked innocently at the inventor.

"Yes, Bud, I do remember the tectonic shifting and how we had to heal a rift coming in, tearing the end of the runway apart."

That was the small end of the story. It had involved a large rift coming in from the mid-Atlantic and might have eventually headed west and done unimaginable damage.

"What's happening over there?"

"We have been invited to an informal wedding. You might also recall the daughter of the airport manager, Darla Digby. She was a rather forward girl of about sixteen as I remember. Well, now she is all grown up, or as Chow might say, 'Growed up,' and her father thinks it might be nice to invite us. It turns out the girl doesn't have a lot of friends, and the area is kind of small. Anyway, Stefanie and Deke Bodack are going with us and we're expected to fly out of here in thirty minutes."

Tom looked down at his standard striped shirt and tan pants.

"Like I said, it is informal. Even the bride is wearing a simple, off-white dress. Bridesmaids are going to be in slacks and no tuxes for the groom and his friends. Come on."

Tom insisted on doing two things before leaving, He went to the lab and apartment down the hall and changed into a button-up shirt and he called Bashalli on their way to the jet they would fly in.

"Oh, that's nice, Tom. I've never met her but your description of how she was a little man crazy gives me an idea about her. Do not let her kiss you in the reception line. Or, if you do, try to break away from her embrace in only a second." She giggled. There was no jealousy in either of them and she liked teasing him about his discomfort when confronted with females who wanted to get closer.

Another woman who knew of Tom's discomfort was waiting for him and Bud next to the SE-11 Commuter jet, otherwise known as the Toad, standing next to a man who might have been two-and-a-half feet taller.

Stefanie Brooks-Bodack was technically a dwarf—a mesomelic dwarf where only her lower legs were affected with the rest of her body that of a woman who might have reached five-feet and one or two inches—but she was also a believer that everybody ought to be her friend and not treat her any differently. She was also given to jumping into Tom's arms and giving him big, sloppy kisses, especially when it might cause the most embarrassment.

She did not disappoint Bud this time practically flying through the last five feet between them and wrapping her small legs and regular arms around the inventor.

As nonchalantly as he could manage, Tom waited her out. He'd found over the years that if she didn't get a rise out of him, she generally stopped within thirty seconds.

"Hello, Steff," he said as she allowed him to set her back on the ground.

"You're no fun any more, Tom Swift," she declared crossing her arms over her chest and pouting.

"You really ought to let the squirt have her evil way with you, *now*, Tom," her husband suggested. "Otherwise, she's likely to climb over the seats and plop right down into your lap as you are trying to fly."

Sensing the logic in Deke's statement, Tom reached out and let Stefanie climb back into his arms.

She climbed back down, now satisfied that she'd had her way.

The flight was fairly quick and pleasant. As they were coming in for their landing, Bud nodded to his left. "See that? Impressive for a small facility like this!"

What he was seeing that everyone got a look at was an older 747 model aircraft painted in white and blue with "United States of America" on the fuselage.

"Is that one of the older Air Force One Presidential jets?" Tom asked.

Deke, who had once worked at the very airport they were touching down on told them that it was one of two jet painted like the famous jets, and operational, but they were more like decoys than actual aircraft a President would fly in.

"If a President was heading for a secret meeting in, oh, say France —"

"France!" Bud and Stefanie piped up.

"Anyway," and Deke rolled his eyes, "he might take off at four in the morning and one of these would take off at seven, in daylight, heading for Seattle or some other place. When the government changed to the new 797s, that one was going to be scrapped, but Alan Digby asked that it be part of the small aircraft museum over there. Only, it can't fit in their space, so it has taken up residence on the side parking apron."

They had reached the turnoff point and Bud, piloting at the moment, turned them to the left and then took another left taxiing past the five large refueling jets the Air Reserve kept at the airport.

In a minute he was stopping them in a parking area in front of a hangar that was empty except for about fifty chairs set up inside.

They climbed out with Stefanie shaking her head as Deke reached out to help her. "Nope. Tom must be punished for his hesitance and this is payback time!"

With an inward sigh, Tom came back and let the diminutive woman latch onto his neck.

"I could give you a hickey and make Bashalli jealous," she hinted in his right ear.

"Don't you dare. Even if it would be rude, I will drop you right here and walk away if you so much as get close to my neck!"

She was already close so she leaned up and planted a bright, red lipstick kiss on the side of his neck where he might not see it and wipe it off.

As she slid back to the ground Deke took out his handkerchief, handing it to Tom and pointed at his own neck making a wiping motion.

Alan Digby looked much better than the last time the inventor had seen him. Back then, the pressure of the rift and potential closure of his cherished airport due to the tear in the asphalt at the start of the runway, had made him seem pale and gaunt. Now he appeared much more robust and was walking around talking to the guests that had already arrived.

Seeing Tom and the others he excused himself and came over to greet them.

Digby appeared to be slightly confused at seeing Deke, almost as if he barely remembered the tall man who had been one of his daytime air controllers.

Things settled down ten minutes later and the ceremony began. It was brief and to the point, and everyone could see how much Darla and her future husband were in love.

The bride and groom had obviously written their own vows and, to Tom's ear, neither of them were a wiz at stringing words together. Even the minister had troubles reading what they'd given him. Thankfully, the ceremony was fairly brief.

There *was* a reception line and Tom's mind flashed to Bashalli's warning.

He needn't have worried.

Darla Digby was holding onto the hand of her new husband and beaming so much he believed she wasn't seeing or hearing anything from anyone. She smiled and nodded when he congratulated her and wished them all the best before looking back, lovingly, at her new husband.

Then, less than two hours later the Enterprises people were back in the air winging for Shopton.

They had a fast and smooth flight and got back an hour before closing time, so Tom thanked his three companions and headed for the large office.

"Your father left for home ten minutes ago, Tom," Trent told him. "Something about a dinner your mother told him about a month ago and he forgot to tell me, and... well, he did rush out of here. Can I get you anything?"

Tom demurred. He had more serious thinking to do and it would suit him to be alone until he went home, in about thirty-five minutes. It was time he put to good use as he'd had a thought on the flight down and wanted to see if there was anything to it.

He scanned through his old files looking for something he had begun while a teen, and before he even had thought about his *Sky Queen*. By the time his watch reminded him he need to leave he was no closer than when the Toad had touched down in locating the sought after files.

Sitting alone in the office five minutes later, the inventor decided he needed to go home. He could enjoy the kids—Bart, Mary and little Anne—and fall asleep later in Bashalli's arms.

He rose early the following morning with an idea of where he might look for the files he had been seeking.

Those had been originated about sixteen years earlier and the automated back-up systems at Swift Enterprises would have noted— without human intervention—they had not been accessed for a long time. So long, in fact, they would have been transferred to the long-term archive system and purged from the computers and normal back-ups at least five years earlier. Even before that.

With nearly all magnetic and even solid state memory prone to eventually fall into disarray, and probably not to be accessed after many years, the only sure-fire method would have been, "Print it out on archival paper and store it in a fire-proof environment."

There was one such place within the boundaries of Enterprises; the purely digital backup was flying more than thirty thousand miles overhead.

Tom hoped the more terrestrial one would prove to be of help.

He greeted the guard at the Executives' gate with a nod and a smile as his TeleVoc pin was registered and he was officially checked in at Enterprises. Once inside the walls he headed along an access road, took a left turn and drove along until he needed to take a right turn. As he approached the far side—the south side—of the buildings he took another right and found himself turning into a small parking lot next to a rather imposing structure. Looking more like a six-story concrete mausoleum or some sort of super secret government building, it was actually the repository for all the inventions Tom, his father and the other developers at the Swift companies, that stored a full-scale version of their inventions.

The few things not inside included active large scale inventions such as his current spaceships, the *Sky Queen*, her larger sister, the *Super Queen*, and a few other things still actively in use.

At some point, anything smaller than an average school bus would find its way inside.

Tom used the scanner to allow the computer to check both his entire face along with a retina scan of his right eye. The surface flipped around showing him a pad of buttons with the alphabetics and the numbers 0-9. Into this he entered a 15-digit passcode.

"*Recognized: Tom Swift. Authorization: full access with no restrictions.*"

He smiled as he generally did on hearing the voice of his own wife coming from the speaker. Since nearly four years ago, Bashalli Prandit Swift had been the official voice of all electronic and even a few mechanical inventions. Her near perfect diction—a byproduct of having spent her first ten years in Pakistan and then coming to the United States where she worked as hard as she could to learn proper and flawless English—meant that just about anyone could understand what she was saying.

The inner door slid open with Bashalli telling the inventor nobody else was inside. He moved to the right and to a metal door set into the side wall. He placed his palm on a spot he knew was a disguised palm-pad and was rewarded by the panel in front of him moving slightly back before sliding to the side revealing an elevator.

"Physical Archives," he said to nobody in the small room. The door slid shut and paused six seconds before opening again.

The scene had changed. No longer was inside a nearly six story tall open area filled with inventions. He now walked out into a room slightly smaller dimensions than the one above filled with more than two hundred and sixty large file cabinets. Each of these was surrounded by a clear enclosure attached at the four upper corners to thin cables extending into the ceiling.

"*Please state needed archive materials,*" Bashalli told him.

He did and was told to please wait. The search could require as many as three minutes. He took a seat on a padded bench next to the elevator.

"*Aisle seventeen, cabinet twenty-three, drawer one and also possibility in aisle fifteen, cabinet eleven, drawer four.*"

Tom got up and checked the hanging signs to make certain he headed in the correct directions.

As he approached, the voice asked him to stand next to the desired cabinet and to touch it with a finger.

This, he knew, would activate the machinery to evacuate the nitrogen gas inside the enclosure, replace it with some of the ultra-clean air used throughout the building, and then raise the enclosure to the ceiling.

It wasn't an immediate process but within two minutes he was opening the top drawer. Inside he checked the tabs noting the contents. He shook his head. What he was seeking was not there. To the air around him he said, "Close and reseal this cabinet. Please repeat secondary location."

The drawer slid shut with a click and the clear enclosure lowered. It sealed with a hiss and the air to nitrogen exchange began.

"*Second location aisle fifteen, cabinet eleven, drawer four.*"

"I love you, Bash," he said slightly to himself and was shocked when the computer responded.

"*I love you too, Thomas,*" and it giggled at him. He would have to ask his father about that as the older Swift was one of only three or four people who might have programming access to allow that to happen. Of course it could never have happened if Bashalli had not recorded it so he'd ask her as well.

This time, the indicated drawer provided what he needed.

As he removed the thick file—likely to be about one hundred pages and as many as fifty drawings—he asked for a materials transport.

"I need this copied and transferred electronically to my personal files."

"*Process will require approximately one hour. Temporary access code will be emailed to your account in fifteen minutes.*"

This time the cabinet did not close and the enclosure did not drop down. Tom knew the copying process would be followed by having a special work robot returning the file to its location and closing everything up.

Knowing that he might need his car again later in the day, he took the time to drive it around to the parking lot adjacent to the Administration building, the single largest building on the grounds at nearly sixteen hundred feet long, more than one hundred feet wide and three floors topped with a multi-sided and glass-enclosed room that had been the original airfield control tower when Enterprises had been built.

He arrived in the office as his father was just leaving. "Oh, son. You're here. Have five minutes for you old man?"

Tom grinned. "I've even got about..." and he checked his watch, "as many as forty-seven of them. What's on your mind?"

"What is there does not concern anyone other than your mother and myself." Damon cleared his throat. "Uhh, anyway, I was just over talking to Harlan Ames. He said to tell you he and his team just ferreted out a possible interloper. Someone who made it past the first round of background checks but fidgeted so much in the personal interview the H.R. person doing that face-to-face notified Security."

"Let me guess. Someone with either a criminal history or a phony background?"

His father shook his head. "Neither. Someone on the Interpol 'Watch For' list. One of the individuals captured years ago when the two planes went down close to Honduras. Remember? One of them carried the daughter of *the Black Cobra!*"

CHAPTER 2 /
REMEMBER WHEN...?

TOM AND Bud sat in the cafeteria discussing what sort of project the inventor might engage in that would keep him on the planet, not underwater, and not likely to get into anything anyone with dangerous intentions might take exception to.

"Only *those* limits, flyboy?" he grinned before sipping his coffee.

"Yeah. Something you maybe started and never got the chance to finish, or have had some little brain worm sitting in there telling you, subtly of course, it wants to come out to play? Anything?"

The inventor shrugged. Over the more than fifteen years they had been friends, there were very few things—other than those that abjectly failed—Tom had not finished in some form or another. In fact, he could only recall a couple and they were so far back in his memory—

"Yes!" he said more forcefully than he intended causing many of the twenty or so other employees nearby to jump. Some of the others just nodded and told their companions, "The skipper's had a brainstorm!"

"Yes, what?" Bud asked now getting excited for his friend. And, for himself because when Tom was on the hunt for some invention or process, he brought his best friend along for the ride.

Tom lowered his voice. "Do you remember what I was doing way back when we first met?"

Bud nodded. "Sure. I was testing my uncle's little, uhh, green jet and got shot down by some bad guy in a really fast, black jet. I barely made it to the Citadel and you came out and took me to see the doctor out there. Then, your truck got blown to smithereens. Not the best of times, but it led me to my best friend and a wife and a lot of adventures."

Tom nodded but said in a sober tone, "Sure, and got both of us clobbered plenty of times, kidnapped, lost in space, and a lot of other nasty stuff."

"Okay, I counter that with encounters with people like The Black Cobra, and his daughter, and some nasty Kranjovian and Brungarians... but the fact is, we survived. Plus, you got married to a woman I introduced you to and you have three great kids. So, what the heck was that 'Yes' all about?"

Tom pursed his lips. "Well, back when we met in New Mexico as dad was building stage two of the Citadel I was there trying to fly my little, poorly named and I admit that now, nuclear hyperplane. The fact is it never really advanced beyond that little jet with its single turbofan jet engine. Underpowered at that." Now, he looked like he was at a loss for something to add.

"And…?" Bud tried to prod him.

"Ahh. The infamous 'And, Tom?' bit, huh? The *and* about this is I have been thinking the past couple weeks I might like to drag that little jet out of storage, give her a larger, or at least more powerful engine, and see if the design might ever be a candidate for an upgrade to give her a reason for the nuclear handle."

"Jetz!" the flyer exclaimed. "Real nuclear power?" Tom nodded but looked carefully around them. A few people seemed to possibly be paying attention, so Tom motioned Bud to get up. They picked up their cups and headed over to a table a bit more private than the one they'd been sitting at.

"Okay. Not so many snoopy ears over here, not yet. So, my thinking is to first wring out the design to see what weaknesses it might have. Then, I plan to upsize it by maybe a factor of one-and-a-half or two, and then see about powering it."

Bud thought a moment about what would be an intelligent question. He came up with, "So, I recall you had your sight set on some sort of hypersonic ramjet or scramjet engine. The problem I recall from military tests is that it takes a heck of a lot of thrust, like rocket thrust, to get up to the speed where the engine can be turned on. Is that still a thing?"

Tom agreed it still was an issue that was difficult to get around other than for missiles. They could be rocket-powered at first, scramjet powered to get them up to Mach 7 or above, and then as their fuel was exhausted—generally fairly quickly—they coasted to their targets or to a splashdown.

The inventor knew that sort of ending was totally unsatisfactory!

"So, what comes out the back?"

Tom shrugged. "Possibly super hot steam and air like the *Sky Queen*. I really don't know right now." He knew his first large-scale jet carried about one thousand gallons of purified water which was just enough to get them to places halfway around the world. He would never have that sort of space or capacity.

If only to get his mind off of the possible project for a few moments, Tom returned to a previous topic and told Bud about the attempt by one of the Daughter of the Black Cobra's former associates to gain a position at Enterprises.

Bud slammed a fist down on the table causing nearby employees to jump and whip their heads around to see what was happening.

"Sorry, folks," he said as he partially stood. "I'm just having another of my little episodes. Once I get back on my pills I'll be fine," he explained only to overhear someone a couple tables over say something about how 'that crazy Barclay needs more than a few tablets!'

Sitting back down he apologized to Tom. "Didn't mean for that little anger explosion to come out, but I still remember how she and those thugs were more than willing to strand us on that little island in the face of a hurricane."

The inventor recalled their temporary capture by the woman they only knew to have claimed to be the Black Cobra's daughter.

They had run afoul of her at a later time when she was involved in setting a series of disastrous forest and oil refinery fires before begging Tom to help save her life; her own men were out to kill her... supposedly.

That had come to pass when someone dumped her from a helicopter within the boundaries of a refinery her team had set on fire and then had joined his comrades in a nearby field giving themselves up to the local police.

"Well, this guy was one of her North Korean people. I believe from the photo Harlan sent me he was one of the men who tied us up in that shack. Anyway," he continued quickly seeing his friend about to say something, "he had some expertly forged papers listing him as a visiting professor from South Korea wishing to experience working at a U.S. company for about a year."

Bud nodded but his face was scrunched up in what appeared to be frustration. A moment later he relaxed. "Okay, but how did Harlan's people get him?"

"Do you know Constance McDavid at our Employment office downtown?"

"Yeah. Met her about a year ago. Nice lady if a bit no nonsense. Why?"

"She spotted this man, calling himself Lon Chu by the way, who kept looking around as if he was nervous about something. She did the interview and said she would forward his résumé to Jake Aturian, and he left.

"She got a call into Harlan a minute later, gave the code for there being a '*problem*'," and Tom used inverted finger quotes, "and he dispatched a Security team. They got the man five blocks away sitting on a bus stop bench. When they stopped in front of him he stood up and tried to run, but the truck had dropped off two men around the corner and they caught him just fifty feet away."

Finally, Bud grinned in relief. "Good. Very good. Is he off to the pokey?"

"He is off to Albany and in the van of the FBI who have said he is wanted on at least seven warrants. He's to be jailed just about forever."

Bud wanted to return the conversation to the notion of Tom's hyperplane.

"So, I know neither you nor your dad had anything small and powerful enough at that time, and you've since created the power pods, but are even those enough to get a jet up to even Mach-3? Or, small enough to fit?"

The inventor shrugged. "I honestly do not know, Bud. I do know that most previous attempts to design or build a nuclear-powered engine have relied on the super hot steam they create in a closed look to spin the turbines. We use a version of that to drive the two *Queens* forward by superheating refined water and letting that steam shove us around. Luckily, those jets are large enough to carry enough purified water to get us to where we want to go in one load. I don't think that is the answer for something that will carry thirty or even up to fifty people at a time."

He told the flyer his father wanted the aircraft research to make money, and that a commercial version was about the best way to achieve that.

Bud looked puzzled. "Why only that small number? Why not two hundred or even three?"

"Mostly because the more people you carry, the larger the aircraft and the more friction you generate necessitating more heat shielding, more weight and more systems to keep those people comfortable... and entertained."

"Ahhh, I see. So, just how large will this *super* super jet be?"

For what he thought must be the fifth time, Tom shrugged. "Certainly it ought to be wide enough to carry four seats in each row. We will need a lot of space in the back for the fuel and the engines, so if we figure four per row, and maybe forty-eight total passengers, that is twelve rows. Given nearly three feet per row that means the passenger compartment is going to be at least thirty-six feet long and probably ten feet longer to accommodate the boarding area and seats for the flight attendants."

"And a kitchen. Don't forget the food!"

Tom only lightly grinned. "Right. So fifteen in front of the main cabin gets us fifty-one feet. Fifteen feet in front of that for the cockpit and nose and perhaps fifty feet behind everything. We're getting into the range of one hundred and sixteen feet or more. That is a lot of aircraft to be shoving through the sky."

He looked a little discouraged, but the flyer had to ask, "And how long was your hyperplane?"

"Sixteen feet or so. Fifteen feet wide. Why?"

"Oh, just trying to figure out the per passenger square footage for something larger. I suppose if you only carried three dozen people and at such high speeds, you could accommodate a lot of passengers in a half dozen of these new jets flying about the same time."

The inventor nodded. "I haven't been giving much thought to anything other than getting something that can carry an unknown number of people at Mach-5 or greater," he admitted.

Their conversation returned to the past as they reminisced about the time they had first met and the adventure they had in avoiding a mystery black jet seemingly out to kill Tom. Or, had it been Mr. Swift the pilot was after? Nobody ever found out.

In any case, that jet had been able to power away from anything the Air Force had in the air, and had a signature maneuver taking it straight up at greater than Mach speeds before simply turning to one side or another and speeding away.

In the end it had been a canny Air Force pilot who recognized what the other pilot was about to do to escape and fired a missile high above that the black jet, which flew up and directly into the path destroying the jet and killing the pilot.

Classified as a Top Secret, no word had ever come to the Swifts about that jet or the pilot.

"I recall we had some fun in our two little jets and even got in a few jabs at my uncle who was such a pain about thinking you folks would steal his small jet design. In the end he never did build another one and abandoned even the improvements your engineers made in the folding landing gear."

Bud now looked sad. "Then, Uncle Des died a couple years later and his company sold out to another aircraft manufacturer. Another pilot crashed the little green jet a few moths after we came back to Shopton. Fortunately, he didn't die. As far as I know my uncle never even took the time to file a patent for those gears the Citadel guys made that folded up then folded again and came up into the small compartments in the jet. Hey! Maybe you should patent that now."

Tom looked at Bud. "Why? It was only the logical thing to do.

Your Uncle Desmond had engineered in about thirty parts more than the gear needed, the struts were thin and it had too much being handled by underpowered springs and hydraulics, and unnecessarily as I recall, twisting around at least twice during the process."

The flyer looked at his best friend and smiled. "And, did you ever look into patenting that process? It could be handy in a few of the small jets the Construction Company has coming down the line I will be testing."

"No. Perhaps I need to think about that. Thanks, flyboy."

Before they parted the inventor promised to look into the situation and to have a chat with either Jackson Rimmer or Patrick Peck in Legal.

"Of *course* we should have patented that," Patrick told him as they sat having tea, Peck's drink of choice, that afternoon. "I've read a lot of materials about your great-great-something grandfather, Barton Swift. One thing stands out in my mind. He said the secret of success is to patent everything before someone like Edison comes along and steals it from you."

Tom grinned. It sounded like something the father of his namesake might have said way back at the start of the nineteen hundreds. That man had been a very good mechanical inventor with a number of patented devices that were still in use in one form or another even more than a century later. He had, after all, created both a steam turbine engine to drive torpedoes at then unimaginable speeds as well as the first nickel-cadmium battery. Even though the United States government had taken possession of that technology, and eventually "leaked it" out through a Scandinavian nation decades later, it had allowed several of the first pre-1900s submarine boats to stay submerged for more than an hour and to not overcome the sailors on board with deadly fumes that emitted from the lead-acid batteries of the day.

That secret type of battery had been installed in a pair of World War I test subs, but had proven to be so expensive for that time, it never saw widespread use.

Tom agreed to contact the engineer technicians at the Citadel who had created those gear systems on the fly to repair Bud's little jet that had taken a hard landing in the desert to the north of the installation.

Once he reached one of them and explained the situation, the man, Chuck Wagoner, laughed when Tom mentioned the episode. "I vividly recall Bud's uncle and the fit he threw when he found out we had fixed and improved those landing gear. I recall I took an hour or so to sketch out what we did, photograph the end results and put it into the computer. Give me tonight to get those found and I'll send them to you," he promised.

Prior to moving on to anything else, Tom dropped Patrick Peck a quick electronic note saying he ought to have enough details the following morning to create the necessary materials to support a patent claim.

"This will be filled in and filed before the end of the day," the lawyer told him by return message.

It was information he passed to his father when they met for an afternoon status meeting.

Damon looked both amused and a little surprised. "I would have thought one of the two of us would have thought about that one at the time. Hmmm? Guess I was slipping in my middle age and you in your youth!"

He asked about what Tom was going to do next. "I mean, you've had a few weeks to get over once again saving the world, so it's about time you got up off your rump and got into something new!"

Tom knew his father was teasing him from the smile on the older man's face. It also was totally unlike anything Damon ever did; he was not one to insist his son was constantly kept busy. Damon Swift knew that in order for the inventive juices to flow, they had to be unencumbered with stress and artificial make-work deadlines.

It was the same with employees; Damon Swift was not a taskmaster!

He next asked about the recent wedding.

"I remember meeting the father but do not believe I saw or heard much about the daughter other than to hear she was a bit of a boy crazy girl. Didn't she sort of make a pass at you or Bud?" He grinned to himself seeing the reddened embarrassment creeping up his son's neck.

Tom was about to give the hard time back to his father with a question concerning Penelope Schott-Partridge, a former Australian Navy Admiral and friend of his father's whom Tom knew had a crush on Damon and he believed there was a little reciprocal affection. He did not have the chance as the company-wide alarm system began blaring the siren that was about to make an announcement of something terrible.

"*Attention! Attention! All Enterprises personnel. Incoming jet aircraft not squawking IFF or answering radio. On course directly for Enterprises. All personnel above ground take shelter immediately!*" It was repeated one more time.

By that point Tom, Damon and even their secretary Munford Trent were jogging to the stairs in the middle of the long corridor. They and more than one hundred other employees and executives of the company headed quickly, but in an orderly fashion, to the basement and the Durastress reinforced concrete bunker thirty feet underground.

Damon stood by the telephone in case Harlan Ames or someone else needed to get word to him.

With walls and a ceiling over three feet thick, it was difficult to know what was going on until the floor beneath their feet vibrated and a distant boom could be heard above them.

They all waited with baited breath for another three minutes before the phone rang.

"It's Damon. What's happening?"

"Damon, it's Harlan. We've just had a major airliner crash out on runway zero-nine-zero south. An old Boeing 727 jet that must have been filled with explosives and a lot of fuel. Emergency crews are responding so you just stay down in the bunker for now. I'll call with the all's clear as soon as I can. I assume Tom is with you?"

"Yes, he is as are most of the people I'd expect to be in this room. *Wait!* I don't see Chow Winkler. Oh, my god! You don't suppose he's still upstairs do you?" He was feeling panic rise in his throat. The older westerner and chef was a favorite of everyone but sometimes was wearing his headphones and was so into his cooking in the little kitchen down the hall fromt he shared office, he missed everything from phone calls to visitors.

"It's okay. He was over here visiting and I made him go into our basement. Got to go!"

Tom was standing next to his father. At the mention of Chow's name he'd turned all around looking for the older man. He, too, had a moment of panic.

"Chow's okay. He was in Security. Harlan could only tell me that an old jetliner, possible a 727, hit the far south runway. I don't have anything other that that, so don't ask right now." He raised his voice and asked for silence before passing the same word to the people in the underground bunker.

"Are we being attacked?" a female voice came from the other side of the room.

"Is that Elizabeth?"

"Yes," she said in a voice quaking with fear.

"The answer is we do not know but it seems to be a single

incident. Now, I know a few jetliners have been used by terrorists in the past but until we hear otherwise, that does not mean it is happening now and at Enterprises. We are all safe and unless I hear otherwise, everyone else is safe as well. So, no more talk of doom, please."

The last was not delivered as a demand or even a rebuke but more as a gentile request.

"Sorry," she told the room.

From closer to the Swifts came a deep voice of Jackson Rimmer, the chief lawyer for Enterprises. "It's okay, Betty. If people will let me get over there I'll sweep you into my manly arms and comfort you."

This made the woman laugh and that broke the tension in the entire room.

CHAPTER 3 /
MYSTERY JET

IT REQUIRED a full hour for the all's clear signal to be given and everyone, many of whom had decided to wait things out sitting on the floor, helped each other to stand and headed back upstairs.

Once again Damon had received the word via the telephone and passed it along to the others.

"We are evidently safe and the fire on the runway is contained. Security wants everyone to stay away. As for myself, I do not care if you are so curious that you just cannot keep clear, but I will warn you that you could be dismissed if you decide to not heed the warning. Besides, the firefighting crews are in full respirator gear because we just do not know if there is anything toxic in the smoke. That is, by the way, blowing to the west and away from all of us and from Shopton. So, go back to your offices, call loved ones if you think they will be worrying—just do not tell anybody anything other than we have had an aircraft crash that is being investigated—and then try to find something to do. Once we get the clearance, you may go home for the rest of the day if you wish."

He thanked everyone for his or her cooperation before turning to Tom.

"I'll contact your sister on the TeleVoc," Damon told his son as they reached the ground floor. That communication system did not work in the protective bunker. Damon had decided years earlier that too many people would flood the system in case of something like today, and that could paralyze communications. So, there were no repeaters in the bunkers.

A moment later, he smiled and gave Tom a thumb's up sign. "Sandy headed downstairs with George Dilling and the others. They are all just getting back to their desks."

"What about the tower people?" Tom asked in a worried tone.

"Hold on and I'll check." A minute later the older inventor smiled. "They are sealed into the tower and it immediately went into air-recirculation mode. No fumes and a bird's eye view. Jerry Stringer up there assures me the crash was both a surprise as well as something they prepped for. We'll find out more in a little."

They got back to their office with Trent retaking his seat and beginning to answer all the phone lines that were blinking.

"Damon and Tom's office. Unless this is a mission critical call, please clear the line and email them. Thank you."

Only one caller asked to be connected. "It's Phil Radnor for you both," he told the Swifts as they headed inside the door.

"Yes, Rad?" Tom said getting to his desk and phone first. He punched the speakerphone button.

"Tom. Is you dad there?"

"Yes, I am," Damon stated.

"Good. Here's what we know. The aircraft was remote controlled and came from almost due east of here. We believe from backtracking the RADAR logs it came from a small field in Vermont. Does the field at Rutland ring any bells?"

It did to Tom. He and Bud had been flying toward there once when they were forced to abandon a test aircraft when an enemy jet, trailing something like a chain, had sliced their tail section off.

"Well, that 727, and it was one of that model, had been parked at the field for nearly a year. It evidently flew in one night, unannounced. All nice and paid for but rarely if ever visited. Then, four weeks ago a truck pulled up and several men in overalls swarmed over the tail of the aircraft. The airport manager thought they were getting ready to remove the engines."

"Let me guess," Tom asked. "They didn't do that but got them ready to fire up."

"Right. Yesterday someone called to ask for a full fueling; the owners had decided to move the aircraft to Pennsylvania. Since it was prepaid, the manager had the jet fueled, noting it took about five hundred gallons more than normal, but put it down to exceptionally dry tanks."

"And, it took off and flew this direction, keeping low enough to not be detected until it was close to the hills?"

"No. It swung south before heading west and then came around ten miles southwest of here. That is when the tower up the hill and our own started to get worried and tried to contact them. Four minutes later it veered around and to the east then came in behind the western hills before it pointed to the ground and hit. There is only a bit left but our people did get water on the tail and managed to pull out the black boxes. I'll have them delivered to you if you want."

Tom asked that they be taken to his underground lab.

"Sure. The cockpit was partially spared which is why we know it was remotely operated. Lots of servos, pulleys, armatures and cables."

The overall damage to Enterprises had been minimized by the aircraft impacting between the actual runways and away from even the crossing taxiways. Phil told them he and Harlan believed the electronic jamming of the drones circling around had kept the operator from aiming it at a more deadly target.

It would take a week or more to bulldoze dirt into the hole and also to replant the grass in the area, but within a couple months nobody would see any indication of the crash.

By the end of the day, things had returned mostly to normal and Tom had visited his underground lab. As he suspected, the reddish-orange boxes had only decade's old data on them. Likely, someone took the time to disconnect them he told himself as he repacked the charred remains in a safety box.

It would go to the NTSB for their check and records.

He TeleVoc'd his father with the non-results and headed for home taking a short detour around the buildings to a point a mile from the impact site. Two of the company's fire trucks remained on the scene watching for any flare-ups under the retardant foam they'd shot all over the wreckage earlier.

At home, Bashalli hugged and kissed her husband before asking if anything on the news had been remotely true. She had not felt anything from the crash and the news generally did not report as many facts as they did assumptions. With the area having been cordoned off by police as quickly as they could drive out there, nobody got their cars or vans to within three miles of the site. By law reporters and the public were not allowed to raise cameras up above the perimeter walls so they had to be satisfied with shots of the rising smoke—black at first and then dull gray—for the hour it took them to figure out that was all they would be getting.

"Not much more to tell except that a very old jetliner, probably far too old to be flying, crashed inside the walls. Nobody was killed and it is being treated as suspicious, but that's all I know."

He assured her he had not called immediately because nothing had been known. "Besides, dad and I were locked in the basement bunker."

The explanation satisfied her, mostly, and she dropped the subject when Bart, their son, came running out of the side room where he and his two sisters, and their nanny, Amanda, had been playing.

"Daddy!" he shouted launching himself into the air a full three feet before getting to Tom and latching his arms and legs around his father.

"Bart!" Tom lightly yelled hugging the boy. "Put me down and let me hug your sisters, then we can talk about how your day was."

"Okay." Bart released himself and slid to the floor standing back and pointing from Mary, the older of his two little sisters, to their father. "Don't take all day!" he cautioned her.

Tom and Bashalli tried to not smile or laugh at his ordering his sister, but both failed in the attempt. It was made even more difficult when the girl turned to her brother and stuck her tongue out at him, blowing a very expert raspberry in his direction before hugging her father.

Anne was given the third hug courtesy of being handed to Tom by their nanny.

Dinner was relaxed and fun for them all with Amanda asking about the excitement at Enterprises. "I regularly ignore anything on the local news because they make guesses, and anything on the national broadcasts because they are never where the action is."

"Well, we had an empty airplane crash but nobody was hurt or killed," he told her sticking with the basic story he and his father had asked all employees to relay with for the time being.

He and Bashalli fell asleep holding hands that night and he woke to the smell of coffee in their room. She was just trying to tiptoe out when he cleared his throat and told her, "Good morning, Bash."

She turned round, came back and climbed onto the bed snuggling into him for a moment.

"Drink your coffee, get showered and come down and waffles will be on the table in fifteen minutes."

When he arrived in the kitchen the two older children were digging excitedly into their waffles with Amanda cutting tiny bites for little Anne to try with her teeth that were just coming in enough to allow her to have small bits of solid food.

His waffles were filled with some of the frozen blueberries Bashalli had put up the previous summer. They were delicious.

Tom kissed his children and wife and got a hug from Amanda before heading to work a little early. The nanny would be packing the two older children up and taking them to their schools where both had only one more week before the summer break.

He came through the main employee gate, stopping to say hello to Davey the guard. It might be farther down the north wall than the executive gate, but it provided an almost straight shot to the Administration building.

"Hey, Tom. Harlan called to ask me to have you swing by his

office if you can. Have a good day."

After thanking the man who was only about a year younger Tom headed for the Security offices.

"Harlan asked to see me," he explained to the receptionist.

"Yep! He told me to send you right in."

"Well, hello, Tom," he was greeted. "I'm guessing you'd like an update on the excitement of yesterday, huh?"

Tom sat down. "Sure. If you have anything solid to tell."

The Security chief nodded. "Well, solid as in what we have been told and some information coming from the FAA. It would appear we were the victims of nothing other than aircraft engine fatigue and an attempt at not ditching the jet. That was a registered flight, by remote control, that was supposed to fly no closer to any town than seven miles."

"So, why didn't we hear about it?"

Harlan looked a little angry. "Because, according to a particular idiot at the FAA, our flight space was exactly one half mile outside of the notification zone." He scowled before adding, "So, they just never thought to call us."

Tom asked about the lack of IFF and also the missing connections to the black boxes. "I'd say that is suspicious," he stated.

Harlan sighed. "Right, and if it had been manned in any way, that would be an issue. Well, the black boxes would be. The IFF was on when the jet left Rutland according to the owner, but failed moments later. We may never know why the FAA decided to not put out an alert, but I have made a call down to all our favorite's senator, Peter Quintana. His assistant said he was in conference with the head of the FAA as I was speaking to her and he'd get back to us this morning."

He added the owner was insisting the reason for the crash had nothing to do with the aircraft or the operator, it must have been forced down into Enterprises by someone out to make his company "look bad."

"What company is that?" the inventor asked.

"The FAA isn't telling me that," Harlan answered looking angry.

Tom left moments later, a little disgusted, heading for the cafeteria. There, he spotted Bud just starting to sit at a table off to one side. He caught the flyer's eye, made a motion indicating he was getting a coffee, and then joined him a minute later.

"What's in the box?" he asked spotting a wrapped package Bud had to his right.

"Perfume. A very special perfume your sister insists will gain me valuable hubby points."

"You need some of those?"

Bud nodded. "Never hurts to set a few away for a rainy day."

"So, she more than hinted it is what she wants? It isn't her birthday, so I'm just guessing she is feeling a little neglected in the gift department." He grinned. Sandy liked flying, pretty clothes and gifts!

Bud looked at Tom. "Sandy is going to love this present," he stated with a nod.

"Why?" the inventor asked skeptically.

"Because she's been after me to get this particular perfume. It's from *Le Laboratoire Spécial Parfum de France*. She told me it is a very special scent all the high class French ladies and world-famous fashion models are wearing."

Tom chuckled. "Does she know that is made in an industrial complex over in New Jersey?"

Bud laughed. "Not a clue!"

Tom had checked out the famous "French" manufacturer almost a year earlier—for Bashalli—only to discover that it had one time been called *Perfumes o' de World* and was, indeed, wholly based outside of Passaic in the adjoining state. Only their advertisements made it sound like it was from the European country, but it was completely without an actual mention—even in the very small print—that it had nothing to do with France.

"I won't tell if you don't," Bud said almost as a request.

With a zipped lips motion, Tom agreed.

It took two days for Peter Quintana to get back to Tom and Damon. When he did it was obvious he was frustrated.

"That old jet was not deemed to be flight worthy and should never have been issued with a certification even for the one-hour flight. And, because it is considered to be a confidential matter, I have been told who owned that jet but have been told to not tell anyone, even you folks. To tell the truth, I stretched things and made a call to the owners telling them they needed to come clean and to repay all your expenses, only to have the woman at the other end laugh, tell me they were a small holding company, and hang up."

"Sounds like something fishy."

"Yes, Tom, it certainly does and especially when I tell you that call went through a computer hookup to an out of country phone. I'll keep after this but for now it might be that you need to bill the FAA for your reconstruction costs. Here's the person who told me to keep mum," and he gave them a name and phone number and the address that person could be found.

After they hung up, Damon told Tom the actual anticipated costs. "Less that five hundred thousand, but that is still a good chunk of change. Go tell Jackson Rimmer to issue to bill and to file a pending suit against the FAA for this and also for any failure to pay it within fourteen days... or to have *them* cross-bill the owners of that aircraft."

Rimmer told the inventor it would be an uphill battle but would file the necessary papers that day.

Tom headed to the lab down the hall from the shared office and sat down at his computer. First, he called up all the files that had been copied and transferred from the archives the previous week. He sat looking them over while his mind tried to spot things he could improve on as he sought to upsize the aircraft.

The actual first jet had been disassembled with many of the parts put in storage out in New Mexico. Truth be told, Tom wasn't even certain anything had been retained after all this time. It was likely a lot of those things had eventually been discarded to reclaim the storage space. A phone call seemed to be in order to determine the fate of his hyperplane.

Nine minutes later he was speaking with the facilities manager, Ruth Jordan.

"Well, Tom, I am going to need to go to the vault to see. You do recall your father okayed the digging of a shallow storage building over behind the first reactor building."

Tom told her he had forgotten about that. "If you could, or if someone could check in the next few days and get back to me, I would greatly appreciate it," he told her.

"Hmm, that might work but I have now left my office and am heading to the back door and to the small hatchway down to the vault. Give me about a minute to get there and we'll see what we still have."

He could hear as she opened a door that groaned slightly at being moved after a protracted period of time.

"Okay, Tom. I'm inside and heading down the isle I believe might be our best bet. And... well... the answer is sort of a yes and sort of a no."

He asked what that meant, hoping it was more positive than a negative.

"There is a large packing case but I doubt it is large enough to hold anything like wings. But, and since it is padlocked, let me get a couple strong people down here to open it up and bring it out. I'll call you in an hour or two."

When Ruth called back it was less than the indicated time.

"You may not believe this, but my people found that inside the case was not just the fuselage with the engine pulled out and packed for storage, there was a note about the wings. They were plastic wrapped and were sitting on the other side of the room."

Tom was excited. "Does that mean you have the entire aircraft?"

"It certainly appears so. Want it sent out? I can get it ready for tomorrow's return of the supply jet."

He asked her to do that and thanked her.

The following late afternoon he was waiting at the Barn as a truck brought both a packing crate and the wrapped wings to offload.

The three men carried the wings to a waiting padded bench and used the truck's hoist to lift the case and set it nearby.

"Need any unpacking from us, skipper?" the lean man inquired.

"No, Steven. I've got it from here. Besides, Bud is coming over from his hangar to help in a few. But, thanks!"

The flyer could be seen driving toward Tom a minute after the truck pulled away.

Together they unpacked everything and began the process of checking all components for wear, age and other possible problems. The dryness of the desert and the tight storage conditions had kept everything pristine. To be certain, Tom brought out a strange device that he used to check each square centimeter. It was an offshoot of the technology he'd developed for Doc Simpson to be used to see inside the human body.

This one was used in the aircraft industry to check for materials fatigue.

The two friends found nothing to indicate any potential troubles.

"Tomorrow we put it together. For now I'll have Dianne Duquesne and her folks come pick up the turbine to give it a check and replace anything they feel is needed."

"When do you want me back?" Bud asked.

Tom thought about his schedule and suggested ten the next day.

By nine that day Dianne—the head of Propulsion Engineering—called to tell the inventor the turbine had to undergo a complete teardown and rebuild. "Unfortunately, nobody thought to totally empty out fluids before it was stored. There is some decomposition of hoses and at least one of the igniters is totally blocked with dried hydrocarbons. Give us three days. Artie Johnson and our two new interns will do the deed. Good learning process for them and Artie needs more supervisor experience."

Tom knew it was going to take a full day and possibly more to put the hyperplane back together and into flyable condition, so he thanked her and said he looked forward to getting it back. "And, have the interns come with it. I want to meet them."

He and Bud met at 10:00 and began the process of reassembling the small jet.

There were rubberized gaskets between most major body and wing components to keep everything sealed tightly and to which sensors could be attached to measure tolerances and movement. All of them were replaced just to be certain of their integrity.

By end of the day, things were starting to resemble the former glory of the misnamed nuclear hyperplane. While Tom checked each of the tires and the brake pads, Bud grabbed a bottle of plastic polish and a buffer and went to work on the canopy.

Unlike more modern Swift aircraft, it had been built before the advent of clear tomasite and so the materials surrounding the single occupant had been hardened polycarbonate.

But, tough or not, it had some scratches and a lot of dust buildup that had, during shipment, added to the micro-etching on the outside.

Within the hour the flyer's efforts were bearing fruits as he ran the buffer back over everything for the third time. With each rub down with the fluid and buffing of the resulting dry haze, more and more of the tiny scratches had disappeared.

Now, the only thing left to do was to add one final layer of a special plastic filling liquid, allow it to dry and then give everything a final buff.

By the time they parted at a quarter until five, there was no visible difference between the current canopy and a brand new one.

And, the next mid-afternoon, Tom received a call from Artie.

"Hey, skipper. Dianne said you wanted to know when the little turbine would be ready. Can you take it at about four?"

"Of course. Always assuming it will be absolutely ready at that time. If you need the extra day she suggested, take it."

"No, I'm really certain we'll be ready. We have it reassembled and it is in the test chamber being given a one-hour run. That will finish in—" and he paused evidently looking at his watch of a clock, "—oh, about fourteen minutes. We'll give it an hour to cool down run the videoscope inside and give it a check, then wheel it over to the Barn."

"It is looking good inside?"

Artie laughed. "It is looking like you never even ran the thing. Dianne okayed a lot of replacements and I had one of the interns give the inside surfaces a really good polish. Plus, it is running like a contented kitten right now. See you in a couple hours."

When the time came for the delivery, Tom and Bud were waiting.

Along with Artie were two young people—both Tom and Bud realized how young they looked and just how the two of them must have appeared to adults over a decade earlier.

To both their surprises, the two interns were young women.

To Tom's true surprise, one of them was beautiful, had a head of bright red hair pulled back and tied with a blue ribbon, and was the one of them who rushed forward to jump into his arms, kissing his cheek!

CHAPTER 4 /
ROCKETS AREN'T ALWAYS THE ANSWER

"OH BOY, but I sure hope you remember me, Tom," she said feeling how he tensed up at her embrace.

It took him about ten seconds to put all the facts together.

"Becca? Becca Carter? From Anchorage?"

She nodded happily. "Yes. It's more officially Becky now, but it really is me." She turned around with her arms out as if modeling something. "What do you think?"

Now, even Bud recognized the young woman who had been a teen when they rescued her after a volcano had inundated her house killing her parents and aunt and uncle. She had been playing in the family rowboat and it had kept her afloat amidst the flotsam and mud for a couple days until Tom, Bud and Hank Sterling, testing what Bud had dubbed the cadaver car for sniffing out bodies after such a disaster, found and rescued her.

She had lived with Damon and Anne Swift for about two months until the draw of her home state had her moving back. Since then she had kept in touch with a few cards each year.

"I had no idea you'd decided to go into this field," he told her. Turning to Artie, he asked, "Is she any good? Like you were at this stage?"

Artie blushed, but he nodded. "Dianne likes her and I think she's..." and he turned even brighter red, "well, I think so, too. So is Valerie over there," he said pointing to the other young woman who was standing a dozen feet to the side.

After suggesting he and Becky get together that evening for dinner, and her agreeing, they approached the turbine.

It was smaller than Tom seemed to recall it to be, but he remembered that he'd been smaller back then as well. It also looked like a brand new jet turbine engine.

Lifting the side cover, Becky showed him the interior. "Val and I took turns cleaning and shining it up. It's a really neat turbine, Tom," she said almost gushingly. "Artie tells me he wasn't here when it was built, but he recognized the design. And," and she looked into Tom's eyes, "he made some improvements," she finished in a hushed tone.

Tom smiled. "What did you do, Artie?"

"Well, since the original got made, some pretty significant strides have happened in things like the igniters. Heck, *you've* made a lot of them. So, inside it has newer igniters like we use in the smallest of the turbines in the Toads, plus higher pressure braided fuel cables and injector nozzles. An all new primary compressor blade set really helps. All combined, I think it gives about nine percent more power for a three percent reduced fuel burn."

The inventor let out a whistle. He recalled the small fuel tank could barely give eighty minutes of full-power flight and had, with Bud's assistance, fitted a slightly larger tank that morning. Now, with the added efficiency, the hyperplane—and he knew he had to give it some other name—should be able to remain airborne for two hours with ease.

The three engineers assisted in getting the turbine carried to and installed in the fuselage. They left as soon as Tom suggested he and Bud could handle the hookups.

"Testing tomorrow for anyone interested." He also asked Becky if she would be ready at 5:45 for him to take home for dinner.

"Love to, but is it okay with Bashalli? I mean, she's got the kids and you and everything to take care of..." seeing his grin, she nodded. "Right. Superwoman I'd love to be like someday. I'll come over to your office it that's okay."

As soon as they left, Bud let out a low whistle. "Wow, she was cute back then, but golly! And did you see the way Artie was looking adoringly at her?"

Now the inventor laughed. "I did. I'll sort of feel her out on her thoughts about that. If she tells me she would rather not get involved with anyone, I'll have a quiet word with the young man."

Bashalli was enthusiastic and asked if the two older Swifts and the Barclays—well, one Barclay and one Swift-Barclay—might be included.

Tom agreed it might be nice to pull out the grill and start off the season with some steaks and pork chops.

"I can pick them up on the way home."

"Nonsense. I am just sitting here, and besides I need vegetables and potatoes and something for dessert."

Tom offered to step down the hall and see if Chow could provide them with a pie or two. She said to call in the next ten minutes if he could not.

He ambled down the hall and into the small kitchen. Chow, hearing something behind him, spun with a bright smile. "Hey thar,

Tom. What's up? I'd-a asked what's cookin' 'cept that's sort o' a chef's joke. So?"

With a smile, Tom told the westerner about the forthcoming family meal.

"I got just the thing. I got a fresh apple pie an' a friend out west sent me a case o' things called Marionberries. Sorta like a blackberry mixed up with a raspberry. Real good, too. I made five pies from that an' you can have one. The others are fer lunch tomorrow upstairs."

"If you can spare them, that would be wonderful."

Chow could and said he'd pack them into a box and bring them to the office in ten minutes.

One the way back down the hall Tom pulled his cell phone out and called to tell Bashalli the dessert was taken care of.

Becky arrived right on time and the two of them headed down and to Tom's car for the short ride home.

"So," he asked as they passed the western corner of Enterprises, "how have things been up in Alaska?"

She hugged herself and told him things had been almost universally wonderful. "I was going steady with a boy named Todd when you brought me down here, then we got back together when I moved back, and then he turned out to be a monumental flake. He now has a girlfriend and they have triplets and he still works in a filing station. I suppose she is okay, but the girl has zero brains. A big chest that got bigger with the kids, but nothing in the noggin."

"You always struck me as about the smartest one in the room, Becky. I'm really glad you have come down here for college and seem to be on your way to becoming a top-notch turbine engineer."

He told her he had a talk with Dianne Duquesne who believed that with one more year in school, and some good guidance she was getting at Swift Enterprises, she believed Becky would be a true catch for any company she wanted to work for.

As they turned onto the final street before the Swift home, she asked, "Could I maybe work at Swift Enterprises?"

Tom pulled over to the side for a moment and turned to face Becky. "As I said, you would be a catch for *whatever* company you set your sights on. Swift Enterprises included."

Her laugh told him that was what she was hoping for. They got to the driveway at the same time his father and mother pulled to the curb in front. Bud and Sandy were just about twenty seconds behind them.

The six marched up the steps, across the porch and into the

house.

Bashalli was coming out of the kitchen wiping her hands on a towel. She walked quickly to Tom giving him a big kiss before turning to hug Becky, giving her a quick kiss on her right cheek before hugging her in-laws and finally Sandy and Bud.

"Everybody to the back yard, get a beer or wine or cola or something and sit. Do not try to come in to help. I'll have the meat ready to go in five minutes. Then Tom can do all the work!"

Her audience laughed and agreed to behave.

Tom checked the fuel tank and started the grill, a combination of gas and charcoal that only required six minutes to bring up to heat.

When his wife came to the back door he jumped forward taking the platter of thick steals and double-cut chops from her. She had expertly coated them all with spice and herb mixtures and as they began to sizzle, everyone's mouths began to water.

When Bashalli came back to the door a second time she asked if Sandy could assist.

"Just the vegetables and the potatoes I have already cooked. But, there are three platters, so your assistance will be nice."

Becky was the first one to pick her grilled item; she chose an inch-thick steak Tom assured her was cooked to medium-rare, her favorite.

"Oh, Bashalli," she enthused after taking the first bite, "this is scrumptious. I mean," she said blushing as she looked at Tom, "Tom obviously did a great job but this rub you made is incredible!"

Everyone at the table agreed and they were soon involved in a combination of chewing and trying to carry on a conversation.

The chewing won out.

Anne Swift was especially interested in catching up with Becky as she felt a soft spot in her heart for the girl who had been orphaned by the disaster and who had declared to her son, Tom, that since he'd saved her, he owned her!

Imagining Tom's face when that happened still made her smile.

Over their desserts the talk turned to the little jet and its rebuilt turbine.

Sandy said, "I remember that little jet. You never did let me fly it." She stuck her tongue out at him.

"I only flew it a few more times before dad and I came back here and it got packed away in New Mexico."

"Why now?" their mother inquired.

Tom scraped his last bit of pie onto his fork and put it in his mouth. "Well, I was thinking about the original intent for the airframe and now think it might be a starting point for some research I want to do into very fast flight. Obviously, with the little turbine Becky here helped fix up, it isn't going to be a speed record setter, but I recall I did a lot of investigation into the aerodynamics of something I had hoped would be at least a Mach-3 or Mach-4 aircraft someday."

Damon spoke up. "Now that Tom has put the whole Wanderer thing behind for the time being, I think it is a good project to revisit."

"For now?" Anne asked. Bashalli looked at her father-in-law and then her husband and then Anne. She also nodded.

Tom explained. "We left everything running up on Wanderer and so far it has done the trick. In fact, the entire field was shut off four days ago now that it has reached a point inside Earth's orbit and the push it was giving is being overcome by the pull of the Sun. But, after it swings around and comes back out I think I'd like to be in a position to remove most of the equipment and bring it home.

"A lot of it can be repurposed or put into storage against a day when it might be needed again."

"And," Bashalli said trying to sound determined, "if you set up a team to go out there and do that work, they can go and you can remain here at home. Am I correct?"

Tom could see the look in her eyes, so he said that was definitely a possibility.

Before it reached ten that night, Becky asked to be taken back to the apartment she had on the Enterprises grounds.

"I do want to be out there when you fire the turbine up and especially when you taxi or even fly that little jet," she told the inventor as they were saying goodnight. Bud and Sandy offered to drop her off back at Enterprises.

In spite of Bashalli's protests, Anne helped her clean up and get the dishes into the dishwasher before she and Damon departed.

Tom called to Propulsion Engineering the following day at around 11:00 to announce his intention to fuel and fire up the turbine. "Anyone involved or curious can come over to the Barn. Showtime's in thirty minutes."

Dianne, Artie, the two interns and one other of the turbine engineers came over and were sitting on a worktable inside the Barn when Tom arrived. Another technician had already put fuel into the two wing tanks and had also taken a sample out for the inventor to check.

It was clean and had no visible water in it, so he smiled at the audience and climbed up the short roll-around steps and into the cockpit.

With a few grunts he finally wedged himself inside.

"Guess I've put on a few pounds," he admitted to the assemblage.

"And, you are taller by six inches and your shoulders are broader than they were way back when," Bud quipped as he stepped over from his little electric runabout in time to hear Tom's comment.

"Yeah. Well, I hope I can maneuver this around; otherwise I might need to let Sandy have a go. She is still small enough to fly this."

"Sure, if her elbows don't get in the way!" Bud stated with a straight face. "I mean, they can't help but jab me in the ribs when we are in close confines, so she might just hit something and end up flying straight up!"

Slowly, Tom responded with, "Ri-i-i-i-ght. Okay," he said turning back to the group. "I am going to do the pre-checks before firing things up, so please stand back." As the others retreated, Tom flipped on the three switches to energize the little aircraft. Even built before he ever created his wrap-around single screen instrument panels, this little jet had everything displaying on a single square monitor. He watched as a progress bar built from left to right with nine small points of light appearing as the line got to that area. These were all green and so, once completed, a master light to the right of the monitor turned from yellow to green.

Two seconds later all instruments appeared in front of them.

"Clear," Tom called out as he pressed and held the START button.

In seconds everyone could hear the electric starter motor as it got the turbine blades spinning. Faster and faster they went until Tom was satisfied they had reached the point he could begin ignition. To do this he released the first button and flipped a nearby switch. With a small cough and then a light roar, the turbine caught and spun even faster.

Three minutes later he smiled to the group and held up his right thumb. Next, he eased his feet from the two pedals on the floor, releasing the brakes, and allowed the little jet to move forward. As it did, he steered the nose wheel using the small knob just to the rear of the joystick.

The jet responded by turning to the left and continuing on for another fifty feet before Tom stopped it once again. Now, he pushed the throttle forward while stepping hard on the pedals. The turbine rose in both pitch and the amount of power coming out from the back of the jet.

He only let it run at this very high idle for a minute before throttling back and making a wide turn to come back to the front of the Barn. There, he shut the turbine off and listened to it smoothly wind down.

"Looked and sounded great," Dianne commented. "No smoke and nothing rattling around. What do you think?"

Tom smiled at her and then gave a small salute to the others. "Great!" he proclaimed as he worked to get back out.

"How the heck did Red Jones ever get into this way back then?" he asked Bud as they walked to the back to look into the exhaust area.

"Giant Red-sized shoe horn?" Bud guessed.

When he returned to the shared office, Tom was elated and was planning on taking the jet up the following morning. His father was pleased the aircraft had passed muster so far, but he cautioned Tom about taking the first flight himself.

"Why don't you let Slim Davis take it up for a quick fly-around? He is about as tall as you but easily thirty pounds lighter."

"And, Slim is slimmer than I am. I guess that would be fine."

Because the other test pilot had come to Enterprises about the time Tom was flying the hyperplane in New Mexico, he had never had the opportunity. Like any good pilot, and specially test pilots, he spent the remainder of the day familiarizing himself with both the specifications as well as the actual aircraft.

"Looks like it will be a blast," he told the inventor when they met the next morning. "And, I like taking these sort of aircraft up when the weather is cool and the air is dense. Better lift. Uhhh, any last minute hints?"

Tom had been thinking back to when he had flown the tiny jet. "I believe you need to let her raise her own nose and do not push to rotate too soon. I'd thought with me, and I was quite a bit lighter back then, I'd need about a thousand feet. It took fourteen hundred. But, that gives you time to get her ground speed up and that is important because she was a little sluggish and tended to need a heavy hand to control and trim her. Get her above one-fifty and you are fine."

Slim went through the same pre-check Tom had and repeated the warm-up and even the high idle runs before he got on the jet's radio and asked for taxi permission from the tower.

"Roger, Slim. Taxi to runway one-eight far east and hold for transiting Shopton to Albany flight just taking off from Regional."

As he taxied, the tower gave him the weather information all pilots relied on. He only had to hold at the threshold for one minute before getting the okay for takeoff.

"Rolling."

There were twenty-seven maneuvers all test flights, or combination of flights, were put through in order to be qualified for anyone other than the test pilot to take up.

For larger aircraft this often required more than two hours of flight time. For many small aircraft of the jet type, this could be cut in half. Propeller driven—and thus slower—aircraft fell somewhere in between.

Slim had the hyperplane back on the ground fifty-three minutes later. On hearing the call for landing permissions, Tom felt a tiny pang of worry. He didn't want to interrupt Slim's concentration so he waited until the little jet pulled up and stopped thirty feet in front of him.

The sun was just glaring enough from the curved canopy to obstruct his view so he could not see the huge smile on Slim's face. At least, not until the canopy was unlatched and rose to reveal a very happy pilot.

With barely any struggle, the test pilot rose and stepped out from the jet onto the steps that a technician had just rolled over.

"Everything okay?" Tom asked.

Slim nodded. "Actually, skipper, more than okay. That little jet might be a bit skittish until you get her flying at a good speed, but man can she do the maneuvers!"

As they walked away, allowing the tech to roll it back inside the Barn, the two men talked about the flight.

It had been, as Tom now recalled, fast to respond and light on the handling—above the magic speed.

"Umm, I hear rumors you want to see if this might finally be taken supersonic... or maybe a little more than that."

"I do. Originally it was called the nuclear hyperplane because that was my intention. Nuclear reactor behind a shield behind the cockpit, super-heated air or some air/liquid mix, and jumping quickly up to Mach-4. Now I realize the structure would never take that sort of stress, but if this design can be proven out, newer materials and an upsizing could give me what I had hoped for all those years ago."

"How about some sort of rocket drive?"

Tom thought a moment. "In all honesty, I believe that rockets are not the answer to all our speed issues. Not in the long run and certainly not for anything other than short flights. I mean, the old X-1 through the X-15 got up to incredible speeds and altitudes, but those rockets could barely run more than eighty seconds at full throttle. One of those pilots, Joe Walker, became the first American to cross into what we now think of as space. With no fuel reserve he coasted back to an unpowered landing."

"Right. Fast but not a lot of longevity in the air," Slim admitted.

Tom chuckled. "It stayed aloft for a lot longer than the stubby little wings might have suggested. Heck, even my hyperplane has wings that are eighteen percent longer in relation to the fuselage but probably can't glide as far."

"Yeah, or go as high and slip through the rarified atmosphere! Don't worry, Tom. If this little jewel proves anything, it is that you are on the right track. You'll do it!"

CHAPTER 5 /
A LOT TO DO FOR A CIVILIAN AIRCRAFT!

SEVERAL WEEKS flew past with the inventor spending his time between his design computers and flying the small jet. Each flight was designed to test one or more small improvements in the aerodynamics and systems. It was, he realized on the second flight, not quite as zippy as he remembered, but then there were a ton of things he remembered one way that proved to be different.

It came down to a matter of degrees.

As a teenager, anything faster than his father's *Pigeon* airplane—which was fairly slow—seemed incredibly fast to him. That all changed with the advent of his supersonic *Sky Queen* and even the small, one-man *Kangaroo Kub* jet it carried in its tail hangar.

Actually, it had been brought home to him when he was attacked by a mysterious, black supersonic jet. His slower speed played to his advantage when the enemy overshot him on more than one occasion.

That notwithstanding, he was slightly disappointed now to conclude the main reason the hyperplane had seemed fast was a combination of his brain telling him it was fast along with the small size combined with the lower altitudes the jet could manage with its small turbojet engine.

"It's like driving down a freeway in a small sports car versus a large sedan," he told his sister as they had lunch one day.

Sandy nodded. "Oh, yeah. Like when the ground is racing past you just a few inches above your butt instead of you being a couple feet up in a big sedan." She turned the subject back to the hyperplane and asked when he thought she could take it up.

"Why not this afternoon," he suggested. "This is Friday and it is your flying afternoon. Do you have many demonstrations to do?"

"Today, just one at 2:00. I'll be free as of an hour later. Can I just go hop in for do you want to give me the thirty-minute tour and details?"

"Let's do the second one. There are a lot of things that little jet requires that someone used to *Pigeon Specials* and even the *Queen* need a refresher course about."

When Tom walked up to the Barn at the appointed time, Sandy was already standing next to the jet having fueled it, made certain the battery pack was charged, and even pulled it out into the open.

She was wearing her official Swift Enterprises' flight overalls.

With a knowing smile he asked if she had already sat in it.

"Well, duh! Of course I opened her up and slipped in. Sort of a tight fit and *do not tell that to Bud*! He'll suggest maybe my hips have become a little wider over the years." If anything, Tom realized, his sister had become slightly more trim over the previous five years. After her teen years and her growth spurts, she had gone on an exercise program for a couple years and had knocked at least an inch from her hips and also her waist.

"Sure, San. So, let's take the walk around now and then you slip those giant hips of yours back inside and I'll have you off the ground in fifteen minutes." She took a playful swing at him and laughed.

"Sure."

It took only seventeen before she had the little jet taxiing away from Tom but she had been completely concentrated on what he was showing and telling her.

At one point she chuckled and asked why he had not replaced the square monitor and panel with its several switches and status lights with a more modern panel.

"A lot of it has to do with dad asking me to keep as much of the cost down on this since it may only get used for a few weeks and then go back into storage."

"Or," she told him with a knowing tap to the side of her nose, "up in the rafters of the museum."

The tower quickly cleared her for a trio of laps around the perimeter of Enterprises.

"When you finish those, we should be able to vector you out for a fly-around of the lake. We will keep a good eye on you."

She made the first lap in shallow turns before taking the second one flying farther along each side and then a steeper bank into the turn. For lap three she climbed from about two hundred feet up to five hundred.

"This is fantastic!" she reported over the radio.

Tom had been monitoring the radio and her comment made him smile.

Thirty minutes later she came in on final approach and he made his first call to her.

"Bring her in low, Sandy, then flare out and bring the nose up seven or eight degrees before you touch down. Come back on the throttle and just let it set itself to the tarmac. Otherwise, you'll continue to float for another thousand feet."

The little jet made a near perfect touchdown and taxi back to the Barn. As Sandy climbed out she had a far-away look in her eyes.

"That is almost better than a hot fudge sundae over coffee ice cream and with extra marshmallow cream!" She patted her hips, saying, "And, less fattening."

When he got her to leave the little jet and he headed for the lab next to the shared office, Tom managed to download the remote data from the circuits he'd had installed. It would tell the tale of Sandy's flight without her resorting to a food analogy.

It was encouraging and showed that she had been a little more reckless than the other three people who'd flown the jet. Her more pronounced maneuvers gave him added information. He put that aside and returned to the design program on which he'd started with a scaled-up version of the little jet.

The stress and maneuverability routines were telling him this was not going to be a good candidate for the larger version. For one, the wings would be far too thick in an aircraft large enough to carry even twenty passengers. Also, it would be prone to yawing in mid air due to the length versus wingspan numbers.

It was something an early "stealth" fighter jet had only been able to overcome with heavy use of multiple computers.

I really don't want this to be a completely fly by computer jet, he told himself as he looked at the numbers for the third time. Now, he would begin the often-tedious task of making small changes to the design and retesting all flight characteristics.

By the following morning Tom had come to a decision.

He was going to need to put the horse before the cart, so to speak. The propulsion method was going to be as important as the shape of the aircraft, and if it turned out to be of some huge dimensions, the airframe would need to be correspondingly large.

The main issue was he had no true idea of how to power his aircraft.

The scramjet technology used by the military for a couple decades had proven to be a little unreliable. It was certainly fuel hungry. He wasn't certain of the actual numbers but recalled reading that nearly ninety percent of the first test jets either disintegrated in flight, had their engines rupture, or just plain shut down. Crashes had been the norm for the longest time.

Then, someone figured out one of the hurdles; bringing the aircraft and drive up to high enough speed to support the supersonic airflow necessary using solid rocket boosters to get the aircraft above Mach-2 before attempting to ignite the scramjet. Still, reliability troubles persisted even though speeds had crept above Mach-5, which was no small feat for such tiny aircraft. Flights had been measured in seconds not minutes, which was a problem for understanding long-term characteristics of flyability and stresses.

He knew that scramjet engines had no moving parts like turbines did. Air was rammed inside the front based on supersonic speed of flight, compressed using a tapered inner conical piece until its widest point where fuel mixed with the thick air was ignited just behind the most narrow point and flowed out over a reverse of the compression piece until it exited from the back at hypersonic speeds.

A bit of research over the next day told him one severely limiting factor had been in the choice of fuels. Liquid hydrogen was to be mixed with the thick, fast airflow taking advantage of the oxygen still available even at altitude.

It was such a hot process that even the chill of great altitude could not keep the first such engines from pretty much melting themselves. The early ones did just that.

Cooling methods had been developed including circulating the liquid hydrogen in a jacket surrounding the combustion area. It was a lesson learned from rocket engines. This had been moderately successful.

"It is still a fuel matter, Bud," he told his brother-in-law as they sat in the lab munching on chicken salad sandwiches.

"What sort o' fuel is that?" Chow, the man who had made the sandwiches and brought them in a minute earlier, inquired.

Tom gave the older man a brief explanation of the principles of scramjets and told him he hoped to turn the technology into something to be used to fly people all around the globe.

Chow nodded as he listened. Finally, he sat down on one of the lab stools and scratched his nose.

"So, if'n I got this'n right, you want to get folks traveling five times faster'n sound?" Tom told him this was the case. "Okay. So the good ole *Sky Queen* can do about half that, an' if ya get inta orbit a spaceship can go all around the Earth in ninety minutes. So, what's the advantage?"

Seeing the downcast look on Tom's face he regretted asking that. He was about to apologize when Tom looked up at him.

"That is a very good question, Chow. If we call the speed of sound, generally measured at sea level, as being a little over seven hundred fifteen miles per hour, that makes Mach-5 something like thirty-eight hundred miles per hour. So," and he did another fast calculation in his head, "something traveling that fast can get an aircraft all the way around the globe in roughly six hours and forty minutes. Of course you'd only need to travel half way around in any direction, so maximum time would be three-and-a-half hours give or take."

The chef was impressed. "That means you'd take off from here an' get ta places like India afore ya even left here?"

Bud picked up on the chef's surprise. "Yep! Tom's going to turn it into a time machine."

Chow's eyes narrowed. He looked at the flyer and told him, "He's already done that with that little time thingie you both brought back from space. So, ha-ha on you, Buddy."

After he left them, Bud asked the inventor, "So, would there be something in building a repelatron people carrier instead?"

The inventor rubbed his chin in thought. "Technically easier, but we still have issues with where we are allowed to fly within the atmosphere, Bud. For instance, China and even Japan have forbidden repelatron flights over their territory at anything under one hundred miles. Even then, the Chinese Ambassador once told our President they would watch for any incursion and would fire missiles immediately if we dipped below that point."

He went on to state he and Damon Swift both did not want repelatron technology open to other companies and nations.

"Oh, yeah. Will there be any problems with this hyper jet power?"

"I've had Jackson in Legal checking and it would appear that if we can guarantee the fuel completely burns, and does not release harmful materials or radiation, then existing treaties and agreements will allow it. Of course it will still be up to national governments, but if I can crack this, they'd be shooting themselves in the foot to refuse to allow their citizens to benefit."

They talked about the previous supersonic aircraft from the U.S., the Soviet Union and the only one to find any degree of success, the Concorde.

All eventually fell to either lack of Governmental support—the United State's SST—to poor design and even less stupendous manufacturing—the Soviet TU-144—and to sheer economics—Concorde.

Of them, the Soviets had lost many of the small numbers they built to accidents while only a few airlines accepted the overwhelming costs of operation of the Concorde. America's attempt had been stymied by lack of support before much could be done outside the design phase.

"And, this HST, or whatever it gets named, won't use any design like those?"

"No, Bud. Mainly because they were at the limits of handing the heat and stresses of just getting above Mach-2. I'm certain that our… HST, as you put it, needs to be three times more streamlined and five times stronger. And that means something for the body and outside that is stronger than even the titanium used by the earlier aircraft!"

With Bud now out of his comfort zone on his understanding of the physics of such a hypersonic aircraft, he left Tom to pursue a few thoughts that had come to him during their brief talk.

CHAPTER 6 /
ENCOUNTERING AN OLD FRIEND

WEEKS PASSED and Tom worked practically non-stop on a rebuild of his former hyperplane. Included in the work was lengthening it by about three feet and adding a second seat behind the pilot. By now he was thinking of it as his Teen Dream Plane or even the Failed Promise Jet. Neither one did him any favors as far as bolstering his attitude about his chances for success.

Bud dropped by every afternoon other than the two days when his test pilot duties had him in the sky. If he were honest with himself, the flyer was a little more satisfied with the flying than in trying to talk Tom into being pleased he had even managed to get the jet in the air after nearly sixteen years.

About every week Tom had Arv Hanson adapt a basic model of the jet so he might test it in the wind tunnel.

"It isn't that I want to get this up to supersonic speeds," he explained. "It is just I am making more and more subtle changes than the CAD programs can give me accurate measurements on."

"And," Arv had told him on at last two occasions, "you don't want one slightly off-kilter change to ruin things. I know, skipper. It isn't a problem. Actually, since all you want is the basic scaled shape and some flight surface movement, I have a perfect 3D printer that turns them out overnight. You clear one to build before five and you have it at nine the next day."

Tom knew this but felt, in the back of his mind, he was imposing on his model maker.

One evening Bashalli noted his slight funk and commented on it.

"I learned a word back when I was about twelve I do not believe I've ever used before in a complete sentence, but why so *glum*, Tom?"

For some reason that made him smile and he was feeling better a moment later.

"I am, or was, glum over my old hyperplane, Bash. When I was sixteen I had such high hopes for it. Now," he shrugged, "it isn't what I remembered it to be. It has made be feel a little down on myself."

She nodded and made a tsk noise. "And, did everything you imagined at sixteen turn out to be exactly that? And, yes I do mean kissing girls and holding hands and... well, *things*."

"Really? Not much. Teens have this idealized viewpoint and it takes a little shock to get them over it. I suppose… no, I know that is what's going on here. Thanks for the little nudge."

He arrived at work the following morning in a better mood. He also arrived with a couple more, and a bit more than *slight,* changes in mind. When he reached Arv in the man's workshop, he told him what he'd decided to do.

"Okay-y-y-y," Arv said slowly, "and that is going to mean major change. Can you do that with the existing plane?"

"No. But, I am now over feeling as if I need to continue with that. It'll go up into the ceiling of the museum in a week or so. I'm going to call Jake over at the Construction Company and tell him I need a few people to hand-build this new jet."

"Come on over when you have the chance and we'll talk about who you want on this," Jake requested when the inventor called him.

Tom obliged him late that afternoon. After they discussed the changes, Jake suggested that one of the current small jets made by the Swifts could be used, with modifications, rather than start from scratch.

"The real plus, Tom, is you and your dad already have it flying at Mach-1.2."

The penny dropped and Tom wanted to slap his forehead. "Of course. The two-man supersonic jet. I've been so tunnel-visioned I forgot we can use that design as a test bed. Do we have one in inventory I can take?"

The manager of the Construction Company shook his head. "Not this week, but I'll have them turn out an extra one in next weeks' run. Can you wait ten days?"

Tom agreed he could and would. It would give him ample time to work with the people in Propulsion Engineering on a new type of power plant.

And that, he realized with a slight grin meant he could go over and visit with Becky for a little bit.

"I have a new project for one or two of your youngest and brightest," he told Dianne when she greeted him with a curious look.

"Okay, I'll bite. I think I can guess the who part of the equation, but it's the what you'll have to fill me in on."

He told her about his plans to outfit one of the already speedy jets with a new type of engine.

"Fine. It sounds like a ramjet to me. Is that what we're talking about?"

"Yes. And, of course, I need it in two weeks or sooner."

She pondered the matter a minute. "Okay. Doable given that it is about the simplest of all jet engines. So much so it was in, unfortunately, wide use back in World War II. If you can shoot over the basic specs we have, along with fuel capacity, I'll assign the girls to this. Maybe let Artie get a few more hours of supervision under his belt." She smiled knowingly.

Tom leaned forward. "And, probably get in a little girl watching at the same time!"

Becky and Valerie Coren came over as soon as Dianne motioned to them.

"It's really going to be an honor working for you, Mr. Swift," Valerie told him with a little curtsy.

Tom looked at her as if the motion had been both unexpected and that he wasn't certain if he ought to respond. So, he nodded.

The four of them went into a conference room where Tom pulled up the diagram of the little side-by-side jet and concentrated on the aft end where the power plant was located.

He asked if both were familiar enough with the concept of a ramjet engine. Becky said she was but Valery sadly shook her head.

"I'm sorry, Mr. Swift. They never taught us about those in school."

Tom was momentarily concerned. As far as he knew all school programs teaching the basics of jet turbine engines included historical classes to demonstrate what had come before. This included ramjet propulsion.

"Oh," he said and even he knew he sounded disappointed. He tried to grin and asked, "What school are you going to?"

Valerie looked very uncomfortable and appeared to be trying to remember something important.

"Rockledge University in Florida. It's south of Cape Canaveral by about a dozen miles. Why?"

Tom looked at her with a blank face. "It's just that I always like learning more about the people I work with. For instance, I've known Becky for over five years and have been kept up to date on most of what she's been up to. Other than, that is, knowing she is in school majoring in propulsion systems. So, let's get down to what is needed."

He further described the airframe, showing them both the strengths and tolerances inside and out, before turning back to the matter of the power plant.

"For this first test version plan on an external power and airflow system to get things running. After that the jet will take off under ramjet power. I need this to fly above five hundred knots and remain airborne for greater than one hour. If you find either of those is impossible, let Dianne and me know immediately and we'll see what a workaround might be.

"I cannot stress to you the importance of this project. It is definitely not make work, nor is it a test of either of you. Perhaps a test of your teamwork abilities, but not individual knowhow or skills. The end result is we have what I need. Keep in mind this project is highly secret. Questions?"

There were none from the young ladies so Dianne told them to head for their shared cubical to study Tom's design.

"And, the two of you brush up on ramjets before the day after tomorrow. Now, scoot!"

One they had left, she turned to Tom. "I'm having some difficulties with Valerie. She has the paper to show her experience with a lot of things, but she seems stumped for what to do if I give her a direct and solo assignment. If she doesn't or can't come through on this, I'm going to have to send her home early. Hate to do it, but the whole idea of an internship is to hone skills and not to pick them up remedially."

Tom understood and told her he and Damon would stand by any decision on her part.

"Just have someone else in mind to step in with Becky if you can."

Dianne smiled. "It'll break Artie's heart if Valerie has to go, but he's a strong team player and can step in with Becky in a heartbeat!"

Tom realized she was being sarcastic. Artie would be over the Moon to get the chance to work closely with Becky.

Tom checked in with Jake at the Construction Company the following Monday and was assured his copy of the jet, minus the engine, would be ready to be trucked over the following day.

"Unless you want a temporary engine installed and have someone like Barclay fly it over."

"No. We'd just have to dismount it and ship it back over to you. Plan on having a truck bring it to the Barn on Wednesday. Thanks!"

Next he called Dianne and told her to expect the jet by ten, two days hence. "Pass it on to the ladies, please, that I'll come out when they start to crawl all over the jet. I want them both to get some hands on time with the airframe and make some of their own measurements."

Then, he asked if the second intern was carrying her weight.

"Well," Dianne started then paused, "she is spending a lot of time in the evenings going over a lot of Internet information, and it sort of is dismaying to realize she might have lied on her intern submission. I went back over it last night and found she ticked all the boxes for ramjets, scramjets, turbine and high bypass turbines, and even stated she had disassembled three types of hobby turbine engines." She sighed. "What am I going to do, Tom?"

"Let's see how Wednesday goes. If she seems to be unfamiliar with aerodynamics and aircraft, then I'll have a talk with Harlan and see if he can look further into this."

She agreed to wait.

Thirty minutes later the inventor got up and headed for the Administration building.

Tom and Bud had lunch in the lab with Chow providing a veritable feast for them.

"Gotcha some fish chowder even though it ain't Friday. I had some really nice cod and halibut and large gulf shrimps. Then, ya get lobster rolls with fresh from the oven rolls split down the top side jest like they do 'em up in Maine."

Bud had brightened at the mention of the chowder. A big fan of cioppino, a west coast specialty, he rubbed his hands together in anticipation. "What do we get for dessert?" he asked as Chow set their soup bowls down on the table.

"How's blueberry pie sound?"

Bud said it sounded great.

"Good, then you get a small slice. Yer wife asked me a few weeks back to cut down on yer sugar intake. Doesn't want ya all soft around the middle like I use ta be."

It was true. Chow and Bud had met Tom within a day of each other and the cook had been about ten pounds heavier than he was now. The thing was, he had ballooned by about ninety pounds over the first eight years at Enterprises and had then started a diet that saw him get back to his weight from his late twenties when he'd been his most active.

He liked his slimmer form; his wife, Wanda, liked it, and he was happy to help anyone who asked for a little assistance. In some cases that was alerting the cafeteria staff to cut someone's portion size down a little or to not give them seconds. In a few cases where there was an attendant health issue, he was happy to provide a special diet or to offer to adapt one of his recipes so that person could make it themselves at home.

Tom had created a special sensor and monitor that checked each person's TeleVoc pin and identified people who had special food needs to the servers.

Bud tried to look disappointed, but the fact was he was enjoying his chowder so much he felt he could do with a little bit less pie when that time came.

Around a mouthful, he asked, "Does that mean she won't let me have whipped cream?"

Chow nodded. "Yep! An' I even dropped the fat level down in the crust. Got it jest about right so it is still flaky, but has 'bout fifty less calories per slice. Eat up, you two. I'll go git the pie."

He left with a spring in his step both men had to marvel at. At his heaviest, the best you could say about how Chow moved was he waddled. Of course that was eleven inches of waistline ago.

After they'd finished Tom asked Bud if he might give some advice. He swore the flyer to secrecy and even cautioned him about being anywhere around Valerie.

Once he heard about her apparent unfamiliarity with some of the basics, he grew angry. But, rather than say something he might regret later he asked the inventor what sort of advice he might provided.

"Well, just am I letting myself, and possibly you, in for troubles if she can't do what she is supposed to?"

"I'd ask Harlan to authorize a little surveillance of the girl. He has those teeny tiny camera bugs he could put into the overhead light in her cube. I also think he might want to monitor what all she looks up online. If it is really *basic* stuff, then Dianne needs to know and take action. If it's something like how to sabotage a jet without anyone being the wiser in five easy steps, then he's going to need to get her out of here."

"And, if he doesn't find anything?"

Bud looked a Tom with his head tilted to the side. "Then, maybe we all need to cut the girl some slack. She might just be really nervous working with and around the great Tom Swift!"

By the time Wednesday came around and Tom was hiking out to the Barn, he had forgotten a lot of his misgivings about the intern and was willing to let her do her best to prove her capabilities.

As he'd hoped, the small jet was sitting just inside the open-walled enclosure. He spotted three people nearby and quickly could tell they were the two young interns and Artie.

"Good morning," he greeted them.

They said hello back before he reached the side of the jet.

"What do you two think?" he asked the ladies.

Becky was enthusiastic. "It's great, Tom! I've seen a few photos of this as it was being extended but you really have to get up next to it to see how seamless the changes are before you came to grips with its aerodynamics. Wow!"

"Thank you, Becky. And, you, Valerie?"

She looked at him a little apprehensively before answering. "It's some sort of engineering marvel. Artie tells us the turbine inside the original version of this is really small and yet incredibly powerful. I was just asking how that works when you came." She turned to their supervisor. "So?"

Artie blushed a little but Tom thought only he'd seen it.

"When Tom designed this—and I wasn't here way back then—he asked for the team to create something running almost four thousand revs faster than anything in the class, and then suggested we could use some exotic materials that can withstand higher pressures and heat. This," he motioned to the jet, "is what it all went into. But, I realized this has no turbine inside so you are both cleared to start measuring and taking notes."

Becky and Valerie took out small laser measurement devices and notepads and were soon doing just that. Becky began in the front at the air intakes while the other girl started from the back.

Artie motioned Tom to come to one side.

"Dianne asked me to keep a special watch on Valerie. Even I can see she doesn't know a lot. I wonder just how good that school of hers actually is. Don't worry. I won't let my infatuation with Becky get in the way of doing my job, Tom."

After saying thanks, Tom walked into the Barn and picked up a chair, which he brought over into the shade. He sat down.

For his part, Artie was walking between both his interns watching and noting what they were doing, and a few things he believed they'd missed.

An hour later it was over and neither girl had much in the way of questions for Tom, other than Becky.

"I was just wondering if a single ramjet is going to be enough, or if we could suggest a pair of narrower ones, or even two staggered so they nest together in a narrow space?"

He answered her question before departing.

* * * * *

Just two weeks later Dianne called to tell him the dual ramjet approach had been completed and tested. "We'll install it tomorrow and you or one of the other crazy air jockeys can take that jet up."

Bud, who always liked the challenge of a new aircraft or power system, was waiting when Tom came back to the Barn to give the jet a preflight look over.

"Okay, flyboy. Dad tells me I can't come up with you today, but if you say things are good, we can take a dual pilot flight tomorrow."

By the time Bud touched back down two hours had passed. He TeleVoc'd Tom over in the shared office to tell him his review.

"I had to eke out a little more flying time by running pretty low on the reserve, but she flies well if not super fast, and lands light and soft. Want to come up today?"

Tom said he would like that and would be at the Barn in fifteen minutes.

"Great. You can take the front seat," the flyer told him.

"How is the exhaust temperature?" he asked as he approached his friend.

"Slightly high but cooling fast. We ought to be safe to fly in thirty minutes. It'll take that long to get her refueled and checked again."

While taxiing to the runway, Bud asked Tom how this size of aircraft might compare to a one- or two-man test model of a jet with both a ramjet and scramjet inside.

"I'd guess this is about a one-quarter scale of that. With two different engine types and two fuel systems, the final one will have to be larger."

They turned and headed toward the coast of Maine. It was a beautiful day and the scenery as it rushed forty thousand feet below them was delightful.

"Oh-oh!" Bud said looking ahead of them and perhaps fifteen degrees to their right. "Look!"

Tom did and was soon smiling. The closer they came the more certain he was of what the very large, ring-shaped flying object was. He slowed them down and set the radio for a frequency he knew.

"HoverCity? This is Tom Swift. Come in, please."

There was a ten-second pause before an older man's voice came back. "Tom? This is Bill, uhh, Smith. Mayor of the HoverCity. I see you on our video surveillance out on about a two-five-five. Can I assume that is actually you?"

Tom and Bud both knew the man's last name was not Smith, it was Boyd and he was the son of the great western actor, William Boyd also known as Hopalong Cassidy. However, when he turned his financial wealth toward the development of the huge floating city, he'd asked the Swifts to keep his identity a secret.

"I am not looking for public recognition," he had said at their first meeting. "I just was to do something for the benefit of mankind, and I foresee the day when livable space on the ground will be quite dear. I also do not see massive spaceships heading to distant stars as our salvation."

Now, Tom keyed his microphone. "Yes it is, Mr. Smith. Nice to speak to you. Are you just in the control room for fun or are you taking a shift at the controls?"

Boyd laughed. "We've had a couple of our pilots fall prey to the old adage about not drinking the water. We just came up from the Caribbean and did a short stopover on an island where a lot of people got off for seven or eight hours while we did some scheduled maintenance in the gardens. Anyway, five of our flyers headed for a small café where they ate some interesting local foods and two of them had fresh lemonade without thinking of the consequences of the local water."

"Oh. Not wise. Are they okay?"

A small chuckle came over their headsets. "Yes. Unable to remain at the controls for more than fifteen minutes at a time, but they'll get over it by tomorrow. For now, I am the unscheduled floater pilot so here I am. And," as the jet flew past the ring about a mile distant, "there you go. I don't suppose that little speedster has vertical landing capabilities."

Tom swung them in a wide arc as he replied, "No. But we spotted you and had to fly past. The place is looking very nice. I'm even seeing what appear to be patches of color. Did you plant something new?"

"Bulbs, Tom. Lots and lots of tulips and iris and other bulb flowers. They don't go down very far, hold onto that soil mix you developed, and do not use much water. As you have already noticed, they provide us a wide array of colors."

They spoke long enough for the test jet to make a full swing around the HoverCity before Tom excused them telling his friend they were on a test flight.

"Well, don't let me delay you. I just wanted to mention we had a visitor about three days ago that gave a few of us the willies. Strange aircraft with peeling and faded paint. Looked a little like a small regional jet from back in the early part of the century. Anyway, it hung around about half an hour and then headed west."

Tom had an uncomfortable sensation as he thought about whether than jet might have any connection with the 727 that had crashed at Enterprises.

CHAPTER 7 /
THE DEMONSTRATOR

BUD WALKED into the construction building to the east of the main buildings at Enterprises one morning. There, he found Tom standing near to a partially-complete aircraft that was so futuristic the flyer wondered if it was meant to actually fly.

Of course he knew that Tom would never build something he had not already tested in the computers. The fact was, he had witnessed several of the wind tunnel tests the inventor had run with various versions of this aircraft.

The only real issue with such tests was that no wind tunnel was capable of providing the incredible speeds, even much above moderately supersonic airflow of about eight hundred miles per hour, and so there was no way to truly test the capabilities other than to understand any aerodynamic weaknesses at the slower speeds.

Tom's *HyperDemonstrator* was an engineering marvel. It was longer than his older hyperplane at thirty-seven feet, but the wingspan was about the same. Just thirty percent of the way back from the elongated nose was the single-occupant cockpit. Because of the great speeds anticipated, the canopy was small, severely curved and only eight inches tall. Behind the pilot were three canard-type wings, one on each side and a third pointing straight up. They were each about three feet in length.

One thing making it unique was the lack of any traditional vertical stabilizer. Instead, and at the end of the forty-five-degree swept wings—more like small deltas—were the equivalent of the vertical stabilizer, a pair of above and below tips the size you might see on a medium range jetliner, which were also just three feet above and below each end of the wings. They were also only an inch thick making them knife through the air.

To complete the set was a single lower fin set to the rear of the boxy structure holding the scramjet engines.

The fuselage behind the cockpit was rather boxy with four low ridges looking more like the top thirty percent of plastic pipes than anything else that all interconnected with sharp angular V-shaped troughs and yet there were smooth transition angles, even on the underside. This was where the four intakes fed into the two engines.

Testing in the wind tunnel had shown the lower profile of these intakes was mandatory to keep vibrations caused by airflow backup from happening. And, since each was only eight inches in height, it meant a pair for each engine was required to scoop up enough air to feed the scramjet engines and to maintain structural strength of the openings.

But, it was going to take something special to get the demo plane up to a high enough speed to start the scramjets. That would be managed via a pair of two-part pods mounted just outside the scramjet housing and under the wings.

The inner portion of these fifteen-inch-tall pods held a pair of turbojet engines capable of getting the aircraft from the ground and into the air, and then up to about thirty thousand feet and over six hundred miles per hour.

They would shut down and the outer portions of the pods, solid rocket motors, would get the jet to the necessary speed for scramjet ignition. This would happen, at least in this test craft, in under eleven seconds. The pilot had to be ready for the 3-G force that would accompany this action.

After that, the pods had to drop away to make the jet as streamline as possible. Then, and only then would the ignition begin and the scramjet engines would send the craft forward at a speed quickly approaching that of four times the speed of sound. The turbojet and rocket pod would float to the ground using two small parachutes and be recovered for reuse.

Tom had worked hard on a proprietary fuel for the jet for three weeks and was only now getting a good handle on the matter. In previous tests, using much smaller aircraft decades in the past, additives of such things as Boron suspended into a more highly-refined form of kerosene—which had proven to give a great boost to the power coming from traditional turbines but at the cost of the exhaust becoming toxic—were tried; the inventor wanted something better.

He had something to his advantage these days in that he could use Boron and even magnesium to create a semi-solid fuel that only liquefied as it was circulated around the combustion area before being injected, and it was also mixed with a non-kerosene propellant. That kept the terrible fumes from being generated while still continuing to give great thrust.

His issues were many, and among them were the handling of the separate ingredients that were still individually dangerous or toxic until his process made them safe, and that the storage of the fuel inside the tanks of the jet had to be carefully balanced between being the semi-solid jelly and being lightly heated enough to flow before it headed into the engine fuel loop.

But, it was inside the engine where great amounts of heat were required to ignite the fuel he had his most difficult task to overcome.

Nothing available in traditional propulsion engines could do the trick.

Nothing other than a fully operational engine could get the ignition process started other than an intense heat source. Tom has chosen to burn a small pellet of magnesium inside the engines to start things. Even with that, it took several seconds for the fire and heat to race around the inside of the engines.

Once it began, it could be maintained by its own heat, but the start was tricky.

It would be, he knew, a nice respite from the acceleration of the solid boosters before the force of the scramjet kicked in.

It left him wondering just how to lessen that stress for any fare-paying passengers.

It was something he needed to work on, just not right now.

The flyer finally broke the silence.

"So, it would appear to be mostly complete, but I'm guessing that is just the outsides. What's left to be built or installed?"

"A lot of things, Bud. For one, I haven't finalized the actual scramjet engines. Once I do that it will take Dianne and her team up to four weeks for the build. It's going to take a lot of specially-shaped tomasite and Durastress to line the insides. And, those take time."

Bud frowned. In a conversation they'd had a week ago when Tom was detailing how the scramjets would function, something was said he now had questions about.

"Okay. So, I understand the high heat and all the powerful stresses, but I thought you told me the fuel needs to be pre-heated. So, how do you use the engines to heat that and also keep the heat inside?"

"Good question. Really good one. Normally, tomasite is very good at keeping every sort of radiation from getting out, including some of the heat... heat I need. So, Hank has created a process that places a number of thin areas in the lining into which stainless steel tubes will be embedded before they get a layer of tomacoat over them. Then the Durastress goes on and the whole sandwich of things gets compressed and set."

The flyer nodded thoughtfully. "So, and see if I am getting this, that thin wall lets just enough heat to get to the metal tubes, they heat the fuel to flow temperature and keep it there, and in it goes and *whoom!* Off we rocket?"

"Nearly. The stainless tubes have a glycol solution in them that circulates into the pre-heater for the fuel. There will be enough heat transferred to do the trick. Assuming, that is, we have nothing to block any of the tubes. Which is why the Chem folks will be creating a super clean form of the glycol solution. No water for a thinner. Everything is eighty percent pure glycol with twenty percent ethanol to keep it flowing."

Both men understood that if that solution leaked into either the engines or even the exhaust, it would burn almost explosively in the lower atmosphere and yet be hardly a bother at anything above about fifty thousand feet.

As they stood there, three of the people assembling the jet came over carrying an empty jet turbine drive and rocket booster pod. It was lifted up—easy for them to do as it was empty and therefore light—and fitted against the fuselage. As two of them held it high, the third climbed up a short ladder and inserted two pins in the front, then repeated the action at the rear.

They stepped back to admire their work before noticing Tom and Bud.

"Oh. Hey there, skipper!" the only woman on the team greeted him. "And you too, Bud. Come to watch us perspire?"

"We came to look her over. I see the pod fits snugly. Is that going to be enough once this is shooting through the sky?"

She shook her head. "Probably not. We're just taking a little break before we get the micrometer probes out and see where it needs to be either shimmed, or more likely retooled to be more snug. Of course, we will likely have to create a heat-proof gasket of some sort and mount these things using a lift, not by hand."

As she returned to her work companions, Bud asked Tom, "How are we going to test that, and by us you know I mean me."

Tom well knew his father's edict that when possible a test pilot and not the inventor would be the first person to fly anything going into the air. It was their job and not his to risk a life on something untried. Not since he'd turned about twenty!

"Yes, I do know. The basic answer is this is going to get its first trials as a glider."

He described how it would be hoisted into the bottom of the *Super Queen* in place of one of her carry bays. It could then be lowered into the airstream below the giant cargo jet and finally be reeled out to follow along like a glider under tow.

"Once we have some data from a few tows at just under the speed of sound all the way up to about Mach-2, we'll go for a tow and release to check glide characteristics. I believe the first tow trial will be unmanned with the others, including the drop, to be yours, if you want it, that is."

He could sense Bud was about to shout for joy, but his friend held his tongue only stating, "You bet!"

The skilled flyer got his first taste of the jet a week later when Tom asked for his feedback on the cockpit.

Bud, whose hangar office was just a mile from the assembly building, beat the inventor there by five minutes. He was practically jogging in place with excitement.

"Have to use the restroom, Bud?" Tom asked with a grin.

Bud stopped moving about. "No. Just anxious and trying to burn off some adrenaline before I climb in. I'd hate to knock the canopy off if I jiggle too much inside."

"Then, lo be it for me to delay you any longer. Let's roll the portable stair overs here and I'll show you what we have."

Two of the technicians had been standing by waiting for Tom's go ahead. In seconds the stairs and the platform at the top were next to the *Demonstrator*. Bud scampered up and was waiting for Tom.

The inventor used a fob he fished from his pocket to open the canopy. It popped up before rising on two small hydraulic struts.

Holding up a hand to keep the more impetuous Bud from just climbing in, Tom leaned in and unlatched the restraint harness.

"If you'd jumped in you would have to jump back out to get those straps out from under you—and they are really uncomfortable for sitting on—and around your body. So, go ahead. Just like a small race car put the right foot in and get it onto the floor before swinging the other leg in. Then start to slide forward and down until your rear end comes in contact with the seat. You need to quickly lift your feet and plop all the way in. Sorry for the tightness, but this is all the space we had left over."

"Okay," Bud said as he followed Tom's instructions and was inside and getting ready to hook the harness over his chest less than twenty seconds later. "How'd I do?"

"Great. You almost look like you've practiced this. But, since only Jake Aturian and I have the proper unlocking fobs, I doubt it. I think you are just too good a pilot. Anyway, what do you think so far?"

Bud said he enjoyed the getting in. "Plus, I feel sort of snug and protected in here. Uhhh," and he looked at his friend, "what's the process for getting out, just in case that is ever necessary?"

"The entire cockpit pops down and out and parachutes down to a safe landing. As we both hope, it should never be necessary."

After a fifteen-minute tour of the instruments and controls, some quite different than ordinary jets or even the various Swift spaceships, Bud stated he believed he understood. "What's next?"

Over the following hour they went over the start process for each of the three methods of propulsion including manual overrides to the computerized systems.

It took Bud almost three times as long to pry himself up and out of the cockpit at the end of his training session.

"How do you feel," Tom asked as the flyer walked around to try to maneuver and stretch his muscles back into working condition.

"I'm feeling like an old man who has been stuck in a wood chair for a few hours. My legs are not actually asleep, but they are feeling pretty tortured right now. How long was I in there?"

Tom checked his watch. "All told, about two hours. That's at least three times what the initial test flights will be. However, by the time we get to much longer flights, we'll need to have a larger aircraft. Two pilots as well." He smiled and pointed first to Bud then himself.

"When is the first test?"

"Five days."

When Bud arrived out near the loading pit for the giant *Super Queen*, Tom was managing the final lift up into the forward pod area.

"How's the fit?"

Tom turned away from the aircraft and smiled. "Fits just as if I'd planned for it when I designed the jet. There's about a foot clearance on each side since the *Demonstrator* fits into a set of padded channels that ease the test jet down evenly and into the airflow. The one thing we don't know is how that first fifteen feet or so outside will go."

Bud thought about it before nodding. "Yeah. A lot of slipstream turbulence to get outside of. Right?"

Tom agreed.

They entered the side hatch and headed up and forward to the cockpit. Already there, running the preflight checks, were Red Jones and Zimby Cox, two of the other test pilots working for the Swifts.

"I'm showing our little test vehicle is a minute from lockdown, Tom," Zimby told him. "We can head out any time after that. Your call, of course."

"Then," the inventor replied, "as soon as we have green lights and the loading crew has moved off, go ahead for taxi to the takeoff pad."

Years earlier the first *Queen*, the *Sky Queen*, used super-hot atomic lifters that would melt ordinary asphalt and do damage to concrete. So, a takeoff and landing area had been outfitted with heatproof tiles of great strength. Today, both giant jets used repelatrons but the pad was there and had become the normal point of departure and landing when vertical movement was called for.

Today, their load was light enough they could use "the elevator" as most pilots called it.

"Ready to fly," Red reported ninety-seconds later. He pressed several spots on the control panel, slid his first and middle fingers up a small touch pad sitting between the pilot positions, and the *Super Queen* gently lifted from the ground.

Their test destination was a known corridor to the west and slightly south of Shopton. All Enterprises needed to do was notify the FAA a day in advance and then they had full access from about ten thousand feet up to one hundred thousand. Below that, private aircraft still had right of way.

As the *Super Queen* entered the test area Tom manned the control panel to lower and fly their cargo.

The dynamics of lowering something below a flying aircraft were known so Tom had decided early on to lower the *Demonstrator* while flying at a relatively slow speed of just one hundred miles per hour. That way there would be minimal disturbances until the aircraft was far enough below to be almost completely unaffected.

"She's looking good so far," he reported to the other three in the control room. All numbers from the sensors in both the *Queen* as well as the *HyperDemonstrator* looked exactly as he wanted them to.

Soon the large jet had increased its speed to five hundred. Still, the little test jet under and now about three hundred yards behind the large jet was flying rock steady.

It continued to fly with easy, albeit unpowered ease, for the duration of the one-hour flight. Soon, it came time to slow down and draw the demo jet into the storage compartment.

It took a little longer than anticipated and required they come to a hover in order to align everything and to not damage their flight model.

Back on the ground and in the shared office Tom reported their near perfect success. He did not hold back on their retrieval difficulties causing his father to laugh.

"I'd have thought it all but impossible without some pilot in there, but I applaud the unmanned test. Do you have a schedule for future tests?"

"I do," and Tom told him about the next three tethered flights, only the final one to be manned.

"Think that one will need to have you drop the jet and let the pilot bring it back down?"

With a shake of his head the younger man admitted he would rather not do that. "Without any propulsion means in there I'd hate to turn this into a glide and land or crash proposition."

It came to pass Tom was right. The total of four tethered flights, only the last one with Bud inside, came off fine, but there were a few handling issues he believed might have negatively impacted the ability to land.

It required seven weeks for Tom to come up with the nine fixes to what he saw as deficiencies, but one final tethered flight showed him the *Demonstrator* was not yet a solid flying machine. It was still a glider, but it was a controllable glider.

He gave the team a two-day notice he wanted to give Bud the chance to fly the jet. It had proved to be stable from one hundred miles per hour up to Mach-2 speeds, about as much at the *Queen* could do with a quarter mile of tow cable training behind it.

The drop was made from twenty thousand feet and at a speed of just four hundred miles per hour.

Bud reported continuously during the six minutes he and his jet dropped altitude and maneuvered until it was just a thousand feet up and a fifth of a mile from the longest of Enterprises' runways.

As the jet came over the western wall and the southernmost west to east runway, Bud reported, "I'd love to take this around again, but I don't think the skipper would appreciate me landing it in Lake Carlopa."

He touched down like a feather and let the jet roll to a halt thirty-one hundred feet farther down.

As Tom stepped up some portable stairs, Bud popped the canopy.

"If you'll give me a hand, I might be able to get out around this smile I have on my face!" he told the pleased inventor.

CHAPTER 8 /

UP IN THE AIR, *MR.* BIRDMAN

"SO, IS our junior birdman ready for this big test?" Hank asked with a smile twenty-nine days later.

"I prefer calling him Young Master Birdman, if it's all the same to you, Hank!" came Tom's suggestion.

Bud grinned, "That's *Mr.* Birdman, Tom. I am getting too old to be called junior or young master anything. Except by Sandy and I don't dare argue with her over pet names."

Hank bowed deeply before saying, "Then, Mister B, how about climbing in and giving me a status check of all systems before your head gets too big to close the canopy?"

Bud grinned and nodded. His head stayed forward and he said, "Uhh, Hank? Can you help me get this large and heavy head of mine back upright?"

Hank laughed and soon Bud joined him before climbing up the roll-around steps and settling into the one and only seat inside.

It had taken a month but the *HyperDemonstrator* now was outfitted with both a droppable pod with a conventional turbojet engine plus it had the first of Tom's ultrafast engines.

This one was not the hoped for scramjet; it was a pair of powerful ramjet engines that he knew could fly the jet to about Mach-1.5. Another advantage was they could be started at a lower altitude and at a slower speed. He'd considered just adding a high-pressure air compressor to get things going, and knew he *could* do this on the ground, but the jet would burn more than half its fuel just getting to the planned test altitude of 25,000 feet.

For this test Tom had decided against using the *Super Queen*. It took just too much time to lower the jet, get it out to a point where the forward speed of the larger ship was not affecting it and then letting it go.

He'd decided to do what the Air Force had done for many of the earlier X planes; he outfitted one of the smaller Swift cargo jets with an attachment point under its starboard wing where the *Demonstrator* would hang with Bud inside until it achieved the necessary altitude. At that time, the turbojet engine would be energized, Bud and the people inside the larger jet would perform their preflight work, and moments later it would drop away.

Before that, more than fifty checks and tests had to be finished.

And, those were just the ones on the ground. Once airborne it would be nearly an hour of further checks before Bud could take over.

"Are you going to have a problem with sitting in the cramped cockpit, Bud?" Hank asked. He'd attempted to get in the small pilot's area once and gave up that futile exercise within minutes. He might get his legs and hips inside but his chest and broad shoulders kept him dangling a full foot above the seat.

"Naw. Tom's had me practicing and I am up to three hours before I get restless. He says it is because of how we were cramped into the *Galaxy Traveller* way back when. Besides, Doc prescribed a tiny pill for restless leg syndrome that really works. No side affects other than the muscles do not get all twitchy."

The small, pointed and rather cramped *Galaxy Traveller* spaceship had been built to get them through a wormhole and into a nearby solar system, not quite living up to its name. They had been stuck—more like trapped—inside that system and their ship for what they knew to be weeks, until their air and supplies gave out.

"I guess that was pretty good practice. Anyway, I'm going to be flying with Red Jones in this one. You'll be in constant communication with Zimby inside the jet and Tom in one of the two chase planes." He nodded to the left where one of the smallest one-man speedster jets produced at the Construction Company sat next to a two-man jet capable of greater than Mach speed.

On the ground were two temporary installations featuring SuperSight systems that would be operated by computers and locked onto the *Demonstrator* throughout the flight. One was on the roof of the control tower in the middle of Enterprises' grounds, and the other was in a special domed pod atop the upper tower situated on a hill to the north of the complex.

Between them they would be able to cover more than four thousand square miles.

The pilot excused himself to head for the employee gym. He wanted to run off some excess energy on one of the treadmills before he had to climb in.

Only then would the small jet be hoisted up and attached to the cargo jet.

Sandy Swift-Barclay met her husband as he came into the main equipment room from the changing room. She locked her arms around his neck and yanked him forward into an embrace and kiss that made him a little dizzy.

When she released him and stepped back with a grin, he looked at her with curiosity.

"I'm not complaining but you rarely do that in public places unless Tom and I are heading out into space. What's the occasion?"

"The special occasion," she told him stepping forward and running her right index finder down his chest, "is that I just received word through Jackson Rimmer our application for adoption has passed the first level of checks. In fact..." and she kissed him again, "he says *they* say we are just what they look for in parent candidates!" She giggled and launched herself back into his arms.

When she released him again she giggled again. "I feel a whole lot better now than I did these past couple of months."

Cautiously, Bud asked, "Do we have any timeframe before they try to match us with a baby?"

Her face clouded a little. "Not right now, but he told me really good candidates sometimes hear within a couple months. Some don't hear for more than two years. I hope we are on the short time list. One thing he says is really in our favor is we are not stipulating we only want one race of baby. Or, that we are not picky about whether it's a boy or a girl. Still..." and she bit her lower lip.

"I would not worry," he assured her. "You come from an exemplary family and I come from people in California. I'm certain your pedigree will win out over mine!"

She kissed her husband one more time, told him to have a great flight and headed back to her job in Communications.

Bud turned on the treadmill and managed three minutes before his glee made him realize he could either continue and possibly fall and injure himself or he could step off and just walk quickly back to the takeoff point.

He chose the latter.

It was about fifty minutes later he climbed up the arched set of steps and slid into the cockpit. Tom, standing on the platform outside, leaned in and made certain Bud had his harness as snugly cinched down as was possible without causing any pain.

"You ready?" he asked.

"As the saying goes, I was born ready, Tom. Let's get this thing in the air."

Tom laughed. "You're pretty jazzed to go, aren't you?"

Bud told him exactly why he was excited. "And, I want to get this finished so I can take Sandy out to a nice dinner to celebrate."

His friend bowed deeply. "Then, let me not take up any more of your time, flyboy!"

The jet was hoisted up and attached to its pylon and was readied in twelve minutes. All radio checks were complete in three additional minutes and the three jets taxied in formation to the end of the runway. The cargo jet with its attachment took off first and began a slow turn to the west. Art Wiltessa followed in the one-man jet with Tom practically on his tail. The two smaller jets made their turns faster and were lined up with the large jet inside of two minutes.

The cargo jet's handling characteristics were impacted by the weight and the bulk under its starboard wing so turns and climbing had to be taken more slowly than normal. This was perfectly fine as it allowed everyone to go through their individual checklists and make certain everything was running exactly to plan.

"Skipper? It's Bud. I'm showing an orange, not red and certainly not green, on the fuel preheat for the system. I'm going to do a reset and see what I get, so give me an extra two minutes."

Inside the cramped space Bud reached over and flipped two small switches down into their **OFF** positions. He counted to ten before flipping them back up with the left one moved a full two-seconds before the right one.

The status lights above turned yellow, paused at that condition for twenty seconds before going to orange and finally to green. He stared at them as if daring one or both to change back.

After a minute he was satisfied they were now working, or at least registering the proper state for the fuel system.

"I've got greens, Bud." Zimby called to him.

"Ditto in here, Zim. I'm showing us about five thousand feet below drop altitude. Do you concur?"

"Four thousand nine hundred fifteen, Bud."

They discussed the final steps for the pilot to take before he and the jet were to be released. One by one, Bud completed the steps and called out readiness on each of the circuits and systems.

Tom had been monitoring the radio communications while he checked his systems readouts for the *Demonstrator*. He'd worried for a moment over the fuel pre-heat issue but could now see how steady the two lights were, so he turned to checking his onboard cameras. There was one mounted in the right wing and another on his helmet.

The wing camera was aimed and its zoom managed by a laser controls system; the helmet cam was aimed by Tom tilting or turning his head. Plus, he could cause it to zoom in or out using commands issued via his TeleVoc.

Each person and station checked in announcing readiness.

Tom got on the radio to them all.

"Okay, we are sixty seconds away from release. Normally I would have loved to keep the two turbojets strapped to the underside of Bud's jet, but it just doesn't have the aerodynamics for that. All calculations say he can get the jet up over seven hundred knots before that fuel is exhausted and then they drop away automatically. The ramjets can begin running just a little above that speed, so once you feel the pod release, Bud, tilt the nose down five degrees and give it eight seconds before you hit the start button."

"Got it, Tom. I'm standing ready."

The other stations gave their final calls of readiness as the clock ticked down the final fourteen seconds.

"Drop happening in twelve," Zimby announced before he counted the final ten. "And," he pressed the master release button, "Bud's away!"

The twin, small turbojets whined up to full power and the *Demonstrator* began pulling ahead of the cargo jet. While it would have been possible to fly the cargo jet and the *Demonstrator* at a fast enough speed to do away with the turbos, Tom knew they needed a successful drop from below supersonic speeds to ensure the process went smoothly.

With his speed approaching the light off point, and the turbos now winding down, Bud pressed the **RELEASE** button. As they dropped away, the jet picked up a small amount of speed; it was now as aerodynamic as possible.

After the one-man test plane dropped its primary engine pod and it stabilized at its current six hundred ninety miles per hour, Bud prepared to fire up the ramjet engines. He flicked the trio of switches to start them, but something was keeping them from working and the jet began to drop toward the ground.

He struggled to go through everything on the emergency check off list. He was not in any kind of panic, but knew he only had enough forward speed now the turbojet pod had dropped away to fly about thirty miles.

It was thirty-six miles back to Enterprises. And, while he could make it to a water ditching in Oneida Lake, twenty miles short of Lake Ontario to the north, he really did not want to do that as the *HyperDemonstrator* would certainly be destroyed.

Tom, in the fastest chase plane watched as Bud's speed dropped and the *Demonstrator* began losing altitude.

He keyed his mic.

"Flyboy? Don't answer if you are busy, but I see there may be a bit of trouble. Can you wiggle your wings?"

He watched as Bud took a brief second to tip the left wing down followed by the right one before he leveled out.

"Okay. I'm here. Not sure what I can do, but at least I can give you a visual check. There is nothing visible at the connection points. Give me a second to think this over."

Bud was thinking, *I hope Tom's brain is working better than mine*. Still, he kept trying everything he could to start the ramjet engines.

It took the inventor three minutes of the very precious time to come back. "Bud? I think the ramjets need more air. Try pointing the nose down again and going supersonic."

As he pushed forward on the joystick, Bud called back, "Just about to try that because I'm now under five hundred knots. Do you think seven-fifty will do it? It'll eat up about half my altitude to get to that speed, and I'd like to reserve that last ten thousand feet to find a place to set down and not keep heading for the ground."

Bud sounded unflappable and it made Tom proud of his friend.

"Yes. Simple answer is we might need to drag you through the sky a little faster next time. And, I see you are going faster. Try the ramjets at seven-thirty."

"Got it."

The little demonstration craft was approaching twelve thousand feet when Tom spotted a white puff coming from the back of the jet followed by it leveling out and then pointing up at a fifteen degree angle.

Bud's voice came whooping over the radio.

"Yes! That's it. Now we'll do some flying."

Tom was about to suggest they all head back to Enterprises when he realized Bud needed to make this flight work. It was a morale breaker to have a test flight cancelled by someone not inside the aircraft being tested. It was akin to being ordered to park a speeding car by the side of a freeway and just walking away without knowing why.

In two minutes the *Demonstrator* had exceeded the speed of Tom's jet and was pulling away and heading up. This is what Tom hoped would happen and he was glad to see the jet was now seemingly behaving.

Tom looked around his position in time to spot a discontinued regional-style jet aircraft following him. It appeared to be badly maintained, distressed and neglected, but it was definitely following him.

When the time came for Bud to turn around, the *Demonstrator* had reached Mach-1.6, a little faster than the inventor had thought it might. Bud slowed the jet back to just Mach-1 and made a sweeping turn getting lined back up toward the home field eleven minutes later.

It was a good indication of a limitation of flying something like this little jet.

"Sorry for the time it took to turn, skipper," Bud came back over the radio. "It steers a bit like a cow on ice skates. It leans over and tries to get around but it is too heavy and can't lean far enough over to go quicker. I only took the horizontal G-meter to three Gs. I could take more, but I don't want the wings to come off."

"Not an issue, Bud. I'd suggest nothing higher than two-point-five Gs in the turns for now but she can handle five. Of course I realize you have to keep up a certain speed to keep those rams running. Let me know your fuel state, please."

"Uhh, sixty-seven percent now that I've throttled back a little. I figure full throttle will be the next test."

"Good call. See you on the ground."

As Tom turned his jet to return to Enterprises, the mystery jet shot past his left wing causing his jet to buck a little. Mmoments later he heard two radio calls from other nearby aircraft complaining about how some small passenger jet had nearly run into them.

His and the other two jets had already touched down as Bud came in from the west to land on the longest runway. As he touched down everyone could see the flameout of the ramjets.

A tow truck met Bud at the midpoint on the runway and hooked up to the nose wheel for the trip back to the hangar.

Another truck had the portable steps mounted sideways in its bed and it pulled close enough for Tom to climb up and help Bud unharness and get out.

"Okay. I'm going to buy you and Sandy the best dinner in Shopton," he promised. "Let's get you over to your office and changed while you tell me your impressions. I'll review the data tomorrow. You'd better call your wife and not argue about me buying. Okay?"

Bud, who made the same as the other test pilots at the company, which was a good salary, was nowhere close to rich, so while he might otherwise argue the point with Tom—he was a very proud man—this time he just nodded and agreed.

The following morning Tom was surprised to find Sandy lounging in the shared office waiting for him.

She got up, hugged her brother and planted a chaste kiss on his lips.

"Thank you, Tom, for being a great brother. And, I don't just mean about the dinner. Bud snitched on you when I balked at the high prices."

Tom gave her another hug and then asked what else might have prompted the affection.

"Well," she told him retaking her seat in one of the comfortable leather chairs in the conference area, "If you will recall I turned thirty at my last birthday."

"Right. Makes sense as I had just turned thirty-one. Go on."

"Do you recall the old Bartle family money thing?"

Tom did. A great grand uncle had endowed his family with money to assure the men and the women could have an excellent education. To do this, he set up a girls' private school where each teen female was expected to attend and graduate. Their mother had but Sandy balked at the very idea of leaving Shopton.

The sad news was this took her out of the running for about a million dollars in inheritance once she turned thirty. The men automatically received theirs at the age of eighteen, ostensibly so they could either go on to a university education or set up a business, and support a family.

The women only received theirs at a point in their lives when Mathew Bartle believed many might become widows and it would help them remain out of the poor house.

Try as they might, Anne and Damon had not been able to convince Sandy the four years of her life would be valuable to her in the future.

Tom knew all about this and had signed his one million dollar check over to his sister in a secret savings account. He didn't need the money; he was making more than a million dollars a year in royalties on several inventions. He also knew Sandy would kick herself over missing out even though it had been her decision.

"Well, the paperwork came through the other morning and that money in the bank is now available to Bud and to me. We're not going to blow it on speedboats or a larger house. It's just really nice to know it is there for when we do need it. Like," she smiled, "when we finally adopt a child and need to prepare for sending her or him to college."

After giving her big brother another tight hug, she told him he was "the greatest!" and left for her position in Communications.

When Damon came in moments later he looked at Tom. "Your mother just told me this morning what you did for your sister with the Bartle inheritance. I am so very proud of you, Tom. I just want you to know that this is one of about ten thousand reasons for me to be proud."

Together, the Swift men reviewed the data from Bud's nearly abbreviated flight the day before. Damon asked about the pod with the turbojets.

"Built in parachute so they came down nice and slow. We had a Whirling Duck on station and they hooked them and brought them home just twenty minutes after Bud touched down. Dianne and her team are tearing them apart to make sure they are ready for the next test in two days."

All was not right with the turbines so the following morning Dianne asked Tom to come over to examine what she had discovered.

When he arrived she took him to an enclosed room where the pod was sitting on a padded mount. The top of the pod was off and both of the turbojet engines had the tops of their cases open.

"That," she stated pointing to a tangle of wiring that had quite obviously been cut. More than a dozen wires from two bundles had been severed.

Tom let out a discouraged sigh. "Time to make it work?"

"Luckily, we have replacement harnesses so it is a matter of a couple extra hours, but I can't figure out how that happened. The pod was delivered yesterday at around four, when all of us were in a meeting, and it was sitting in the other room at five when we all went home."

Again, she pointed to the damage. "That happened some time between five and eight-ten this morning when I came in."

Tom shook his head as he reached up to tap his TeleVoc and say the name of his Security chief.

"Harlan Ames."

CHAPTER 9 /
HARLAN IS DISCOURAGED

"SORRY, SIR, but that is confidential information and it may not be distributed to your organization at this time. Good day!" and with that the line went dead.

It wasn't that Harlan expected his call to the FAA was going to get immediate results, but to have been cut short by a mere assistant to an assistant was galling.

The conversation had started with him asking if the FAA was aware, yet, that Tom Swift had been followed and harassed by an old and unmarked regional jet with distinctive peeling paint in the skies over central Pennsylvania...not to mention the 727 crash into Enterprises. Or, that the reported jet nearly hit him.

"Erm, that has not been brought to the Under Secretary's attention to my knowledge. Is it germane? We can't just go reporting every tiny thing happening in the sky, you know!"

After waiting five seconds for the man to say more, Harlan asked, "Don't you think it is something the Under person needs to know? It is, after all, a sky-borne stalking that could have been precursor to an outright attack, in FAA-controlled airspace, on an American target by an aircraft definitely not squawking any identification. One, I will add, that evidently left the area at very high speed causing two separate civilian aircraft near-miss encounters to be registered. That alone is reason enough the FAA ought to be very interested! So, what is your organization going to do?"

That was when the irritating man made his feeble apology and hung up.

The news there was not going to be any immediate attention paid to the unregistered and unfriendly jet shook Harlan and it made him acutely aware there were people out there trying their level best to make him fail at his job, and to harm or even kill Tom or Damon Swift. It was times like today he practically yearned for the days when the worst thing his position fought against was industrial or even international espionage.

But, to have the faceless, nameless person who'd sent the old jetliner to crash at Enterprises—and worse, to have someone or someone's protecting that person's identity at a Federal level—was so aggravating he wanted to explode. Now, this incident had occurred, and his mood was not made any better.

Fortunately for his heart, a heart that had attacked him in the past, his medications and the pair of spring-like stents that had been inserted to open blood flow through one mostly cogged artery were still working for him.

He even had felt well enough to begin some light jogging the year before.

Harlan pushed himself up from his desk and headed out the door into the reception area.

"I am going to head over to talk with the two big cheeses," he told the girl there who grinned up at him

"Have a gouda time!" she punned making him groan and reach up to his forehead.

"Nacho-rally," he told her before leaving with a chuckle that he had given her a pretty darned good comeback. As the door was closing behind him, he heard her state, "I'm really fondue that man!"

The little exchange had lightened his mood a bit so he arrived in the outer office in somewhat better than a foul mood. "Are they in?"

Trent nodded. "Yes. Both of them, but I believe they are still on a video call to Senator Quintana. However, you look as if that might just suit you. Go in."

Harlan still gave the door a slight knock before opening it and sticking his head inside. Damon looked up, smiled grimly, and motioned with his head for Harlan to come in and take a seat.

"I'm sorry, Senator, but Harlan Ames just came in. Could you say that last bit again, please?"

"Certainly. And if it is just Harlan with you two..."

"It is."

"Then let's go back to Peter for now. If you call me Senator again I'll know someone else has come in. So, as I was telling Damon and Tom, we have a real mystery and a maddeningly frustratingly aggravating situation here. That old 727 that crashed in your back yard was not an accident. It is an old aircraft that was located out in the California dessert up until five years ago. Then it was torn apart for scrap!"

"But—"

"Yeah... but! It was one of twenty-seven of that model that had outlived their usefulness even for spare parts. The crew out at the Mojave facility stated at the time they lost track of the actual number of airframes but one man believed they ended up one short."

All four men were silent while they thought about this turn of events. Finally, Tom asked a question they were all thinking.

"How could they lose track? Wouldn't they have had checks and balances and even an inventory before and after the work was completed?"

The men at Enterprises heard the senator in Washington take a deep breath and let it sigh out. "The problem is they started work on a Thursday, had it about three-quarters complete by Friday and then took a three-day weekend off. Now, according to a report from one of the groundskeepers at the time, something *might* have taken off early on Sunday morning. He could not be certain because he was drowsing at the time, was in a building on the opposite side of the facility, plus nobody expected anything to be going on."

"Senator? Or, Peter if you would rather. I spent a very discouraging three minutes on the phone to the assistant to the assistant to the phone answering individual of the Under Lesser Assistant Associate of something at the FAA fifteen minutes ago. He was supremely disinterested in hearing that Tom and Bud had been harassed during a test yesterday while on their flight, and I'll assume that is one of the things prompting this call."

"Yeah," Peter replied wearily. "It was the start of today's bit of *fun*, once Tom called me after his flight yesterday, and I have to tell you all I have been running into blockades all along the way on this. It took some personal interviews with people who know people who worked in the Mojave facility back then to get what I have. Now, I'm worried that it will all disappear down the back of the political sofa if I let things be known until I can locate the top person in all this obfuscation."

"Could this go all the way to the top of the FAA?"

The senator paused. "I don't think so... but I don't know."

He asked that the Swifts, and Harlan, keep the information to themselves for the next several days. He promised he would get back to him as quickly as he knew anything else.

When the line was cut, Harlan gave Tom and Damon a briefing on the exact dialog he'd had with the person at the FAA.

"Did you get his name?" the older Swift asked.

"Barry Pepperson, or so he identified himself before I told him why I was calling." He shrugged. "Doubtless if I were to call another number within that organization I'd learn there is no such person there. I feel impotent over this and not being able to get it through at least one person of average intelligence that this is a crime and needs stopping!"

They agreed to table the discussion until Peter Quintana could get back to them.

Harlan left the office and trudged back to his building.

Even the receptionist could see something terrible was weighing him down and did not attempt to crack a joke as he came back.

Tom informed his father he was headed to his laboratory down the hall.

"I'm really close to having a handle on the necessary fuel for my full-size hypersonic jet."

Damon, as always, asked to be kept apprised of any successes. Or, any outright failures.

But, success eluded the inventor that day and for eleven more weekdays after that.

At last! Tom had come up with the fuel he knew could drive his hypersonic aircraft at speeds up to at least Mach-5. Highly compressed Hydrogen-infused fuel with dissolved boron and sodium. It was necessary the fuel be kept in a semi-solid state until moments before ignition to keep its ingredients stable and non-toxic.

But it was so much more than just the right fuel.

Of course, that mixture had undergone almost hourly tests in order to "dial in" the absolute best combination of ingredients along with the proper handling of them and adding certain ingredients to buffer the toxicity or the explosive nature of a few of the things in it.

It was that explosive nature to the mixture and individual components that made it so powerful.

Then again, if simply used in a standard off-the-shelf design for a scramjet, it would have burned through in minutes rather than the two hours Tom believe was a must for a commercial version of the jet.

The concept of a radically new technology came to him as he and Bud sat having coffee in the underground lab one afternoon.

"Does it have to be an air breather?" the flyer asked. "I only bring that up because I did notice the power curve started to drop the higher I got in the *Demonstrator*. Especially on that fifth test flight when I got to one hundred fifty thousand feet."

This made Tom think and think a lot. He thought about it that day, that evening and even the following five days, right through the weekend. He thought about it even at home, mostly in silence, during meals and as he and Bashalli were trying to get to sleep.

Finally, on the next Monday morning she took him aside and told him she was becoming unhappy.

"This is only because you seem to be in the house, and yet even little Anne can tell her father is not truly there. You must get whatever it is on your mind out of it, Tom."

He grinned weakly at her. "I'm so sorry, but I believe it finally came to me this morning in the shower. I won't annoy you with it now, but if you can plan to go to dinner with me tonight, I'll let you in on things."

Giving him a resigned sigh, she told him she would be ready at six. "Not later."

He arrived at Enterprises and went to the shared office where he told his father his ideas. The more he laid out in his thought processes, the more the older man realized this was a great leap ahead on previous attempts at harnessing the hypersonic aircraft.

"Plus," Tom told him toward the end, "it is able to be throttled up or down which means it can also be used to get the aircraft from takeoff to the kind of supersonic speeds necessary for the scramjet to be started."

All his father could do was shake his head and smile. "I don't know how you do it, son, but that is a brilliant solution if you can pull it off."

Tom was fairly certain he could, but it would take some additional testing to fine tune his ideas.

He was in his large lab and preparing for this when Hank found him the next afternoon.

"Oh. Sorry if you're busy but your dad said you were here," the big engineer said as he began stepping backward to leave the lab.

"Huh? Oh, no, Hank. Come on in. I'm getting set to try something on a very small sale I'm going to require your assistance in scaling up. Possibly in three stages."

His pattern maker would be involved in anything that would be mass produced, for certain, but he also had proved time and again his ability to assist in Tom's test mechanisms. He often told the other people with whom he worked it helped him understand more of the operational dynamics so he could do a better job when the time came to make more than one of something.

He stepped over and looked over Tom's right shoulder.

"Okay. That would appear to be something I've got a notion I've seen before, but can't pull out the memory. What is it?"

The object on the inventor's screen was about fifty percent longer than it was tall, started out about a third as wide and featured ten small tubes with flared ends pointing into the curved side he could see. At the top—or what was sitting at the upper part of the CAD screen at present—were ten not-quite-square and not-quite-round *somethings* that were three times as wide as the flared openings below them.

"That," Tom told him sliding his chair back and pointing at the entire assembly, "is what was once called an Aerospike rocket engine."

The basic design and operational statistics had been developed by one of the preeminent rocket and missile propulsion companies as far back as the 1960s. It was meant to replace the standard bell-shaped rocket nozzle with something the individual outputs of multiple smaller motors could slide down on either side, combine their effective power into something quite strong, and use less fuel.

For Tom's purposes that was very important. This type of engine used a lot less fuel for the amount of thrust it produced, and could—as he'd told his father—be used in places where being able to be turned up higher or lower by a mechanical or even electronic throttle was very, very useful.

"Oh. Right. That was around when NASA and others were trying to build Single Stage To Orbit rockets. I recall they had one but it got cancelled for some reason and the technology sort of was abandoned."

It was true, and if the planned replacement for the original Space Shuttle had been built and flown, it was likely his father would not have been hired by NASA to work on the Shuttle Mark II project and would have been spared having been part of the program that had so many ignored troubles it had ended in the explosions on two of the four shuttles and eleven deaths.

"The company that engineered the first of these developed this wide version along with a few circular versions with varying degrees and lengths of conical spikes poking out the end."

They discussed the basics of the thrust to size ratios along with the amazing fact this could replace not only the solid rocket boosters to raise vehicle speeds to those requires, they could be used at lower power settings to get the jet rolling down and off the runway and into even high altitude.

It was when he told Hank he believed such engines—or a single, wide one featuring between ten and sixteen small motors per side, would be all that was necessary to get even a full-size hypersonic airliner up to more than Mach-3.5—was going to be a game changer.

The engineer agreed that from all he understood of the scramjet technology, that speed would be sufficient to get the super fast engines into operation.

"The wonderful thing is it will do away with the slamming into the seat acceleration I was worried about in using solid boosters. Those will be fine, and have some good qualities for test flights, but once we try to get this certified for passengers, I fear not even the friendliest of FAA inspectors would okay it."

And, he thought ruefully, *right now the FAA is anything but being a kind organization toward we Swifts!*

Hank remained in the lab for the next half hour as Tom prepared to test his small version in the explosion-proof booth to one side of the room.

"Oh, wow! I thought you were still in the drafting process. I had no idea you had that small version ready to go. Where," he asked with great curiosity, "did you get it?"

Tom laughed. "You do realize that you and Arv are not the only people around this company who have or have access to some pretty nifty 3D printers, right?"

Hank pondered what his response should be. "Well, I've heard rumors, but never thought you'd exclude your old friend, Hank!"

They both chuckled over this. In truth, Tom had borrowed one of Arv Hanson's printers, the one he had set to one side of his workshop that worked with both metals and glass.

"I used that one to create the outer shapes from a high-heat alloy and the insides with volcanic glass that won't melt under the heat and pressures these will run. Don't worry. When it comes time to make the flyable test version and then at least one more size, I'll rely on you and your expertise!"

Moments later Tom attached the fuel lines from a pair of pressurized and heavily shielded tanks in one corner of the test booth to his engine input. For this lets he was using a premixed combination of LNG—liquified natural gas—and liquid oxygen. The idea was not so much to get high thrust from this small unit—barely eight inches wide—but to prove he had the basics of the design, build and operation right.

Tom pressed a button next to the control computer and they watched as a portion of the outer wall of the booth swung open. It was the emergency exit point for anything that built up inside so that pressure did not rupture the outer building wall. There was a distinct lack of light coming in as this outer area was covered by a square steel tube that forced everything down and into a pressure relief pit away from the building edge.

For added safety the two men donned heavy, leather aprons running from throat to knees and also shatterproof goggles.

"Ready?"

"Yep!"

Tom pressed another button causing a pre-recorded announcement to be broadcast throughout the building.

"Attention. This is Tom Swift. An experiment is to commence in my second floor lab in thirty seconds. It should be perfectly safe but if there is some sort of explosion please call Emergency Services and do not enter the lab room."

The two men watched the timer counted down. When it reached 5 Tom activated the extractor pumps and also remotely opened the fuel valves.

At the zero mark they spotted a small puff of smoke—mostly unburned fuel—of a fifth of a second followed by light blue flames shooting down both sides, around the concave curves, and into a heat-resistant baffle below.

The inverted cone began to glow a dull orange and remained that way for the twenty seconds of the test.

The inventor shut things off and smiled.

"I was honestly prepared for it to make a little boom sound and sort of explode. This is better than I'd hoped."

He suddenly laughed as he reached up to tap his TeleVoc button. "It's dad."

"Since I heard the announcement and did not hear anything else other than a dull roaring sound coming from outside, I want to conclude the first test was a success?"

"It sure was. Hank is here with me and we'll be going over the numbers before he tells me what he can do to make it even better."

Inside his head his father now laughed.

"Tell me about it tomorrow. I'm off to DC to meet with Pete Quintana and at least three other politicos to try to find out who hates us. Talk to you in the morning."

He looked at Hank.

"I've got nothing to say other than I'd like to see those power numbers. Oh, and get an ideal of the fuel consumption. Am I going to have to account for additional fuel load over what you had planned before?"

"I don't think so. I like my current mix for the scramjet and this will use... oh. Right. This will use both a fuel and an oxidizer. But, we will not have any turbines to carry or have to store fuel for. So, the answer to your question is likely to be yes. Even if I had a notion we could rely on ambient air for takeoff—which we do not—to get up to speed this will require about a fifty-fifty mix."

Hank stood there thinking before he asked, "So, do you change things to carry along this rocket into higher and faster flight, or is it going to be dropped like you planned before?'

"Dropped, but I'm trying to decide whether to add flight surfaces and to fly it back to the airport of origin. Of course, in a final production jet it would be carried up inside the fuselage and not dropped off, but for the smaller, test version it'll need to be jettisoned for both weight and drag reasons."

"Then, I'm looking forward to working with you to see that comes to life. As for now, I am going to go check your design files for that marvelous Aerospike engine and see what I can tinker with." He smiled, saluted the inventor and walked from the lab.

Tom decided to not make another test with the engine but knew he would be trying several other fuel mixtures inside the test booth before taking the engine outside to the far test area of the grounds, and giving it a full throttle test for up to a full hour.

He would need to know any vulnerability in the design and testing up to, and perhaps beyond, the point of destruction was about the best way to find that out.

CHAPTER 10 /
GOOD TEST FLIGHT; BAD LANDING

BUILDING THE different type of rocket engine had been much easier than anyone believed. And, while there were still pumps and fuel lines and combustion chambers to be dealt with, and in greater numbers by far, the fact each one was a smaller unit working together as a whole and could be handled by individual technicians rather than use gigantic gimbaled mounts, hoists and micrometer precision measurements, meant the basic engine was ready just five weeks later.

"We had a huge advantage," Tom described to his father and Bud at lunch one Monday. "We aren't rediscovering the physics behind the wheel or building a faster-than-light drive with our eyes closed."

What was going to take longer than he felt he wanted to wait was to come up with a manner in which to mount and test it at high altitude on the aircraft. It would, he knew, not be the final version and the time and cost of adapting the *Demonstrator* to use it was looking a little prohibitive.

"Why not test it on one of our sounding rockets?" his father suggested. "They are mostly reusable and if it becomes a matter of lifting capacity, we have those strap-on booster solid rockets you can add. Up to five in the current configuration."

That, Tom realized, was a great answer to his needs and so he arranged for one of the forty-six-foot-tall rockets to be pulled from inventory at Fearing Island, outfitted with the five external boosters, and that the second—top—stage be kept mounted, but the payload cone left aside for the time being.

"I will want to use the liquid hydrogen and liquid oxygen tanks so leave them in place in the small flying test vehicle." He did outline the needs for a splitter to feed ten separate small combustion chambers in his test Aerospike and the fuel line setup needed to feed the engine that would be inside a small dart-shaped airframe.

About a week before the scheduled transport of the engine to Fearing, Bud sat on his favorite stool in the large lab in the Administration building watching Tom finalize a small design change.

"Just how much thrust do you hope to get from that small rocket engine, anyway?" He asked. He was looking at the actual engine as it sat inside the test booth to one side of the room. Barely fifteen inches wide and two-thirds that tall, it had a strange appearance that looked, to Bud, as if it would not work. Even if it did send out rocket flames, it certainly did not have the appearance of something capable of lifting much more than its own weight.

"On paper and from previous engines of the type, I'd say we'll get about four thousand pounds of thrust. It ought to keep the rocket heading up another five miles above the first stage separation. Of course, that will be fourteen miles above the booster separation point. All total I would say we are looking at a flight of about nineteen miles. About two hundred thousand feet."

Bud grinned. "Now, I have been told by a reliable Hank… I mean *source*… that this isn't just a new engine strapped to the bottom of the second stage. He tells me it is sort of a foldable aircraft that comes out the back end and then detaches and flies on its own. Any truth to that?"

"Yes, there is. The second stage of the rocket we'll use is, as you likely know, only nine feet tall and generally only has enough fuel to get the rocket and a light payload to forty miles. Or, thirty if the payload is greater than fifteen pounds. Our payload will be fifty-six so I believe we are looking at a total of less than twenty miles. The little aircraft will be fired up two seconds after second stage cutoff and a nitrogen charge set off that helps with the separation. It will carry enough fuel for its own final burn once the second stage fuels are spent so there is enough for it to get another four miles at top speed and then scoot off to the side for its final glide down."

That evening when Tom mentioned the forthcoming test flight Bashalli suggested it might be nice to take the family to Fearing.

"It will be Saturday, Tom, and you know how much Bart loves rockets. He's even convinced Mary they are fun and I'd like to see what she thinks. Then, Amanda could use a break so we could give her the weekend off… or take her but let her enjoy herself and I'll watch the kids."

He looked at her, asking, "And, do you suppose Sandy and Bud want to come and we can make it a day out for everyone before we head to the mainland for dinner?"

"Your sister, who is my sister as well, is spending each and every night studying for what to do once you adopt a baby. She is so nervous even though I have told her it is not as hard as she might think. So, we can ask but I expect she will have some excuse to not go."

Bashalli was correct. Tom called Bud who set the phone down to ask his wife. He came back a moment later. "Sorry, Tom, Sandy says she's going to be tied up. If you need me she says I can come."

In a low tone Tom asked, "Is she standing near you?"

"Nope."

"Okay, then I know why and that's her way of coping with the stress. If you want an excuse, come along. If not, I've got this covered."

By way of an answer, Bud said, "Okay. I'll see you at work tomorrow. G-night."

"Good night, Bud. Best to Sandy," Tom answered hanging up.

There was a furry of activity at both Enterprises and in the Swift household the following day as everyone got ready for the trip and rocket test.

Tom had the new Aerospike engine taken to the test area in one corner of the facility and given a ten-minute test run at everything from barely putting out enough flames to keep the combustion going to full throttle. Each and every stage of the test went as hoped and the inventor declared the small engine ready for its high altitude test flight.

At Fearing another team was installing all the instrumentation necessary to test the Aerospike and to both send data streams to the ground as well as storing it all in a trio of data banks onboard.

Tom woke on Saturday morning at about five and tiptoed out of the room and down to the kitchen. There, to his surprise, Amanda and Bashalli sat having coffee while bacon was cooking in the oven.

"Bu— That is, I thought—" and Tom stopped. He was certain he'd felt his wife's form in the bed behind him as he eased out, but here she was with a bright smile on her face.

"I stuffed my pillow under the covers and against your back to give you comfort and to make you remain in bed. I see it did neither of those." She sounded disappointed.

"I just didn't want to wake you, Bash. I figured I'd come down and make the coffee and bring you a cup."

She held her cup in the air in salute. "Got my own, but I do thank you for the thought."

Once Amanda and Bashalli got the kids up and ready for the day, the family had scrambled eggs, bacon and toast for breakfast before heading for Enterprises and the *Sky Queen*.

They landed at Fearing Island just two hours later. As Bashalli and Amanda got the children organized, Tom worked with a small team of technicians to unload the Aerospike engine and get it over to the launch area and installed in the lifting body style air vehicle that would be perched atop the second stage.

The main body of the rocket was still in its cradle on its side with the second stage waiting twenty feet away. It took very little maneuvering to get it into position and bolted into place at the rear of the small dart-shaped test airframe that would glide back for a soft landing on the island after its flight.

Tom went off to find his family and to get them heading for the launch site and the special, tomasite-enclosed safety stand to watch the forthcoming flight while the techs got the rocket assembled and the fueling finished on the test craft.

Fueling for the first stage would not be undertaken until the rocket was tipped upright into position, and even then it required less than ten minutes to complete.

As everyone settled into their seats, Tom explained how they would want to use the sound-proof headsets so the noise did not bother them, and then he showed Bart and Mary the special monitor to one side where they could see the rocket after it left the pad and got so high they would not see it with just their eyes.

The Launch Coordinator's voice came over the speakers above them.

"*Skipper? We are at four minutes to launch. Do we have the go-ahead to continue?*"

Tom picked up a handset and clicked a button in the handle.

"Yes. We are go for launch. Let us know if there are any glitches, please." He must have liked the response because he thanked whoever was on the line and hung up.

"We're going to hear some more things come over that speaker system," he told his guests, "right up until you hear the famous words, 'T-minus ten, nine, eight, and so on until it gets to zero and then the rocket takes off."

When Mary asked what the T stood for, Bart leaned over and whispered into her ear. "It means take-off, dummy."

Mary looked seriously at her father before asking, "What does the dummy do after it takes off?"

Tom suggested Bart tell her that and said to his son, "And, do not call your sister any names!"

As Tom, his family, and the team inside the control room watched, the Samson VII rocket—the newest in the series of liquid-fueled rockets named for a very good friend of the original Tom Swift, Eradicate Samson—headed skyward. Inside the nose cone that would separate at about twelve miles in altitude, sat the *HyRider*, Tom's test vehicle for the prototype of the forthcoming hyperplane's Aerospike engine.

Once in the air it would head up to an altitude of only fifteen miles before releasing the test plane, continuing to run the new engine and zooming—in Tom's hopes—to greater than Mach 4 during its minute of powered flight.

The final version would try for Mach 6 or even Mach 7, something that would be necessary to realize the potential for an in-air to space plane and back again capable of travelling half way around the Earth in under three hours from takeoff to traditional landing.

"*She's passing four nautical miles altitude and downrange two miles, skipper,*" the man on the tracking board called over.

"Great. How are the interlocks and all the separations for the boosters looking?"

"*All green. Booster cut-off in eleven seconds and separation charges two seconds after that. Standby...*"

Right on time, the five lights on their monitor representing the solid rocket booster pods surrounding the bottom of the rocket flashed red before going out. Also on time, the orange LEDs under those flashed three times before going green.

"*And, we have clean separation! All boosters away; clean separation with recovery chutes deployed. Second stage coasting and... now going to full second stage power for its seventy second run... yes, we have separation of the outer shell. Stand by for the HyRider to separate... It's free! Aerospike coming on line and we have ignition.*"

Tom and family marveled at the beautiful picture the SuperSight feeding the monitor to their right was showing them. Guided by computers, it maintained focus on the *HyRider* with that craft right in the middle of the screen.

The inventor realized he had been holding his breath for the best part of a minute and was getting light-headed. He let it out in a whoosh and heard the same sound coming from next to him as Bashalli exhaled finally.

They sat in silence for fifteen seconds before Bart turned to his father, asking, "Is it supposed to just fly straight like that, Daddy?"

Tom nodded. "Straight and on that course, Bart. It will only fly that fast for a few more seconds before it shuts the rocket motor off. After that it will curve around and come back to this island to, and it is all just a hope right now, but it should land on the same runway we did this morning.

The SuperSight was doing a remarkable job of showing them the little aircraft as if it were only a few hundred feet away from them. All eyes were glued to the monitor except for Mary's. She was scanning the sky trying to see the *HyRider* for herself. A moment later she shrugged and gave up, joining them all in watching things on the screen.

"No more exhaust," Bart declared as a tiny puff of white came from the rear of the little craft. "Where does the other rocket stuff land?" he asked without looking around.

"It comes down by parachute that can steer it back this direction before releasing it at about one thousand feet, then it lands softly on that concrete pad to our far right. That way we get to reuse that first stage."

Bart looked up to where the rocket had disappeared. "There it is!" he practically squealed with delight. Indeed, the bright red and white para-foil chute was easy to spot as it was completing its turn to come back.

The boy was having a difficult time choosing whether to watch the main stage or the small test craft. Tom came to his rescue.

"The *HyRider* won't land for a full minute after the first stage does, so keep you eyes on that rocket."

Down it continued to come until the women and children gasped. The parachute came loose from the rocket body and it started to pick up speed. Within seconds it seemed like it as going to crash, but then the rocket motor fired up and it lowered down to the ground as softly as a feather.

As that engine was shutting off and the smoke started clearing, all eyes turned back to the monitor.

HyRider was finishing its final turn and would soon come down onto the longer of the two runways running primarily north to south.

Something about the attitude of the test craft made Tom apprehensive. It just did not look right. Soon he realized what it was. One wing tip had torn from the craft, likely from the high acceleration. At top speed it had not made much difference, but as that speed diminished to below three hundred miles per hour, it destabilized the craft.

Then, it happened.

The *HyRider* spun swiftly to its left, flipped tail over nose and broke apart just a quarter mile short of the end of the runway.

It splashed down into the ocean no more than a hundred feet from the north shore.

"Oh, Tom!" Bashalli had tears in her eyes for her husband's now destroyed aircraft.

Tom, smiled, a bit sadly, but it was a smile. "Hang on, everybody." He picked up the phone handset and was soon speaking with the Launch Coordinator. When he hung up he had a better smile on his face.

"We have all the data from the flight and other than the wing damage we had just proven the Aerospike engine we tested worked like a champ!"

At that news Bart cheered, Mary clapped and little Anne looked up at her mother in wonder. She was just beginning to realize this was a special occasion and she let out a giggle and then a burp.

Amanda, who had not spoken since the four-minutes to launch notice had been given, laughed. "I guess that means Anne thinks this was great fun. Congratulations, Tom. I am sorry for the breakup, but if you got the data you wanted, that is great!"

While they began to pack up to leave, Tom explained that the *HyRider* had been considered expendable, but a team was already leaving the harbor in a speedy recovery boat to see if they might pick it up.

"If nothing is on the surface," he explained, "they will have a couple divers who can go down and bring things up. It is only about fifty feet deep where it splashed."

Before they returned to the *Sky Queen* for their homeward trek, word came to Tom via his TeleVoc pin the recovery had been made.

"They got back just about everything, skipper. Want to hold for it so you can take it back to Shopton?"

Tom decided to let the Fearing techs do the post mortem on the craft. "Just, have them send the Aerospike to my lab in a day or two. Thanks."

* * * * *

He reported the near-complete success to his father once he and the family got home that afternoon. The older inventor was philosophical about the loss.

"If you get back even a fraction, that is more than the U.S. military did from its first four hypersonic launches. I am looking forward to hearing a rundown on the data."

When they met on Monday, Tom filled in both his father and Harlan Ames.

"The reason Harlan is here, Son, is that word from Fearing tells us there was some small amount of sabotage to the engine. Not enough, as you witnessed, to cause it to fail, but some."

Harlan spoke up. "Someone snipped through five of the retaining nut safety wires, Tom. Looks as if they hoped the nuts would vibrate loose, letting those nozzles wobble or break away, and that would destroy the whole aircraft. The good new is you and the team built that engine so well it didn't need those wires. But, it makes me now have another thing to investigate. So, with that I shall leave you two and head back to the office to review the security camera footage."

Once he had gone, Tom filled his father in on the test results.

"Excellent. Positively stupendous. And, you say it ran nearly nine percent more powerful than it had on the test stand?"

"That's right. I believe our testing of it ramping up and down didn't give us the full results we got from running it all out from the beginning of this flight. The only disappointment is the new engine burned through its fuel load four seconds earlier than I anticipated. That's about five percent."

"Meaning what sort of loss of burn time in a full-sized version?"

Tom had to think about it. The results might have been from the slight loss of aerodynamic integrity when the wingtip broke away. He told Damon of his thought.

"I can see that as one distinct possibility," the older man said. "If I might make a suggestion regarding costs, is it possible to redo the engine tests on our stand without resorting to another rocket launch?"

"Sure. Now I know not to fiddle with the throttle, I can give the test engine a good cleaning and set up for a local test by this time next Tuesday. At least I got some good data the engine runs well at both sea level and at altitude. What we got I do not believe we might have achieved here. Thanks, Dad!"

Damon had to chuckle inwardly. The only reason he believed—and believed strongly—that Tom would find the fuel consumption would be better had to do with his own father, George, who had constantly been on Damon's back over his way of driving the family car as a teen.

"Just keep your darned foot steady on that gas pedal!" he'd admonished the boy. "You keep pumping it like that and you'll run through a tank of gas faster than corn goes through a goose!"

It had never been clear whether corn went through a goose any faster than any other type of feed, but he understood the actual meaning.

So did Tom.

The engine was in amazingly good condition given its drop into the ocean and brief stay in the briny water. Luckily, the Fearing Island crew had quickly rinsed it with clean distilled water and dried it thoroughly even before it was unloaded back at the docks.

Only two of the combustion chambers showed any appreciable damage and of them, just one had to be replaced. The other had simply been twisted in its mount, likely to be the result of that retaining bolt having loosened... and *that* was likely to have been caused by the sabotage.

The inventor sat morosely staring at the engine. All he could think about was there was a saboteur—and he desperately hoped it was a single individual—possibly at Swift Enterprises, and that person was out to hurt someone and that someone was most probably Tom Swift!

CHAPTER 11 /
EVEN MORE TESTING IS WARRANTED

A FEW small instances of what must be sabotage happened in the next three weeks, but Harlan was frustrated that he could not find any hint of who might be doing it.

These problems were considered minor to Tom so he chose to mostly ignore them. He did, however, closely examine everything he was about to test for any signs of tampering.

Twice he found very small things that, if he chose to think of them as problems rather than man-made damage, could be ignored. Fixed, for sure, but they only impacted his design and testing of the next version of both the Aerospike engine as well as the larger aircraft.

What he could not ignore happened to Bud when the pilot took up the *HyperDemonstrator* for another powered flight using an even larger Aerospike.

Just like the previous drops from the cargo jet, Bud climbed into the cockpit, strapped himself and began all his preflight checks while they were sitting on the tarmac at Enterprises. Also, like previous tests the lights that needed to turn green did and he soon declared to Zimby—again in the lower fuselage of the large jet—he was satisfied and ready.

It was an eerie feeling to see the taxiway and then the runway move under him. His brain told him it was too far below for this aircraft and so he closed his eyes until they were several hundred feet into the air. After that he had a lot to concentrate on so he was completely lost in his other work to notice a small and unmarked airliner that was shadowing them just below the right wing so the pilots would not be able to see it.

Painted in a mottled gray—or with badly peeling paint—it was an older regional jet once built in South America but that factory had been destroyed in a fiery explosion six years earlier and never reopened. Replacement parts became scarce and nearly all airlines abandoned their jets in favor of ones built in North America.

Of the over fifteen hundred aircraft of the type built, only seventeen were known to be still in operation by a small airline in Southeast Asia. They had purchased about fifty of the disused aircraft, had them taken apart and shipped to their headquarters where the parts were used to keep their fleet in good condition.

More than one thousand were known to have been broken up for scrap with the rest sitting in the desert in eastern California.

What nobody in the cargo jet or Bud in the *HyperDemonstrator* knew was that three of those aircraft had disappeared during a one-month period a half-year earlier.

Now, one of them was flying along, just below and behind them, close enough to not be seen or picked up as a differentiated contact on RADAR.

Tom was too busy back at Enterprises to be flying in the one and only chase plane and that pilot, Slim Davis, was just a few hundred feet too far forward of and above the cargo jet to see any hint of it. To make matters worse, the jet had flown up from behind the hills to the west of Shopton at just the right time to not be seen by either of the towers because of the placement of the hills and trees, and managed to get close enough to only give a hint of a ghost image on RADAR.

While the test team was in the air, Tom was in the large lab working on a variation of the rocket fuel the Aerospike engine was burning. In his mind he knew there was still more power to be eked out but it was going to be down to the fuel used and not something to change the actual engine configuration.

He was more certain of the fuel for the scramjet engines than he was for the rocket that would propel the final aircraft up to the speeds and altitude needed.

Up until now he'd tried super-oxygenating the liquid oxygen by adding ozone to it. He'd attempted to use nearly pure hydrogen peroxide as the main fuel along with the liquid hydrogen, and had just completed a small batch of a propellant he had first created for small rockets flown from Fearing Island. It consisted of highly pressurized kerosene into which hydrogen gas had been percolated until you had a very fizzy kerosene that burned with about a forty percent higher heat and greater power.

This test was being performed using a very tiny rocket engine connected to a test rig inside the lab's sealed chamber that featured both the instrumentation to measure the power generated from moment of ignition right to the end as well as five high-speed cameras to watch every part and function of the engine.

At only four inches in length and little over an inch wide, the entire engine had no pumps for the fuel and oxidizer; it used high-pressure nitrogen gas to force the liquids through a pair of small but accurate valves.

Standing with the inventor was Dianne Duquesne who had come over to talk to Tom about another issue.

"Just about ready to go," he explained, "and then we can talk. Okay?"

"Of course."

Tom's prerecorded announcement sounded within the building—something that had become standard protocol so nobody would be startled by a sudden noise—and the inventor did a short countdown.

A small amount of vapor came rushing from the small rocket nozzle before the sparker set it to light. The flames quickly went from a more billowy form to a tight point of blue and yellow flame as everything came into balance.

Tom watched the instrument readouts while Dianne stared at the blue and orange flame cone.

Eleven seconds later it all shut down.

"Fuel is exhausted," Tom announced as he turned things off. "It will take ten minutes to cool down so let's take a look at the numbers and the video."

The numbers, while promising, were not quite as high as Tom hoped they would be. The high-speed video showed a good, tight cone of flames he knew would be good at low altitudes, but it would spread out at high altitudes due to the lower air pressure not shoving in on it.

The one thing they both noticed was at the end, during about the final quarter second, and that was the flame turned a reddish gray and sort of sputtered out. It was just at that point in the measurements the thrust dropped by three-quarters and then to nothing even as the final one-tenth of a second still showed some level of flames.

"What could cause that, Tom?" she asked.

"Well, my guess is that far too much of the nitrogen was mixing with the fuel at that point. It sort of began to snuff out the flames and that meant we lost a small percentage of the overall power we might have managed otherwise. I guess more testing is called for. Maybe I ought to switch out the nitrogen to pressurized hydrogen. Some of it will be absorbed into the fuel over time so perhaps there is something else to do. Maybe not on this small rocket, though."

Up in the air and as they passed near to Buffalo, New York, Bud was preparing to fire things up. It was a tricky part of the flight as the drop had to occur a split second before the engines fired, or in this case the Aerospike. A computer could handle this, but both Tom and Bud decided they needed to see what a pilot's tender touch and sense of timing would do.

Tom wanted Bud's judgement to dictate the firing of the rocket motor to best balance forward velocity with proper separation from the cargo jet.

This manual approach is likely to have saved both Bud and the *HyperDemonstrator*.

Because there was no telltale puff of exhaust just before the test plane was dropped, and no other outward sign other than it actually dropping away, the pilot of the mystery jet did not have any warning and was unprepared for what happened next.

He had maneuvered to a point one hundred feet under the cargo jet as Slim's chase plane had moved into position above and ahead so as to be out of Bud's way when he went zooming off.

"Ready to go," Bud announced via the wired connection going from his headset through the pylon and to Zimby's headset. For his part, Zimby passed the word to Red and Art in the cockpit. Red told him to leave it all up to Bud.

"You are go when you want to, Bud."

"Okay... and... I'm... outa here!" Bud stated as he pressed the release, dropped immediately down from the cargo jet and he started the rocket engine.

Unfortunately for his would be attacker, the *Demonstrator* dropped to a point thirty feet directly in front of the regional jet just as the rocket came up to power. The scorching flames raced back covering the front of the small jet causing the windscreen to immediately shatter and implode into the jet.

"What the hell was that?" Slim called out as he watched below while Bud began his acceleration away.

"What was what?" Red radioed back.

"We had a shadow and I think the *Demonstrator's* rocket engine just knocked it from the sky. It is spiraling down and starting to break up. Yep! There go the wings and the tail. Oh, man. If I'd see that jet I'd have called for a halt while I went under and buzzed him... or her. Sorry, guys. Someone make the decision whether to call Bud and tell him. I don't want him to think of anything other than the flight!"

While Art maintained contact with Bud, checking that all parameters were in line with expectations, Red radioed to Enterprises and the control tower to report what had happened.

Everyone was stunned. The control tower operator immediately called up the recording of their RADAR to check. A moment later he reported, "I only got the occasional single blip on the screen. They must have been tucked up pretty close."

With no backward facing camera and the cockpit canopy not allowing anything more than straight out and up viewing, Bud was unaware of what had occurred. He was monitoring everything and preparing to make his sweeping turn back toward Shopton.

"Everything is running smooth and normal," he radioed to Zimby.

Trying to keep his apprehension out of his voice, the other pilot radioed back, "That's great. I show it is about turn time. Report your fuel level."

"Sixty percent, Zim. Tom'll like that. Starting turn now." As he said this, the small craft tilted to the left and slowed down to under Mach-1. The turn took three minutes but that was well within the acceptable time. He sped back up to Mach-1.7 once he was back on course. It wasn't quite the top speed Tom had said he wanted, but given the current fuels it was about all Bud and the jet could manage.

The arrowhead design cut through the air with barely a hint of sonic boom. In fact, on the ground a measuring station had been set up and reported only a ten-decibel increase in sound levels after Bud passed overhead.

At the point he was twenty miles to the direct west of Enterprises, Bud cut the rocket back to its minimum setting and reduced his speed to about three hundred knots. It was still too high for landing but that would be done on the glide.

The shutdown point came at three miles out and everything stopped making sounds immediately. Now, Bud's precision piloting skills really came into play as the craft started to drop down in both speed and altitude. He had a grin on his face as he passed over the outer wall just sixty feet up; he'd been hoping for anywhere under one hundred feet.

The landing gear came down and the *HyperDemonstrator* settled to the asphalt with only a slight bump. The braking chute popped out and opened further slowing his speed until he was traveling at under fifty miles per hour. The chute dropped away and he applied the brakes bringing the *Demonstrator* to a halt just thirty-seven hundred feet down the long runway.

The usual trucks with the stairs and the one to tow the craft back to the hangar approached as the flyer opened the canopy.

Tom came up to help him out and they headed down the stairs.

"Is Zimby all right?" Bud asked with concern.

"Why do you ask?"

"Well, just after I dropped away he sounded nervous about something. Did I make a goof?"

Tom suggested they head for the large office so Bud could make his report to both Swifts, "Then I'll fill you in."

They entered the office ten minutes later. Damon was sitting at his desk talking on the phone. He saw them, pointed to the conference area and finished his call by thanking whomever he had been speaking to.

He joined them. "So, how was it?"

Bud gave them both about a five-minute rundown on the flight including his pleasure at using less fuel than before while achieving a slightly higher speed.

His joy was punctured when Damon told him about the mystery jet that had been following them.

"It is my belief that pilot was going to try to knock you from the sky, Bud. I don't know how, but we have a recovery team heading out to pick up the pieces along with an NTSB team and a five-man team from the FBI."

"Jetz!" the flyer exclaimed. He sat back in thought. It never had occurred to him he might be in danger from an outside force.

Two hours later, and after Bud had returned to his Hangar 6 office, Tom received a call from Security.

"Hey, skipper, it's Phil. Got some news about that small jet that crashed. As we believed from Slim's description, a regional jet out of that Brazilian manufacturer that went out of business. It didn't so much burn up on impact as it did explode. We think—based on what the on-scene investigators have told us so far—it probably had less than a half load of fuel. Apparently to make it fly and maneuver faster. It also had no seats or bins in the passenger area."

Tom thought a moment. "You say it exploded? Not from fuel?"

Phil now paused. "No. They have located the remains of casings for three air-to-air missiles in the wreckage. The FBI thinks whoever is behind this wanted to knock Bud and the *Demonstrator* out of the sky."

He continued, telling the inventor there was no sign of a fourth missile and that one of them was inside what amounted to a launching tube. It was similar to a torpedo tube in a submarine.

"It probably would have had troubles had they fired anything. Oh, and when I say they I mean two bodies were recovered, both in nearly unrecognizable condition. Sorry to have to tell you that."

"So, they didn't get anything launched and with one in their launcher could it have exploded should they have had the opportunity?"

"No way of telling from what the investigators have found. Not yet. Harlan is on his way and will be on scene in about ten minutes. The one thing I ought to tell you in case a certain nasty woman might come to mind is the two occupants were not of any recognizable foreign nationality. Post mortem results will tell us if they were suffering anything like the terminally sick men the Black Cobra's daughter used to hire. I'll keep you posted."

Tom sat back to digest what he'd just been told. It sent a chill up and down his spine. First, the 727 crash within the grounds of Enterprises, and now this.

Someone, obviously, had it in for the Swifts, or perhaps only Tom. Whatever and whoever and for what reasons were mysteries he hoped Harlan could solve.

That, along with the sabotages.

He launched himself from his chair and strode from the office. On the way out he told Trent he intended to take a long walk to clear his mind and to forward any important calls from his father, Security or Bashalli that might come in.

"I should be back in about two hours."

The secretary looked at him with a small grin playing around the corners of his mouth. "That's a lot of mind clearing, Tom. But, you go ahead and I'll try to keep people from bothering you."

"Thanks. You're great, Trent," Tom complimented the man who kept Enterprises running at peak efficiency.

As he headed out from the side of the Administration building Tom encountered Hank Sterling.

"Going someplace, skipper?"

"Just a walk. Want to come or didn't you have anything for me?"

"I will and I have. Given the great numbers Bud's recent test gave, I have been working on the plans for the final version for your full-sized… uhh, whatever you will be calling it. Or should I say whatever Bud forces on everyone?"

The both laughed.

They began to walk along the meandering pathway that ran between all the buildings in the center of the facility.

"So, what I have come up with is a set of questions. For instance, do you have any idea how heavy the final jet is going to be?"

Tom puffed his cheeks out. "Not precisely, but I do have some numbers from the CAD program on likely weights. Empty it should be between sixty-seven and seventy-eight thousand pounds. That is dry weight by the way."

They both knew that aircraft were often measured in both dry and wet rates with the wet rate meaning it was fully fueled, outfitted with all other fluids—from oil to drinkable water—which was often much heavier.

Hank nodded. "Okay. Thanks. The other thing I need is to know the theoretical top speed this needs to travel under 'Spike power alone." Tom smiled at the simplification of the full rocket style name.

"I want Mach-1.8 to Mach-2.2. Also, I need to have the entire jet get to at least sixty thousand feet before we kick off the scramjet engines."

"Fine. Now for the tough one. How much space do you plan to have for fuel for the 'Spike?"

Tom informed his engineer the idea was to have most of the fuel for the 'Spike engine to be carried in the ejectable pod while the actual engine would be drawn up inside. Every cubic inch of space could be used other that where it would be just too hot from the combustion process.

"Okay. Let me look something up. Hang on a sec." They stopped and Hank pulled out his tablet computer. Two minutes later he looked at Tom. "I'm showing we need to either upsize that pod or plan on only achieving Mach-1.7 and fifty thousand feet. Is there any way I can take about ten percent of the space inside the fuselage for additional rocket fuel and oxidizer?"

Tom explained that now *he* was going to go back and compute several things before he could provide answers.

They continued their walk with Hank asking if Bud had any feedback. He had not heard about the near attack. Tom knew the big man could and would keep a secret so he filled him in on the small jet, its weapons and the destruction of just about everything.

"But, our plane jockey came through everything? Right"

"Yeah. He didn't even know about the incident until after he landed back here."

As they came around one leg of the path that was close to Hank's building he begged off and said he looked forward to anything new

Tom might be able to tell him.

"One thing is certain," the inventor told him before they parted company, "we are going to have to perform several more tests. These next times I want to see if we can get some Air Force or Air National Guard protection."

Tom continued on finding himself coming close to the museum building. With a slight grin he let himself into the secure building and walked to the center of the main floor. Looking up, he spotted his Nuclear Hyperplane now hanging from six cables and dangling close to his old space kite.

It looked pretty good up there. Much better than he remembered until he realized someone would have sprayed a protective coating of liquid wax over the entire thing to protect it from dust and even the dry air.

All in all it was slightly shinier than he remembered, even though this underside vantage point was not one he generally had spent much time enjoying.

While looking up and the jet tilted as if in a turn, he thought quickly of everything that had happened in the ensuing months since he had it pulled out of storage. One thing popped into his mind and he said loud enough so anyone in the room might hear:

"Do you see all the problems you've caused? If I'd just forgotten all about you I would not be having the troubles I'm having right now. Thanks!" He gave the little hanging jet a rather sarcastic salute.

In his mind, even though he had admonished the inanimate aircraft, Tom knew this project was just what he needed at this point. It might even be the turning point in his life that kept him grounded with a very happy wife and children.

As he left the museum he also had a brief realization that if the saboteur or this flying enemy had their way, it might be his very last project.

Ever!

CHAPTER 12 /
THE ENEMY ENCOUNTER

TOM ATTEMPTED to put the recent events from his mind as he concentrated on both improvements as well as new items necessary to devise his final hypersonic air transport.

He was only partially successful on either front.

The two things bothering him most were the crash of the old 727 right on Enterprises' grounds and the close encounter Bud had with the old regional jet. As for the first one, there was no indication unless you got right out to the site anything untoward had occurred near the east-west runways.

The Facilities team had cleared all the wreckage within a few days and the work to clean up and patch the area begun immediately thereafter. Because this was an unmanned crash, the NTSB and the FAA had ceded the investigation to Enterprises even though they both requested to have a small team on site for the first two days.

Within two weeks the area had been filled in, graded and replanted with fresh sod so now it was difficult to see where the aircraft had impacted.

On the other side of the coin, Harlan and his Security team were allowed a courtesy presence by the NTSB for the crash site of the jet that had been tailing Bud and the Swift cargo jet.

From that crash—and even with the explosion of at least one of the missiles and the ripping apart of the other two—some clues began to emerge as to the origin on the aircraft.

"That regional jet was once owned by a company out of Bogota, Columbia, Tom," Harlan briefed the inventor.

Because he now looked slightly uncomfortable, Tom asked, "Operated by what company?"

Harlan shook his head. "That's just it. It was a phony company called BoGAir owned by one of the big heroin operators down there and seems to have only flown charter flights and cargo ones at that. I guess we both understand what that cargo must have been."

Tom nodded.

"Anyway," the Security man continued, "they had three of those jets that were impounded by the United States over a four month period when they used them to try to smuggle huge loads of drugs up into Arizona. Supposedly more than three hundred million dollars worth. Those jets, by the way, went to the storage facility in the California desert and those same three are believed to be the three jets of that type to have disappeared recently."

"So, they somehow got a pilot or pilots into that place, managed to get the jets fueled, and took off in the middle of the night." Tom raised his right eyebrow. "Do we have any idea where they headed?"

"We, or I, did not until this very morning. It would seem a scan of the entire Central America and northern part of South America by our old Outpost's SuperSight spotted something both curious and suspicious down in Honduras."

"Honduras as in the place the two transport aircraft of the Daughter of the Black Cobra headed," Tom stated sadly. "I am liking that country less and less."

"Well, in their slight defense, the Honduran government tries to keep things clean, but they struggle finding enough money to do a thorough job. But, back to this story."

He told Tom about the sweep, captured on video, of a city in the western part of the nation, about half way between the Atlantic and Pacific oceans by the name of Gracias. It was not a large city—there were only about forty-eight thousand people in the surrounding farming and light business community—with an old airport that had been closed in the early 2000s due to lack of business.

Once the state-owned highway had been completed, people found it about half the cost to drive to the places they needed to go than to fly. Sometimes it was faster as well.

"So, there is the old single runway field with the parking pad and there wasn't supposed to be much of anything else. Except, now there is. Nestled up into the surrounding trees are three buildings, estimated at about two thousand square feet each. But," and he paused with a small grin, "that is not the very interesting part. Or rather, *parts*.

"On the parking pad are two old regional jets of the type that BoGAir once owned and that same type involved in the crash when they followed too close to Bud!"

Tom let out a low whistle.

"So, do your instincts tell you these are connected? And, I mean both to the drug trade and the stolen jets?"

Harlan nodded but he did not look particularly happy.

"I made a small call to someone I believed was on the side of good within the FBI to ask and also to provide them the video. While I didn't so much get stonewalled, my suggestion they investigate this was… well, deflected. He went so far as to tell me this is all nice and such, but it is more likely that local business people have reopened the airport, and since this is an international thing and not domestic, they couldn't, et cetera, et cetera."

The inventor took a couple breaths before continuing. "What do we do now? Go to the CIA?"

"Did that and got primarily the same thing. 'It's the local's bailiwick so we can't get involved.' Hogwash!"

They talked for another eighteen minutes about what might be done with the only thing coming from it to be more surveillance.

Tom thought about what form that might take after Harlan left and came up with three things.

1. Fly down there and take a look.
2. Get something in the air nearby—or slightly above that—to look.
3. Continue with the SuperSight at the old station.

The third one did not satisfy him in the least. Tom knew the limitations of his system and especially when the camera was some 22,300 miles away.

The first one seemed to be both dangerous as well as requiring an agreement by the Honduran government as well as the local governing body. And, what if the locals were controlled by the very drug people he believed to be stationed down there?

So, it appeared that number 2 was the thing to put into action.

It was relatively easy to do. He made a call to the Construction Company to ask if they had a spare Attractatron Mule available.

"Well," Jake Aturian told him, "we don't have a new one, but we are performing a refurbishment on one of the earliest ones that sort of got an electronic hernia."

He explained that in deflecting an object some two hundred and thirty feet across from getting into a position where it would have hit the Moon, the Mule in question had raced out, grabbed the thing and strained to get it moved to a trajectory where it would miss the Moon and the Earth by more than a million miles.

It had pulled and strained until it was nearly seventy percent of the way before several key power circuits had melted.

Somehow it had limped back to Earth and made a semi-soft landing at the Construction Company but had been torn down and was near to being rebuilt.

"Day after tomorrow and she goes up for tests. Or," and he

chuckled, "do I detect a question about whether you can take it for something else?"

"You do." Tom explained the basic situation and how he wanted to outfit the drone with a version of the SuperSight.

When he thought about it there was no reason why he could not just mount a Digital BigEyes instead. He only wanted to fly above sixty thousand feet and the resolution on the portable version of the SuperSight should give him a look down from that height as if he were just a thousand feet up.

When he told his father his intentions, the older man cautioned him about causing an international incident.

But, he also suggested Tom look into some very recent improvements in camera lenses.

"I understand that German company that produced the original lenses has a new precision grind capability to give about a fifty percent higher zoom with high-definition resolution. I'd give them a call."

Which is exactly what Tom did three minutes later. It was nearing four in the afternoon in Dusseldorf when the call was answered. He identified himself and was immediately transferred to the *Vorstandsvorsitzender*, or Managing Director.

"Ah, is this the senior Swift or the junior one, please?" the man asked.

"I am Tom Swift, so that makes me the junior one. I hope you will still speak to me, sir. This matter has nothing to do with my father."

The German man laughed. "*Nein*... or no. I have no issues with speaking to you, it is just I wanted to be certain to thank the correct man for the fine work you did with our Venus probe several years ago. And so, that was you and so I thank you most sincerely! Now, what is it I might help you with?"

Tom asked about new lenses in the size and optical strength he hoped for. There was a shuffling of papers and then he heard a keyboard being used to look up something. He waited.

He was rewarded for his patience with, "Ah, yes. Yes, yes. We do have just what you ask for. You say you need two of them. Is that all?"

"Truthfully, for this use I need the two, but if the pricing is favorable we might wish to offer the enhanced version of the optical system using these better lenses to our customers. In that case, it could be in the hundreds of pairs over the coming one year."

"Then, and to thank you for rescuing the Venus probe—which

used, I am certain you are aware, our lenses for the five optical systems—I will send a pair of the lenses in your size by overnight courier. You will install and test them for us in your system and for that we shall call the deal even. Our hope is you find them to be what you need and there will be a forthcoming order."

Tom offered to pay for the lenses but the man at the other end would not hear of it. Finally he accepted and gave the specific address.

"I believe we can send these out tonight in the late shipments, so let me get to that, please."

When the box was delivered to Tom's desk by Trent at eleven the next morning, the inventor opened the inner cartons eagerly admiring the lenses encased in tight, plastic covers. These would not be opened until ready for installation in a clean room to avoid even a single mote of dust to be attracted to the precision lenses.

He would know how good the lenses were by the following afternoon. For now he wanted to ensure the Mule was going to be ready to receive the BigEyes and transmit what they saw back to Enterprises.

While some of Tom's quick projects had small troubles, it seemed this one, the one to create a "spy" drone to fly over the area of Honduras in question, was going to go smoothly.

Within just six total days he had the drone ready to send up. He'd created a navigation program based on GPS satellite inputs and could steer the Mule anywhere he chose on a global map.

Bud stopped by the underground lab where most of the work was happening the day before the planned launch to ask about the name for the device.

"Surely, you can't just call it a Mule, Right?"

The inventor pursed his lips as he thought about it. Finally, he brightened and said, "Well, I planned it to be sort of an inside joke about the drug trade, Bud. You know. People who transport drugs are called mules and so this is sort of a slam at the drug lords. If, that is, the people behind both the attacks and also that suddenly reopened airport are in the drugs trade."

The flyer nodded and admitted it made a sort of perverse and ironic sense.

The next morning, he accompanied Tom as they rode the passenger elevator up to the surface and were soon standing between the reconnaissance Mule and the *Sky Queen*. Once at ground level they rolled the Mule off and about fifty feet away so it could launch without any danger of clipping the right wing of the triple-decker.

A TeleVoc beep in Tom's brain had his finger hover over the button that would send the aircraft skyward. He answered it.

"Son, I was wondering if I might have a short word with you and with Peter Quintana? I can send it to your TeleVoc so you don't have to run over here for what is likely to be a two-minute conversation. Okay?"

"Sure." A few seconds later he "heard" a pair of clicks indicating the call was connected.

"Okay, Pete. Tom is on the line now. Go ahead and repeat that little tidbit, please."

"Sure, Hello, Tom. So, there is a little bit of a hint of a rumor of a possible fact that a small faction of Kranjovian militants, the ones who just could not live in that nation once it started to behave and play nice with the world, who have moved operations off the European continent."

"Uh, could they be in Central America?" Tom asked.

"It is not outside of reason they may have moved to that very area. Possibly down in Nicaragua or Costa Rica."

Tom knew he had to ask this next question. "What about Honduras?"

The senator paused. "Now, why would you ask about that nation, Tom?"

Damon came to his son's rescue. They both knew the planned flight was to be taken in absolute secret.

"I believe Tom is wondering why the list seems to head south and not north. Could they have ended up in Guatemala or even Belize, for that matter?"

"Ahh. I see. Well, the short answer is yes. The long answer is three stolen military jets transports were plotted leaving the airspace of Kranjovia and heading to the southwest. Their last known plotted position, before their IFF transmitters suddenly shut off, had them heading in the basic direction of Guatemala City and possibly their La Aurora airport. No record we can find of their officially landing, however. I suppose it is not outside of reason they changed course for one of the surrounding countries."

Tom felt he needed to know if the senator had any idea of their plans, but the man finished the call quickly with, "Just tell Harlan about this and let him know someone from the CIA will be in contact directly later today. I hate to keep ending calls this way but I really do need to run. Bye!"

One click told Tom the phone call had been disconnected. His father then asked if he was going ahead with the flight?

"Yes. I am and in about five minutes, Dad. The drone is RADAR invisible and it looks a lot like our restyled security drones so if anyone asks this is just a new one on a long range test flight with the intent to bring it in late at night and nobody will see it then."

Damon's chuckle came through the electronic communicator. "Fine. Give it a pat on the nose for me, then."

Tom scanned the sky before calling to the lower control tower.

"I've got a new drone to send up on a two-day high altitude flight at least around the state. How are things looking for it heading to fifty thousand feet?"

There was a slight pause. "Clear as far as we see. There is a flight heading into Buffalo that will be at under five thousand in one minute, the usual traffic south of us so if you can launch on a two-two-zero up to three-zero-zero heading you are clear."

Tom thanked the woman and clicked off.

"Get ready, flyboy. The Mule is about to go take a look at Honduras!"

Harlan received the call from a CIA operative recently returned from assignment in Costa Rica.

"Mr. Ames, I am Douglas Carter. We met years ago when you were the Vice President's assigned Secret Service lead."

"Of course. Call me Harlan, please."

"Fine. Well, I hope you were expecting this call because I only have a couple minutes but have some interesting info for you and your employers. There is some trouble brewing down in Either Guatemala or Honduras. And, personally I believe it is the latter. A militia team of Kranjovians who either left or were expelled once the government there settled down headed for the Central American Coast.

"I strongly believe they ended up in a small city called Gracias in Honduras. The reason behind my belief is that there is some known activity at the airport there, one that was closed down and fenced off fifteen years ago."

"I assume no airline is doing that."

"No. To add to the situation several known drug lords have made peace with each other and likely moved into that area. The locals have been studiously ignoring what is going on because some of them have found employment in building structures at the airport, grinding down some of the bad asphalt and filling in that and other holes and generally getting the runway ready to handle flights."

Harlan asked if the CIA knew of any aircraft down there.

Agent Carter told him at least one satellite overflight spotted three aircraft, all of the same approximate size, sitting there a month earlier.

"Now, there are only two. We are not certain what happened to that missing jet, but I think you and I both have an idea about *that*!"

Harlan did and it sent chills down his spine. The attempted attack on Bud's test flight.

"I have just two more things to pass along before I have to leave for a new assignment. First, there are at least four small concrete pads arranged near to, but tree-hidden from the ground, that would make great hiding spots for missile launchers. The final item is the North Koreans have been chattering about some new super recon jet the Swifts are building. One they believe is meant specifically to spy in them and what they are doing. I don't know if there is anything to that, but I'd be letting your people know they might run into troubles if they make any flights in that direction. After all, the regime over there boasts they can shoot anything out of the sky out to about twelve hundred miles."

The *Drug Mule*—Bud had finally announced his intention to call it by that name twenty minutes after it took off—made it to its cruising altitude of one hundred thousand feet in just six minutes. By that time it was over Scranton, Pennsylvania and heading in the general direction of its forthcoming patrol area.

It would fly on a heading of two-one-five until it passed Savannah, Georgia before turning to two-zero-zero and its track to Honduras.

Just two hours later it streaked over the long and thin island of Jose Santos Guardiola where it started to slow down to a cruising speed of just three hundred knots. The course was also adjusted to be more direct to Gracias on a heading of two-four-two degrees.

Tom received a notification over his TeleVoc of the approaching time for it to park high over the small city and to begin looking down at what might be going on. He'd already notified Security and Gary Bradley joined him in the Communications building and the room where everything was being fed.

For nearly ten minutes they were treated to scenes of the city and the surrounding area before the Mule found the airport. As reported by the CIA man, the airfield looked as if it had been patched from end to end. There were three fully completed buildings and a fourth one under construction, all of them close to the stand of trees on the southeast side of the field.

That wasn't what caught the Security man's eye. What did made him let out a swear word.

At the corner of the parking area and almost exactly east of that by perhaps fifteen feet sat a missile launcher system. What was worse, they could see four surface-to-air missiles mounted on it and an active RADAR dish searching the skies overhead. There were signs of at least three more small areas similarly prepared for something, like more launchers!

"The good news is," Tom told him, "The drone cannot be detected by RADAR and it is too high for anyone with anything other than a powerful telescope to see visually."

He left Gary to keep a watch on things and to check the rest of the area carefully.

Back in the shared office Tom filled his father in on the initial discovery in Honduras.

"Sound as if they are very serious about protecting their new airfield," Damon stated with a weary shake of his head. "What can we do about that?"

Now, Tom shook his head. "Not an idea. I suppose we can come clean and get the video to the CIA or the military or even Peter Quintana and hope for the best."

Ten minutes later it was decided that talking to the senator was the best first step.

He was not at all pleased at the news. "I am not displeased with you two for finding this out, however. Is there any way to couch the video and having come from your old Outpost and their equipment?"

Damon answered. "We can have them use the Space Prober now we have a specific thing to look at. I'll arrange that and have the video ready for you this time tomorrow."

Tom was only partially hearing this exchange as his mind had turned to something he'd believed would be necessary for his hypersonic aircraft.

I'm going to need to build a half-scale version just two people can fly in to test the final arrangement of the Aerospike engine and the scramjets.

As soon as the call to Senator Quintana finished, he slipped out of the office and headed to the lab and his CAD system next door.

CHAPTER 13 /
TAKING A GANDER AT...

WITH THE basic design finished and the build of the full-size hypersonic jet nearly ten percent complete—with the majority of that framing—it only left Tom to do the scaling down for the proof of flight model he intended to fly at least to Europe with Bud by his side. While he might like to have the final scramjets available, this one would have two-third-size engines so he might evaluate their performance.

It wasn't so much a task of having to do a lot of things over again or differently, it was more an exercise in having enough fuel space along with providing for the comfort and breathing needs of the two-man crew.

Of these, the fuel situation was the most critical and of a particularly tricky kind.

Like the final version there would be two very different types of engines to deal with, each having special fuel and handling requirements. Of these, Tom felt the fuel situation for the longer burning scramjet engines would take the most fuel and therefore the most space within the fuselage.

He toyed with the idea of drop tanks for fueling the Aerospike engine and nearly had a good appreciation of that until he realized he might need to burn that engine again once the jet dropped to below about Mach-1.5. It would be especially critical if they had to do a go-around before landing.

Otherwise, he might have a jet that landed like an old Space Shuttle, meaning it would glide only and not have the ability to take a second shot at a missed landing.

One time and one time only! That might have been acceptable in the small one-man version Bud had tested, but he knew the final jet had to have something more functional for commercial flights.

Since that would not pass muster with his father, or Bashalli for that matter, Tom had to deal with carrying enough fuel to get them off the ground, up to altitude and speed, and then have enough in reserve to run the Aerospike for at least an additional thirty minutes of powered flight.

A great many computations went into his final decision to downsize the Aerospike by eleven percent over what he had originally wanted. It would give enough thrust to achieve his needed goals while burning a surprising sixteen percent less fuel.

In one of their frequent talks regarding Tom's project, Damon inquired about whether or not Tom had decided to take off from Enterprises or from Fearing Island.

"You do know that getting permissions from the FAA for a New York takeoff might be tricky, don't you?"

"Honestly, I hadn't given it much thought. Why difficult for this? We won't hit even above Mach-1 until we are getting to within a few miles of Maine. I suppose I can throttle it back until we pass over land."

"I was thinking about the somewhat adversarial relationship we seem to have developed with the FAA lately. You will need to file a flight plan with them and they could demand a subsonic flight over land. Which reminds me, just how fast will you be coming back in?"

Tom told him his plans were to brush the lower end of Nova Scotia in Canada before crossing the coast about ten miles north of Portland, Maine, and at about 700 knots.

"Just above sonic speeds but slowing down quickly."

Damon suggested they table the idea until Tom was closer to actually having a flying craft. He also decided to have a private conversation with Peter Quintana to discuss just how hostile the FAA might be.

Using the notion the hypersonic test jet had to be capable of one hour of flight using the Aerospike engine and then about two hours of total flight time using the scramjets, Tom concluded the jet was going to need to be about a 6/10th size and not half-scale. It could still be perfectly scaled down, just not quite as small as he'd wanted.

Now the jet would be able to fly just under Mach speed until it reached the coast and then could quickly come to speed before firing up the scramjets.

"We can and should end up with about a sixty percent fuel load for the Aerospike when we are crossing back over the Atlantic and that gives us plenty of reserves," he told Bud as they stood at the entry of the construction building on Enterprises' grounds where the jet was taking shape.

"When do we travel?"

"In just four weeks, flyboy. This is actually a fairly simple jet to construct. The full one will be a little trickier with the passengers to contend with and the structure to provide for that open space, but Hank has vacuum formed and prepped all the outer panels and it's just a matter of finishing the interior skeleton, adding the fuel cells, and skinning her. A couple subsonic tests and maybe one out over the ocean to Mach-1.2 and then you and I go for the civilian non-stop Atlantic crossing record!"

Five relatively local test flights complete, the flight day came with Tom and Bud sitting in the cockpit performing their checks by ten in the morning. Everything pointed to a great flight with no complications.

Since he needed to get the full "feel" for the craft so he might judge what was not quite perfect, Tom would be pilot for most of the flight starting with their being towed into takeoff position.

The Aerospike flared to life and the jet picked up speed rapidly before the nose rose on its own and the rest of the jet followed suit. They were at sixty thousand before they both realized it and Tom had to pull back of the throttle to keep them under supersonic speeds.

Then, the coast of the U.S.A. was below and quickly behind them. Tom opened the throttle and they surged ahead getting to Mach-2.5 in another minute. The scramjets had just enough airflow to get started and by the time they were pulsing out power, the Aerospike was shut down and was drawing inside the jet body.

As the Hyperplane streaked across the Atlantic Ocean, Tom and Bud were being kept busy plotting their turning point and eventual return to the East Coast. At Mach 5, it was not the sort of thing you did in your head, nor did you wait until the final minutes to get started.

"I really do not want to come within one hundred miles of Northern Africa or even the coast of Portugal, Bud. I'd like a three hundred mile buffer. So, we either slow down starting in about two minutes or we *began* our turn three minutes ago!" He raised an eyebrow to his copilot.

"Oh, then I'm in favor of slowing enough to keep the hypersonic engines running and also start the turn," the flyer responded as he checked his instruments. By this time they had reached Mach-5.2.

Tom carefully ran his index and middle finger down the speed scale until the readout stated **SLOWING TO M-3.5**.

"Okay. Give us ten degrees per minute port turn, Bud. We'll increase that a little as we get to the slower Mach speed."

Bud slowly adjusted the automatic pilot computers with the new turn information. As he did, the jet shuddered slightly and began to tilt a little left wing down. It was just as planned. The jet began its "slow" turn to the left.

By the time the jet was heading slightly away from Europe—although it would pass within eighty-seven miles of the southernmost tip of England so Tom had to radio their air control for permission to enter their controlled airspace—they were almost even with the northern part of France.

Minute-by-minute the jet streaked around finishing its turn, now at a rate of fifteen degrees a minute. Sooner than either young man would have expected it, the jet was pointing on a course of two-eight-five and was heading back mostly toward Canada and eventually the United States.

That was about the instant when the first alarm went off.

"Rats!" Tom exclaimed seeing the heat sensors for their wingtips and nose. "We just took on too much air friction in that turn. We have an overheated starboard wing tip. Now I have to slow us down under Mach-2 to give things a chance to cool."

"Uhh, that means we have to go back to the Aerospike rocket motor, right?"

The inventor nodded, a grim look of determination on his face. "Yeah. We might have to do that. The problem is in how long it is going to take to cool things down. We also have to come back down to about forty thousand feet to give the wings enough air density to give us lift without using too much of our fuel reserve." He shrugged. "Well, nothing else to do, so let's start dropping speed and get off the autopilot."

Bud slid the speed controls down further and as the scramjets sensed the slower speed, they announced—another loud alarm—they were five seconds away from disengaging.

"We're gonna have to glide this beast until we drop some more speed and get lower," Bud declared. He understood that to try to restart the Aerospike at both the altitude and the speed they were traveling would mean a waste of precious fuel and that would mean even more troubles for them.

"I know." He reached into the pocket to his left pulling out a laminated card. "Let's go over the changeover checklist."

Item by item Tom read out the procedure and Bud responded once it had been attended to. Several of the items were only manageable from the pilot seat so Tom did those. By the time they were just south of the tip of Greenland everything had been accomplished and the jet was at forty-two thousand, three hundred feet.

"Starting rocket motor fire up sequence," Tom announced. He

could see the heat problem had dissipated, but it would burn far too much fuel to try for a restart of the scramjets now. They had to either stretch out their rocket fuel or gamble on getting fast enough for the scramjets, but likely having to glide into Shopton.

Tom did not want to be in that position.

"Fine, I'm going to need to get us pointed to a good landing spot because I'm seeing a sad lack of our Aerospike fuel. As in, we have enough to run the rocket at seventy percent for about thirty-six minutes and that is not quite enough to even get across Maine!"

Tom yanked out a map and placed his right index finger at an angle to a spot he believed would be okay for them. "Bud, turn left to new heading two-five... uhh, let's call it five for now."

Next he set four switches and grabbed the manual throttle levers, making certain they were in the idle position.

Not wishing to bother or distract his friend, Bud remained silent as he worked to get them to the indicated heading.

A moment later, they both breathed a sigh of relief when Aerospike motor fired and began to increase its output. Seconds later Bud happily reported he had better control.

"Please give us seventy percent throttle, skipper. I positive we can hold this altitude with that setting."

Tom did it and then leaned back. "Aren't you going to ask me where we're going?"

Bud shook his head. "Nope. I figure you'll tell me before we get there and also will pull up the area charts so I know how to approach."

Tom could not suppress his grin. "Well, in case you come up with any level of interest, we're heading for Gander, Newfoundland."

"Okay," the flyer said slowly, "and why there?"

"The only spot with a long runway, emergency equipment and within our range, Bud. Does the name ring any bells?"

"Honestly? No. Is that anywhere close to a big city?"

"Not really." Tom told him the story about Gander and how it had once been the stopping over for almost all trans-Atlantic flights before any of them had the fuel capacity to make it across the ocean on one tank and to airports in New York and Boston. And, during the emergency and airspace shutdown in the United States following the attacks on September 11th, 2001, Gander had been the place more than three dozen airliners coming across the Atlantic had been sent.

"They have one runway long enough for the heaviest passenger jets to land without having to use their reverse thrusters. And, since we do not have those in this jet, we'll need that real estate!"

Tom got on the radio and made a call out to a general emergency frequency. A half-dozen years earlier it would not have been possible from their current position, but a recent satellite in geosynchronous orbit, put up by another company, now made radio contact a seamless and constant possibility across the entire Atlantic Ocean from Greenland down to about the east coast of Brazil.

"Swift Test Jet Two requesting contact with Gander Approach. We have a possible low fuel emergency and wish to declare a Pan Pan at this time."

He had to make the call twice before getting a response.

"Roger, uhh, Swift Two. Understand possible low fuel emergency and wish to declare Pan Pan? Is that correct?" The man's sing-song vice almost sounded Irish.

"Roger. Declaring Pan Pan at this time. We are an experimental jet with..." he looked at Bud a second, "partial engine flame out. Still have remaining smaller engine but low fuel state. Can we get contacted with Gander?"

"Uhh, yeah. Hold on... try frequency one-three-six-point-three. I'll stay on this line until you acknowledge contact."

"Thanks. Switching now."

Tom reached out and set their radio for the new frequency. "Gander Approach? This is Swift Test Jet Two with a declared Pan Pan, low fuel emergency. Request vector to your long runway."

The call back came immediately. *"Boy, you're lucky you called just now. I was about to head home for my dinner. Umm, sure, come on in. Where are you, by the way? Must be out of RADAR range."*

Tom had to chuckle. "We are on your approximate zero-six-four heading two-three-five approximately eight hundred miles out. We are squawking seven-seven-three-eight on the Pan channel. Over."

There was a pause so Tom switched back to the previous channel and said they now had contact with Gander and thanked them. When he switched back he only had to wait nine seconds.

"Okay, Swift, umm, Two. I gotcha on the beam. You're gonna need to turn back to about two-six-five for five hundred miles before turning to our approach on two-one-zero. That's our long runway. Are you gonna need the emergency vehicles called out?"

Tom paused. "I don't believe so. We just need a safe place within our current range and you are close to the outer edge of that. We are traveling at Mach-One-point-six so we should be at your facility in about one hour. And, yes, we realize we need to slow down, but please call me when that time comes."

"*Oh, wow. Are you some sorta military jet? We've never had anything more that the Canadian Red Arrows here and they don't go all that fast even with a tail wind.*" He chuckled on the line before adding, "*About the slowdown point, please slow to six hundred when you are ninety miles out and also come down to altitude two zero thousand at that time.*"

Tom told him they would comply with that and asked if the man could stand by. He said he definitely would.

Bud, while this was going on, had pulled up a satellite map of the area around the airport.

"Lots and lots of lakes and ponds," he reported. "A lot like Minnesota. By the way, she is responding nicely and the drop in speed is working in our favor. Not enough to get to home with any reserve, but we will have a pad in case we need to execute a go-around."

Forty-two minutes later Tom called the tower at Gander giving their position and suggesting they could start their descent early.

"*Roger but can you wait five minutes? We got a Aer Lingus heavy traversing the area eastward approaching altitude three five thousand.*"

"Absolutely," Tom told the controller. And, when the man called back five minutes later with permissions, Tom thanked him. "Starting down now. You still want us at twenty thousand?"

"*If possible, sir. Otherwise I can clear you for fifteen in seven minutes.*"

"We'll head for twenty. Thanks!"

Their approach was smooth and steady and as they came down under four thousand and within visual distance of the airport Bud let out a whistle. "Jetz! That's one large airport for being in the middle of nowhere!"

Tom reminded him about the airport's history.

"Sure. It's just that I've never been right over the area before and it sort of is impressive!"

Gander Approach gave them permission to come in as soon as they got to the outer marker.

"I've been looking at you in the binocs, and you're one impressive-looking jet. Is it possible once you're down to come meet you?"

It made Tom smile. They were not exactly a secret project any longer, but he had hoped to minimize the number of people getting a good look. "Sure, but can it just be you, please. We are not ready for public viewing."

"You got it, sir. See you on the ashfelt in about five."

Bud brought them in smoothly and there was barely a bump when the wheels touched down. He had to lightly use the brakes but they only required two-thirds of the runway before he turned them off to the right and headed for the terminal. He did stop at the cross runway point when the tower man announced there was a small business jet on final.

It crossed in front of them and they hurried across getting to the terminal and position 24 as the controller had told them.

Running across the tarmac was a man holding onto his knitted cap and waving at them.

Tom got up heading between the seats and down through the lower hatch where a ladder automatically extended. He met the man under the left wing.

"Martin MacAfee, Chief Controller here at Gander. Welcome to Newfoundland," the man said extending a hand.

"Tom Swift. A pleasure. Thanks for standing by. I guess the field closes up around five?'

"Oh. No," the man stated in what sounded a lot like a light Irish accent. "Just my dinner time. I'd have been back in an hour and a recorded response would have told you ta come on in using the radio beacon, just to be sure ta watch out for other traffic." He was looking at the underside of the jet. "This sure doesn't look like a conventional jet or even military. Uhh, can I ask?"

Tom told him about the jet being a hypersonic aircraft they had been testing when they overheated their wings. They might have made it back to Shopton, but nobody wanted to take a chance.

"Hey, I gotcha. So, what kind of fuel do ya need? We got Jet A-1 fuel and we gotta keep some JP-8 on hand in case a military jet has ta land. Which one do you want? I can call the proper truck over in less than five minutes."

Tom said that either would be fine and knowing they were about the same cost he was happy to agree to a partial fill with the JP-8. It was a pure and powerful version of kerosene and would do temporarily as their Aerospike fuel.

"Can we also get a tanker out with liquid oxygen? We are going to need about eighteen hundred pounds of that as well."

"Well, that should be no problem. I'll call my brother-in-law and the welding supply company and get him out here. Listen. If ya want it I can have my field guy give the windscreen a good cleaning. Or, if ya don't need that, how about a cup of coffee? Coffee's horrible at the airport, but we got a Tim Horton's three minutes away. You can borrow my car if ya want."

Tom thanked the man and asked if they could borrow the car just to drive a bit around the community.

"I've heard all about the 9/11 event, and have taken my wife to see the play about it. Made her cry like a baby," he said with a wink telling the man he had also shed a tear or two over the emotional effects the play had on him.

"Oh, sure. Listen. Could we drop by my house and let me off. Then you can come back and get me in half an hour?"

"That would be fine, but unless you have a wife waiting for you, we would be happy to treat you to something a little better than a doughnut at Tim Horton's," Tom told the man.

With a smile, he nodded and suggested somewhere called Lily's.

Bud came down the ladder about this time and Tom filled him in on their host's offer.

"Neat! I'd like to see this place. My wife saw some sort of musical about Gander a couple years ago when it was revived on Broadway. In fact," and he turned to Tom, "you and Bash took her when I was out visiting my folks."

The trip to the restaurant was a fast one and straight down the street coming from the airport, Airport Way. Martin explained, as they were parking, that Gander was about seventy-five hundred people and, "Darned little to do except wait for the next big airline diversion. Or, golf."

After their steak sandwiches arrived he admitted they had a good course. "It's actually sixteen fairways and you play two of them opposite ta get the full eighteen! Ya gotta watch out for the other guys coming your way, but it's never really crowded. Other than that, we don't have a lot. Next closest town is small, that'd be Appleton and then Glenwood." He took his last bite. "So, can I ask anything about that neat jet of yours?"

Tom told him about his desire to create a hypersonic aircraft that could be scaled up for passenger travel. He mentioned his hope to cover the Atlantic in about one hour and the Pacific from the West Coast to Australia in just under three hours.

Martin let out a low and appreciative whistle.

They got back to the airport forty minutes later and drove right to the jet. The fuel and liquid O2 trucks were gone and a pair of charge slips had been taped to the ladder. Tom signed the two multi-part forms and handed the top copies to Martin.

"I want to thank you for the hospitality, Martin. Someday soon I hope to come back under slightly less emergency circumstances."

The air controller stood on the parking apron until they had taxied to the runway and headed into the air.

When they arrived in Shopton, four hours later than planned—but Tom had called Enterprises before they set down in Gander—it was to a small gathering of family and a couple Enterprises employees.

Tom got out first and gave his wife a hug and kiss, kissed his mother on the cheek as he also shook his father's hand and then turned to Hank.

He briefly mentioned the wing and nose heating and asked for the jet to be checked over.

"I have the feeling we need something more to dissipate the heat of fast turns. I should be able to get something designed and be back to you in a couple days. Thanks!"

"I have a notion that includes a small loop of coolant out there," the engineer told him before heading back to his workshop.

Tom hoped that was all it required!

CHAPTER 14 /
SUPER QUEEN PROVES HER METTLE

TOM SUPERVISED a team of technicians that went over every part of the two-man test jet. There were some signs of normal operational wear and tear, but the wing tips were not in as bad condition as he feared. There had obviously been some heating beyond the normal structural tolerances, and that was witnessed by the fact the hypersonic air had pressed the evenly-curved leading edges in by about a fifth of an inch for the last two or more feet at the ends.

"Is it as bad as we assumed?" came Hank's voice as he stepped over beside Tom.

"Well, everything held together and there is no sign of impending rupture, but we definitely picked up a lot of heat, even as high as Bud and I were flying." He pointed to the right wing. "I've been trying to imagine what it will take to keep that from happening in the full-size one. We can't have any commercial pilot getting into trouble with something overheating."

With a grin, Hank asked, "Don't you mean *ones*, as in plural as in everyone and their brother is going to want to travel in one of them?"

The inventor nodded. "I sure hope so. But, not until we can crack that heat issue. I was just trying to think about using the liquid oxygen for the Aerospike to run through there. I've decided to keep as much of that fuel duo in the wings as I can so they lighten up during the flight."

"What's keeping you from— oh, wait. If you use the LOX it will heat up and boil off and that will cause a lot of pressure buildup and that would need to be bled off and *that* will lead to a loss of valuable oxygen. Right?"

"Yes. That's the conclusion I came to only a bit more slowly than you just did. So, I'm afraid it is back to having a separate closed loop cooling system. I just have to figure out what to use."

They discussed liquid nitrogen, liquid helium and even a wide hollow sheet of circulating glycol with an associated radiator at the back of the wing to dump off the heat it would carry away from the tips.

It was something Tom knew he needed to spend a few days or a week or more on.

* * * * *

Something even of greater importance was happening while Tom was working to perfect his hypersonic jet.

Harlan had been secretly feeding some of the more damning video evidence of the situation down in Honduras to key contacts in both the CIA as well as Interpol.

He hated acting all bad spy movie secret agent, but a couple years earlier he had, using his own cash to keep things from being traced back to Enterprises, purchased fifty disposable cell phones, and he had taken three of them—so far—to make the calls and send files he had downloaded to them.

Once used he carefully made certain each phone was completely erased and destroyed.

The positive about it was he was getting the right materials to the right people and keeping Swift Enterprises completely out of things.

On a call to a man he'd once worked with—David Puddleston-Corbett, who held the rank of Inspector Chief within the Interpol international police agency—he had managed to get the agent very excited about information regarding the former Kranjovians and what appeared to be a major illegal action in Central America.

"And, you can assure me these videos and images came from a source that is reliable and no attempts have been made to acquire them through illegal means?"

Harlan grimaced on his end of the call. "David, I can assure you these are real and true images acquired from a known means located in high Earth orbit. It is not illegal to look down from space."

"I shall not ask the question that begins with, 'So, how did you know…' and finishes with, 'and can you guarantee that?'"

"And I appreciate that, David. So, is there anything I can do to make your work of trying to get all this to the powers that be interested easier for you? Frankly, I'm running into a bit of trouble over here as different agencies keep pointing me to the others and those point right back. Nobody seems to want to tackle these people."

"Have you attempted to get the country in question interested?"

It was a flat question and one that could not be ignored.

"Yeah," the Swift man said wearily. "The person I spoke to stated they had no reports from the locals anything untoward was going on and they do not have the manpower and no, they would not like to receive the videos proving what is going on!"

"It is the same the world over, my friend. If we just ignore it, it will not be happening, which works until it rears up and starts slashing at people and then all hell cuts loose!"

A minute later the Interpol man was wishing Harlan a better day, adding, "I will try to get these in front of the appropriate people in the next day or two. I'll be in touch."

Harlan suggested an alternate number, one from a different "burn" phone from the one he was holding.

"Will do. Cheers!"

Harlan decided that if he was going to contact the Swift's primary political ally with the latest news, he'd best do it with Damon's blessings.

Tom's job of developing a heat wicking material and system went amazingly well and he concluded his investigation with a small-scale test only four days later.

He was describing it to Chow as the chef was setting up his lunch when Bud walked into the underground office.

"Well, now you are here let me begin again," he offered.

"Begin lunch again or whatever you were telling Chow?"

"The second one, flyboy. So, Bud very well knows about the tremendous heat we built up on the wingtips of the smaller hypersonic jet, and I was filling Chow in on that and why it is vital to overcome it. I've hit on two things that will help."

He reached over his desk and turned his monitor so they could all see what was on it.

"This is the current scaled version we flew... and this," and he pressed the Space Bar, "is what I plan to do to the airframe."

As the image changed, only the wings seemed to move. They angled back another four or five degrees, shortened by perhaps a foot and the leading edges curved back earlier.

"Was it that easy?" Bud asked.

"Well, yes and no. That change in the wings means the super heated air molecules that come off the nose of the jet do not hit the tips where we don't have the same internal space as the nose with its four-inch-thickness of the fuselage materials. In fact, the wing tips need to be made with just under quarter-inch materials.

"That is the structural change you can notice. It is inside where something Hank suggested finishes the job."

He told them about a one-sixteenth-inch gap inside a very wide and flat tube of Durastress that started on top of the wing beginning just be two inches above the forward edge, curved over the front and back under the wing another three inches. It would extend from the curved tip to a point just sixteen inches across the wing front. Coolant would continuously be pumped through that space.

"It sits right up against the inside of the wing skin and is filled with a solution we've used before for cooling; it's seventy percent pure glycol and thirty percent pure ethanol. There will be a small pump in each wing to circulate about two gallons each through this flat tube and to a very small radiator that sits about half the way to the back of the wing with just a very thin piece of tempered glass between the bottom of it and the outside."

Chow was scratching his head.

"An', that'll keep things nice n' cool inside?"

"And, outside, Chow. In the computer simulation I did earlier this morning I can get the temperature down from the approximately seventeen hundred degrees it took to deform that wing material down to under six hundred and keep it there no matter what we do. At least, above forty thousand feet; under that and the air is just not quite cold enough to do the trick. But, by then we will be slow enough to not build up more heat."

"Wahl, I don't care a hoot what Buddy says about you, Tom; Yer a surefire genius!" With that and giving the inventor a sly wink, he picked up his Stetson hat and left the office.

Both young men heard him chuckling as he left.

Bud turned to Tom. "I said no such thing. He's trying to get me in trouble!"

"No, Bud, he is trying to get back at you for all the teasing you do to him. Live with it. And, by the way, what is it you say about me?" He grinned and the flyer blushed before also grinning.

More seriously, Bud asked, "So, does making these changes mean the next flight in the final test model is delayed?"

Tom shook his head. "I don't believe so. We are going to have new wings built for the two-man unit and will fly that in a week. Unless you have another pressing engagement."

Bud shrugged. "Only that Sandy and I are supposed to meet with the head of the adoption agency next Wednesday. I can do any day other than that. Or, possibly Tuesday or Monday when I am certain Sandy is going to be almost a mental case and I should be close to her."

"Thursday it will be, then."

Beginning late that afternoon Tom worked with Hank and the

structural engineers to redesign and then replace the existing pair of wings. Now, the vertical wingtip extensions were to be gone and the actual covering of the wings was going to be in the flat black of the possible final materials.

Bud was holding Sandy's ice-cold hand as they sat across the desk from a woman who seemed to have one expression, and that was a constant smile. It was meant to defuse nervous jitters in the people she met with, and worked on Bud and long as he ignored his almost bloodless fingers, but Sandy was close to breaking down she was so nervous.

"Mrs. Barclay? I can see you are close to panic so let me assure you this is not a, 'We have found very bad things about you,' sort of meeting. In fact, we find only the most favorable of reports including all the efforts you two have gone through to conceive a baby of your own. We, I, admire that in perspective parents."

Sandy released her vice-like grip on Bud's fingers and he had to give them a small shake and the returning blood made them ache.

"So, to continue, this meeting is to let you both know we want to continue the process and get headed toward the day when we can sit here, you signing the appropriate spaces and me the ones for which I am responsible, and then you can officially be the parents of the baby or infant we will have worked to match you with."

"When do we meet him… or her?" Sandy gushed out.

Mrs. Gabriel, the agency manager, smiled. "You are pretty anxious, and we like that to a point. I will remind you this is not an instant thing. We are several months to a year away from that day. In the mean time we would like to have you come to one of our private visitation rooms and to have a few of the very young children brought in to you. Just to see how you react and hold them and talk to them." She raised an eyebrow. "Would today be okay?"

Sandy nodded so hard her hair, not in a pony tail today as she believed worn down looked more mature, swung around and bounced against her face and forehead. "Yes, please!"

By the time Bud caught up with Tom around four that afternoon, he was all smiles.

"Gee, skipper, you ought to have seen your sister. She was incredible. They brought in a little girl, just four-months-old, and Sandy cuddled her and whispered soothing noises to her and that baby just settle in and fell asleep in her arms. I had to wait for the agency lady to bring in another baby so I didn't wake her up."

The visit and meeting with three possible adoptees had gone very well. The first two had been baby girls and the third one was a nine-month-old boy named Samuel. His mother had father had divorced with the father disappearing a week later. When the boy's mother perished in a car crash he was left with no parent and no other known family. So, he was part of the program and had been for nearly a month.

"He's got dark hair and dark blue eyes and by golly, he could be my own son. Not that that is important. I really kinda took to the kid. Sandy could see that and when we left she told me he was her favorite even though I think she liked the second girl better."

"Yeah, I've suspected Sandy's saying she doesn't care if it is a boy or girl is to try to convince herself. I get the feeling she started out wanting a little girl... someone to dress up and almost play with like a living doll. And, I know mom thinks you two would do better with a boy for starters. Always nice to have an older brother to protect a little sister."

The next morning Bud met Tom at the place where the *Sky Queen's* elevator would normally rise. Sitting just to the east side was the *Super Queen*. Under her was the loading pit where the various interchangeable pods could be set, the jet towed over them and then they were lifted up into the body.

The very bottom of the scaled down hypersonic jet was disappearing up inside to forward pod area.

Bud looked like he was puzzled about something so Tom asked him what it was.

"Well, I know the jet is smaller than the final product and all that, but even with the wings slightly modified aren't they just too wide to fit inside?"

Tom clapped his brother-in-law on the right shoulder. "Well spotted, Bud. The first ones were, but these have fold-up tips so they do fit. For this run I had the Aerospike engine taken out, the turbines put in, and extra fuel for the scramjets put in. Also, these wings fold up enough to give us the right space. We'll get the *Queen* up to about Mach-2 before we climb in, seal up and drop away. That'll start about seventy thousand feet. The wings immediately come down and lock. so I believe by the time we get down to about fifty thousand we'll have a speed of Mach-3 and a pretty easy time of starting the scramjets."

"How long will we be flying?"

"Over an hour. We're heading for a turn point just south of

Greenland. Wide swing to the right and pretty much straight back here coming to about Albany as we slow down and shut things off. We glide that last twenty thousand feet and seventy miles."

"So, back to no reserve power again, huh? Guess we make this a good landing first time!"

They climbed up a short ladder and into the side of the giant jet heading forward along the left passageway until they reached the first stairs up. Taking that one and the next got them to within thirty feet of the cockpit.

Deke Bodack sat in the pilot's seat with Zimby in the second seat. Tom and Bud took the jump seats behind them.

Clearance to taxi was immediately given along with all the salient weather conditions. They held at the end of the runway for less than a minute before being given permission to take off and turn to the left for a quick transit to the East Coast.

As they headed up Zimby turned to Tom. "We had a bit of a discussion with the FAA about going supersonic." He shrugged. "I had to remind them of their own FAA Directive stating that both the *Sky Queen* and this baby are always cleared for up to Mach-2.2. They grumbled and sort of grumped but in the end they said it was okay. Go figure. Anyone know what sort of bug they've got up their hind ends?"

Tom suggested he'd fill them in once they all got back to Enterprises before he and Bud headed back to climb into the jet for their flight.

Eleven minutes later Zimby called back to them with the information they were initiating their wide circle just offshore while they gained altitude.

"Give us six minutes, skipper, then you and Bud can do the magic thing!"

When the time came, the two men felt the big doors under their craft open and the winds enter buffeting things a little. It also became very bright inside.

Zimby gave them a one-minute to go signal and then counted down from ten.

As he spoke, "One," Tom pressed the disconnect button and the hypersonic test jet dropped like a stone.

Fortunately, it was a stone with wings that came down in about two seconds and started providing lift and maneuverability.

"Switching on the pre-heat for the fuel," Bud announced.

Forty-five seconds later they were down by about three thousand feet but their speed had climbed to Mach-2.6. Now, the wings were providing enough lift they stopped losing altitude. In order to get the speed up a little more, Tom tilted the nose down about three degrees.

"Coming up on Mach-2.9, Bud. Go ahead with the start sequence."

More felt than heard came the rumbling of the scramjets as they sucked in huge amounts of air, mixed it with their fuel and it ignited sending them surging forward.

While Tom concentrated on piloting, Bud radioed to the *Super Queen* of their success and that everything was running as expected.

"Yeah, Bud," came Zimby's voice. "We sort of saw you shoot ahead of us and into the wild blue yonder and figured you guys had things under control."

Bud turned to Tom. "You know, getting dropped at this higher speed from a good altitude beats the hot snot out of my first drop from the cargo jet. This jet just cuts into the air and flies!"

Their initial course of zero-five-five would bring them to within four hundred miles of the southern tip of Greenland where Tom intended to slow to Mach-4 before making their starboard turn. That would complete with them nearly due East of New York and a pretty much direct flight back to Shopton.

"Keep a close eye on the new temperature gauges for the wings, Bud," Tom requested. "Any hint of an overheat, you sing out loud and clear. I'll straighten us out and cool things down if needed."

Bud kept a close watch on the temperatures both at the tips of the wings as well as for the coolant system.

A quarter way through the turn he reported, "Tips at seven hundred eighteen and internal coolant underneath running seven-sixty-five. Coolant coming back from the radiators at two-sixteen. Jetz! It's working!"

By the time they completed the turn the numbers were not much different.

Tom was very pleased and knew he had just about the final piece of the puzzle completed. Once they landed he would have only three very minor things to look into—two from a programming standpoint and one having to do with a small aerodynamic reconfiguration he wanted to make to the scramjet exhausts—before he would feel comfortable releasing everything for the final prototype completion.

They were now just about the same latitude as the southern part of Ireland and heading toward Montreal.

To position them for a better approach from the south, Tom turned them to the left heading directly toward Manhattan. He would adjust their direction again when they were six hundred miles out.

The jet was slowing down to under Mach-2.1 as they came even with the outer bank of Massachusetts. At the same time Tom had descended to just thirty-two thousand feet and had reported in to Eastern Control.

"*Swift Experimental, you need to drop to below six hundred fifty knots immediately. Do you read?*"

"We read, but as filed we are in a jet that does not fly well under about Mach-2. We are configured to build up no forward pressure so no sonic boom issues. Also, we need to shut off our main propulsion in order to descend and slow any further. We are doing that right now."

There was a twenty-second pause before the controller came back on the radio.

"*Swift Experimental. You cannot enter U.S. airspace at this time. Turn around and go back to wherever it is you came from.*"

Now, the inventor was frustrated so he looked at Bud to take over the communications.

"Hey, FAA guy. We came from upstate New York and that is *exactly* where we are heading back to. I don't know who is pulling our chains or your strings but we are heading to our home field as planned, as filed and as approved!"

"*Swift Experimental. Until we get verification from our management, you need to turn around. We can give you a racecourse pattern to fly where you are out of the way. If you fail to comply an air intercept will be called in.*"

"Be advised, we are unpowered at this time. This is an experimental aircraft making an *unpowered* approach for Shopton, New York. We do not have the ability to relight our engines at this time."

"*Sorry Swift Experimental, but you are going to have to go around. You do not have permission to descend and land at your home field! US airspace is closed to you!*"

CHAPTER 15 /

BLACK BEAUTY

BUD SWITCHED to the Enterprises' control tower frequency and quickly outlined what they were up against.

"Roger, Bud. We are calling the FAA to state you are coming in without available power and any interference will mean a crash. I'll tell them our lawyers want names so we know who to bring into court."

A minute later, and with the jet now under thirty thousand feet and slowing as it glided to about Mach 1.3, the radio came back to life.

"You have immediate permissions to come home. I repeat, come in now."

With a rueful grin from Tom, the flyers began a sweeping turn to their right to line them up with the longest runway at Enterprises. By the time it was in plain sight they had dropped to just three hundred twenty knots and were heading down through two thousand feet.

"We're gonna make it!" Bud stated gleefully. "Piece of cake."

A moment later they crossed the western wall and set down. It was a little bumpy but they remained heading straight down the asphalt. A switch flick saw the drogue chute coming out to slow them to the point where the brakes would be most effective.

"Look what the tower called out," the flyer said pointing to their right.

The full compliment of Enterprises' crash trucks were heading for their final position, lights flashing. As soon as they stopped Tom opened the canopy and stood up, waving with both arms to show they were just fine.

As he looked up at a whooshing sound, the entire set of drones flashed by overhead. They all were heading to the east.

"Tom? Bud?" the tower man radioed. "There are five fast jets heading our way. They must have been the intended escort for you guys. We're broadcasting on all their frequencies to not try to come overhead. What do we do if they are friendlies that won't take no for an answer?"

Tom immediately told the woman to radio a new message. "Send the following to them: 'Swift Enterprises is a U.S. Government contracted facility with strict and enforceable air restrictions. Do not cross within two miles of our facilities. If you do, your electronics will be jammed until you turn away. This is a one and only time warning!' "

Over the hyperjet's radio they heard Tom's voice and message going out. At the same time the small squadron of jets came into view over the far hills. It was evident they were slowing down as the drones approached. Then, and to Tom's satisfaction, they peeled off, three to the left and two to the right and quickly headed back the way they had come.

Tom called to the tower. "Send another message to them, please. 'This is Tom Swift and I thank you for turning away. No matter what you believe, we were on a sanctioned flight that the President of the United States knows about. Do not return with any intent to land.' That'll be it for now."

No further transmissions came from the FAA control center.

Harlan was incandescently angry on learning of the approach and demands by the FAA and their notification of the Air Force. He made two calls, one to Jackson Rimmer in Legal and the other to the office of Senator Quintana.

Jackson assured him a formal complaint was about to be filed.

Peter Quintana was even more angry than Harlan had been on hearing the news.

"Someone is going to lose their job! Those morons were ordered to back off and leave your flights alone. If the FAA can't keep its own house clean, by God I'll do it for them!" he promised before hanging up.

Tom had been sitting quietly across his Security man's desk. Now, he stood and headed for the door. "At least those Air Force jets turned away. I really do not want to get into a position where we force one or more of them down or damage them." As he opened the door, the phone rang.

"Hang on, Tom," Harlan requested.

"Harlan? This is Peter Quintana. I just got off a short but sweet call with the head of the FAA and reamed her severely. She says she was unaware of anything you have been encountering going back to even that 727 crash. She also assures me she will get to the bottom of this and thinks she knows where to start. Just thought you and the Swifts would like to know. Got to go and shout at an Air Force General now. Bye."

The man at the desk looked at Tom and Tom looked back. Both

sighed.

"I find it a little difficult to believe the head of a national agency can be blind to what is going on," Tom stated.

Over the coming weeks the last components of the framework for the full-size hypersonic aircraft took shape. Inside it still was an empty series of beams, braces and interior panels, but both a manufacturing line at Enterprises and the ladies—and the gentleman—of the Uniforms Department were hard at work creating the seats, storage units and even the video systems.

With an understanding of the level of stresses it would encounter, it had been engineered for great strength with more bracings and structural parts than any other aircraft coming from Enterprises. And, it was being built entirely at the large facility rather than partially built at the Construction Company and finished at Enterprises.

Tom spent at least an hour every day working with the engineers and builders making small tweaks when necessary and approving each step of the build.

One day, Hank approached him with Arv in tow.

"Skipper? Arv found a possible issue with the mounting hardware for the initial thrust pod. Seems that for this size, it might be dangerous to go the current route."

The inventor's head turned to his model maker. "Oh?"

Giving his left eyebrow a little scratch, Arv began. "I was going back over the wind tunnel results for the final model of this version. Something in the buffeting and airflow coming from under the jet struck me as not perfect, so I did some further investigation and a few computations." He shook his head. "That retractable pod, at the size it will be in real life, is just too disruptive of the smooth air flow. There is a vibration that will be felt at between eight hundred and nineteen hundred knots that is not what any of us expect… or want."

Tom nodded. "And, smooth air flow is mandatory to get this up to the proper speeds to light off the scramjets. What can be done?"

"Fix the mounting for that pod or downsize it and completely draw it up into the fuselage when not in use. The problem is I can't see a way to engineer it to be smaller, less of a problem and still give you enough power to do anything meaningful."

Tom responded with another understanding nod. "Okay," he said finally. "I suppose I need to go back to the proverbial drawing board… except, I may have a good idea what to do to fix this. Give me a couple days and we'll meet on Thursday afternoon. I should have something solid by then. Oh, and thanks for bringing this to me as soon as you could."

Even though he had thought to avoid it in the final jet, Tom brought back all the plans for the Aerospike engine. Obviously, it would need to be made larger. Or, and as he considered it, it became clear there was another way; he could replace the dangling ramjet and jet turbine's pod with a lower profile pair of the Aerospikes.

They could be the same size as the first production one, just sitting under each wing as separate propulsion units. And, combined they would use about the same amount of fuel—different to be sure—as the turbojets might have so there would be no need to reconfigure the main body or its tanks.

No, that wasn't correct he told himself. The turbojets used a single fuel while the rocket engines used two.

Obviously some testing was in order and that meant, at this stage, more computer programming.

Tom got to working on it and had the simulator program well on the way to being adapted for the new systems to be tested before he left for home that evening.

When he got back to the lab the following morning he looked back over his work from the previous day. To his dismay, he spotted at least two errors in the programming that took him another three hours to fix and test. However, in the end he knew his test suite was going to give him the results he required without the costly and possibly dangerous physical testing.

Besides, such testing would need to wait for the next month or more before the jet was in any shape to fly.

By that time, and because of the nature of the build, even a small error in the design would be both costly and time consuming to find and repair.

Arv came to see the inventor that afternoon with a scale model of the final hyperjet.

"Brought this over in case you wanted to give it a short and hopefully sweet flight test, skipper," he told Tom.

Sliding his chair back, and standing, Tom's response was to give out a small whistle of appreciation. The model, a beautiful matte black and looking more like a sleek, futuristic fighter jet, was just about six-feet-long and appeared to be true to his design.

"You say that is flyable, but how? I mean," he said, "there is no droppable pod with turbine engines and I very much doubt even our folks in Propulsion Engineering could make something to fit into the scramjet pods in the wings. So, what's the secret?" He was grinning because he knew full well there would be an easy answer.

"Only has a single turbine in it."

Tom looked at his model maker waiting for more information. When it was not forthcoming, he leaned his head forward and said, "And...?"

"Oh. And, it is inside the fuselage in this model. The intakes on the pods are sufficient for what the turbine needs and that gets routed up and around into the front of the turbine with the exhaust routed via tubes back to the rear end of the pods. We lose about nine percent of the thrust, but overall this thing flies—on paper—at a scale five hundred and sixty knots."

Tom let out another whistle. As he was doing this Bud walked in.

"Spot a pretty girl, Tom?" he asked.

With a small blush, Tom responded, with, "Nope. Pretty model from Arv. Come on and take a look before we go outside for a test flight."

Bud's appreciation of aircraft in general and this design was evident in his reaching out to stroke the jet model.

Within fifteen minute they had headed over to the taxi and test area close to the Barn. Arv had already positioned the fueling equipment and also the pressurized air cylinder needed to spin up the small turbine inside. Another two minutes and everything was ready to go.

While Tom checked all trim and control functions, Arv attached the air hose. He gave the others a thumb's up sign and in return, Tom nodded. "Go ahead. Get her running." He had already TeleVoc'd the control tower for clearance.

The hiss of air came to their ears along with the start of the turbine, which was a sound that was familiar to them all. After five seconds a small readout on the remote control told Tom it was time to add some fuel and electricity to get things running.

A small roar was added and the turbine sped up to about twice its former speed.

Arv had headed to the back and was standing with his legs sideways so neither was being directly hit by the exhaust gases from the twin scramjet outlets, holding the model so it did not scoot away.

"Let her go!"

Arv did and the jet rushed forward as Tom worked to keep it heading straight. It soon lifted from the ground, albeit slightly sluggish. A single button raised the gear and, once the doorways snapped shut, he gave it more throttle and also put it into a starboard turn. Moments later it rushed past them overhead at least one hundred feet up.

By now the speed was up and the handling was responsive and accurate.

"You have about nine minutes of fuel all total, skipper," Arv warned him as he watched minute three slip by as fast as the little jet model raced over their heads for the third time.

From the corner of his mouth, Tom asked if he might try a straight vertical climb.

"Hmmm. Not certain there is enough power to weight for that, but I suppose you are quick enough to tip out of that if it gets into trouble. So, I say go for it."

Tom did. He knew the more momentum he had at the beginning, the more likely if was to be a success. However, it took all the available power to get the model with its nose pointing into the sky and fifteen seconds later it had slowed to the point Tom was concerned it might go into a power stall.

He really did not want to try to recover from that, so he brought the nose over and had the jet in a forty-degree downward tilt seconds later.

He brought the jet in for a landing with about a minute of fuel in the small tank allowing it to roll close to them before flipping the cutoff switch.

As the turbine wound down he turned to Bud and Arv.

"I guess that tells me what I needed to know about the airframe and the shape. It would seem we have something capable of cutting through the air nicely. I'll review any data from the sensors I know Arv will have put in that and see if we need any minor adjustments. In all, I'd say we are a big step closer to having a hypersonic jet."

Two weeks passed with no further mention of the recent FAA threats. Peter Quintana had also been mostly quiet although he did come up to Shopton on what he termed a "fact finding visit," during which he briefed the Swifts on some things he had discovered.

"The Assistant Deputy Director—basically the third man down the food chain, has been stonewalling things going up and coming down. I have to believe the actual agency head has effectively been severed as far as reporting and data go, and Director Caperna is in the dark." He looked disgusted. "I'm having a private meeting with her tonight with none of her other people. She told me this must be something designed to discredit her, and I'm going to lay it all on the line that her people are damaging her reputation and that of her agency. We'll see what happens."

He departed after making them the promise he would bring Federal charges against whomever was out to damage the Swifts either physically or do harm to their reputation.

The next Thursday Bud met Tom at the large hangar where the full-size prototype of the hypersonic jet was being built. They stopped just inside the partially closed doors and stood watching as another pre-shaped panel was lowered into place just forward of the vertical stabilizer.

The flyer looked fondly at the aircraft now taking shape inside the construction building on the east side of Enterprises and looked at it for a full minute before he thought he'd noticed something unusual.

"No windows for the passengers?"

Tom shook his head. "No. With the jet moving through the air at hyper velocities, regular windows would either melt or rip apart. That, plus things are going past so quickly and at such a distance, Doc and a Psychologist he hired to consult on these things tells us that it could be disconcerting or even disturbing for about eighteen percent of the flying public here in the U.S. and up to fifty percent in less developed countries."

"Ahh. So, they climb in and look at the pretty wallpaper for the hour or more of the flight?"

Tom had to laugh at that mostly because he'd never considered that sort of scenario.

"No, Bud. Every seat on the outside will feature a monitor built to look like a traditional window, and that will show them what is outside. Only, there will be just six cameras on the hull providing those views and a computer to parse it out so no matter which window you look out, you see what you might expect. A little wing, a lot of dark sky above and a blue planet below. Even up in the cockpit we will not have direct view of anything. Sort of like the seacopters with their screens or the flying saucers."

Nearly sixty percent of the inner, light blue panels had been installed so far. Only the tail had already been sheathed in a light white materials Tom said was an insulative layer.

"The outside will be a new material I am still perfecting, but you can lay down a pretty good bet it is going to be very dark. Perhaps even black."

Now, Bud got a mischievous smile telling Tom he was thinking of a pun name for the final aircraft.

"Can we call it the *Black Beauty*?"

"I'd really rather not," the inventor told him. "Firstly, ask your wife what her favorite book was as a young girl."

"Wait, wait. I know this one. Was it *Black Beauty*?"

"Nope. In fact she hated that book with a sort of nine-year-old's cold vengeance. She absolutely destroyed the Shopton Library's only copy and had to give over her allowance for five months to pay mom back for buying them a replacement and bailing her out. So, if she were to hear this might be called... uhh, by *that* name, she would likely explode. I would not mention that idea to her if I were in your shoes, my friend."

Bud was crestfallen. But, he rallied. "*Black Ghost*? *Space Ghost*? *The Phantom Air Spear*?"

Tom stood up. "Keep thinking, flyboy. You'll come up with something that is both descriptive and a real groaner. I have faith."

With that, Tom left the construction building and headed back to the big office.

He was only mildly surprised to see Sandy sitting on the edge of their father's desk having a conversation.

"Oh, hey, brother dear. Daddy was just telling me you've started to fill in the outside blanks on the new jet. He was also telling me," and she turned to give her father an unhappy look, "that I am not going to be even in the first ten people to fly it." Now she got her lower lip quivering. "Do you also hate me, Tom?"

"Knock it off, my overacting daughter," Damon directed. "Tom understands how dangerous this flying at hypersonic speeds can be. He's not even going to take it up until it's had a good shakedown flight or three."

Sandy sighed and stopped the lip movement. "Do I get a shot at naming it or has my husband already dubbed it something like the *High Altitude Steak*?" She rolled her eyes. "Daddy tells me it is going to black or nearly so. Please, please, please tell me that bonehead flyer I share my bed with is not suggesting the *Black Beauty*!"

If the younger inventor had a mouth full of water, he might have spit it out, but the kept his face neutral.

"I don't think even Bud would try to come up with something like that, San. Doesn't he know about your—shall we say—intense dislike of that novel?"

She stood up. "Honestly? Over the years I've told Bud so many things and yet I might have glossed over memories of ripping a certain and *unnamed* book apart and attempting to flush the pages down the toilet. Must have slipped my mind. Well," she looked at her watch, "got to get back to the desk. I take it we are all meeting at your house for dinner tonight?" she asked her father.

"Promptly at seven. I have been reliably told that a five minute delay will absolutely ruin the planned chicken noodle casserole!"

Sandy had reached the door but spun around. "With peas?" She had a hopeful look.

Damon looked at his daughter. "You will have to ask your mother about that. I am only a dishwasher and food consumer in the Swift house."

She snorted. "Sure. And Tom and Bud and I learned how to grill steaks to perfection from... let me see... was it *Mother*? Hmmmm. No, no. Don't try for a comeback. Too late!"

With that she left the office.

Tom looked at his father who was keeping in a laugh.

"I guess Sandy has reached that point where all those things she remembers from years ago are starting to come out. I wonder what she has in her Tom file?"

"No woman remembers more of the day-to-day inequities she's perceived in growing up than your sister. I am certain if you look carefully into the distant past of your memories, you will find something you did years ago to make you quake in your boots just waiting for her to bring out."

CHAPTER 16 /

BICOASTAL RUN, or
"WE ARE APPROACHING SPOKANE"

WITH THE full-size prototype for Tom's hypersonic airliner at the stage where the partially-skinned lower half and the rest of the framework was hinting at the eventual size and shape, the modified and more powerful half-size ramjet drives they would test were finished and Dianne was calling about what to do next.

"They've been static tested and we even trucked them out to the rocket test stand and fired them off last night. If you didn't hear anything at home, then I am very pleased. The team has done an incredible job of fine-tuning everything for the best sound dampening possible. It'll be more like an older turbojet aircraft than one of the QuieTurbine jobs."

The inventor told her he'd had no indication the previous evening or night. Even out on the patio where the family had their dinner.

"What time were you running things?"

"Between nine-thirty and eleven-ten. So, nothing?"

"Not even a subsonic rumble. How'd it measure next to the stand?"

When she gave him the numbers—ten percent lower than even the most heavily sound-deadened standard turbine jet engine—he let out a whistle.

It was what she told him next that made all the good news disappear from his mind.

"The only issue we have is this morning I came in to find that two of the stainless steel fuel conduits had been crushed. Likely it happened when the night team was dismounting things, and I have replacements already installed, but I had a few Angry Dianne moments."

Tom reviewed the design in his mind. "That would be nearly impossible. Those tubes are on opposite sides of the engines so someone would have to be very clumsy and knock the whole rig back and forth into the test stand. I'm going to ask Harlan to go out and take a look for obvious contact or damage out there."

When he spoke with the Security man two minutes later, he got back a heavy sigh. "I hate to keep making that noise, Tom, but this is about the fifth little *oopsy* incident in the past three weeks. Nothing is obvious man-made damage, other than this fuel tube trouble, and none of it is directly attributable to any one person or team or group. But, it is aggravating and also dangerous. I'll go out there myself and check things. Be back to you in an hour or so."

When the call came, the Security man had nothing to report other than there was no evident damage to the test facility or to any of the mounting hardware.

"It would seem this happened post test, Tom. Damn it! I'm going to have to spread my Security force all over the place for now."

Tom asked him about the status of using the small camera bugs.

"I have about a hundred of them on a shelf. Jackson Rimmer has been checking the legality of spying on our own people. More than one company lost its shirt to disgruntled employees who took legal action for such an intrusion. I'll appreciate it if you or your dad could light another fire under those folks upstairs."

Jackson responded to the younger Swift's call.

"We have a Constitutional Law expert digging into Supreme Court and other Federal court decisions. So far it looks like as long as we do not plant anything in a restroom, locker room or any other place people expect absolute personal privacy, we are clear. Especially in anything having to do with a Government or other contract of a confidential or secret nature."

"This is pretty much company secret right now, Jackson. It won't be in the end. In fact, the flight I want to take in three days is just about going to put an end to that secrecy.

Of nearly the final design and holding not just Tom and Bud but enough fuel for a transcontinental flight at Mach-4, the newly christened *TranSpeed TestLiner*—one of Bud's plays on multiple words combined into what he felt was a little flashier—the slightly modified test jet sat near the Barn and the entryway to the *Sky Queen's* underground hangar. It looked to be sleek and dark and incredibly speed capable to both men.

"What's the black skin made of, Tom?"

"For this go-around, magnetanium with a surface coat of a new liquid Durastress. It is dull as heck and you might be forgiven for thinking it is rough, because it looks like it is, but once you run a finger over it you'll see that is an illusion."

Bud reached out and lightly stroked the right wing front and pulled his hand back. "Jetz! And I haven't used that term for a while. But, that is some smooth surface. You don't even have to use your positive to negative ionization trick, huh?

"No. It is naturally that smooth. I've tried over the past couple months to make it glossy, but nothing works other than to reduce the strength and turn it sort of a dingy gray."

"Well, I like this look. A bit industrial and a bit like that old Air Force and CIA surveillance jet, the Blackbird. In fact, as I look at this design I'm seeing just a hint of that jet in this. Only, the fuselage is taller and wider and the engines are mostly inside and not shoved inside big tubes in the center of the wings."

He walked around to the back of the jet.

"Is that tail cone for aerodynamics?" he asked pointing at the eight-foot-long piece sitting directly under the vertical stabilizer.

Tom nodded. "Sure. It will smooth out the air flowing over the body and around the stabilizer. Without it Arv, Hank and I found the jet has a rather sour spot between about Mach-2.6 and Mach-3.4 where the whole tail tries to vibrate. Not a good thing in an airliner. So, that does the trick. We also," he said with a small smile, "found we can fill the widest area, about fifty percent of its length, with additional fuel and not cause the aft end to want to droop."

It was very much a blended wing design so there was no definite point where the fuselage ended and the wings began. This would, Bud knew, mean much better airflow and an incredibly low drag or friction rate for the overall craft.

As they were looking, both men saw the first drip. It was coming from the joint between the tail cone and the rest of the body.

Drip... drip... drip.

In the large, outdated spy plane, the SR-71, dripping fuel had been a normal thing as the tanks and the skin were porous while on the ground. They only heated and tightened once in the air and at speed.

This was not supposed to be doing that.

Bud jogged back inside the Barn to grab a canister of absorbent beads and a fire extinguisher while Tom TeleVoc'd for a fire truck to come. While the flyer sprinkled granules over the small puddle and stood watch over the leaking fuel, Tom raced over to bring out a portable electric tow device. If nothing else he wanted the jet to be away from any fuel that might ignite. He was hooking it up when they both heard the fire engine siren and Tom stopped what he was doing. At best he realized he might be about to spread out the fuel leak.

While they waited, Tom mentioned his mother called the previous evening to say Bud and Sandy were thrilled... about something she could not tell him.

"What gives?" he inquired.

Bud had a slightly goofy grin on his face when he told his best friend the news. "The agency called Sandy just before I got home to tell us we can take that little boy, Samuel, home for between a week —their required minimum—and two months—Sandy's demand. So, once you and I get back, she and I will go pick him up."

"And, I'm guessing my sister is suggesting a major shopping trip to get everything. Right?"

All the flyer could do was nod.

As the large truck arrived, a smaller fuel truck did as well with the two people inside clad in fire and toxic materials suits. They quickly dragged an armored hose over and got it mounted under the right wing.

One man went back to the truck while the other waited. He made a motion and everyone heard the pumps begin to draw the fuel from the most likely leaking tank.

The drips stopped within five seconds.

While this was going on the firemen and women sprayed a thick layer of a fire-retardant foam over the spot Bud had already spread the clay-and-cellulose based absorbent.

The lead firefighter gave Tom an OK sign as his people brought out a simple broom and wide dustpan into which they scooped the wet material.

They were finishing their cleanup when Harlan and Phil Radnor came over at a very fast walk.

Tom told them what happened and both men looked stricken with anger.

"I'm going to get to the bottom of all this if it kills me!" the older man stated. "Who had access to this jet since it came out of the... no, wait. Who had any access to this jet all along the way from the first tiny brace to what it is today?"

Everyone could see how angry he was and Phil touched his coat sleeve telling him to take a few deep breaths. "We'll get to the bottom of this, Harl. Let me and Gary and a few others take this. I don't want to have to send you to Doc Simpson's naughty step if you make yourself sick."

That broke the mood and Harlan nodded, a bit sadly, at the logic of his second-in-command's admonishment.

By quitting time Phil had a list of more that one hundred twenty people who had anything to do with the jet. Nearly half had not been involved in anything dealing with either the engines or the fuel systems. He called Tom and Damon admitting that he disliked having to do it but he was investigating everyone else, including people like Artie Johnson, Dianne Duquesne, Hank and Arv.

"I'm going to call them tomorrow morning to tell them it isn't a personal thing, just what we have to do to make it fair for everybody."

Damon said, "They'll understand. They are good people with nothing to hide. One thing, though. Dianne is concerned about one or even both her interns. Now, Tom and I have known Becky Carter for years but the other woman—and I know she has been on your RADAR—is a strange one. But do not let me influence you at all. Go and do your special level of checking. I'll deal with any hurt feelings if it comes to that."

Tom made a call out to Washington State and to the Air Force base near Spokane. He asked to speak with the base commander and was soon transferred to the man's desk.

"Yes, Tom. We're standing by for your arrival in an hour or two. The fuel tank your people dropped off is here and ready to go. Is this a status call?"

"No, sir. It is a call to say we have to postpone this for at least a day." He told the Major of their small fuel leak and his desire to take no chances.

"We'll have the leak identified, stopped, and systems checked before the end of today. If it is okay with you, we'll leave here about our zero eleven thirty and be there about an hour after that or your zero nine thirty or nine forty."

The officer said that was fine and he hoped the simple-sounding leak could be attended to.

"We'll have one of our aircraft conflagration abatement vehicles—a fire truck—standing by for your arrival. We will see you and this intriguing sounding jet tomorrow."

By the following morning the source of the leak had been found and fixed. A small nick was discovered in the gasket sealing the conical external tank from its feed tube into a splitter valve and from there into the main tanks on the left and right rear wings.

Unfortunately, there was no way to determine if it had been a manufacturing fault—it had been ordered from a company specializing in odd-shaped gaskets—or if it had been a victim of tampering.

Tom chose to believe it had not been any attempt at sabotage, but neither Harlan nor Damon were convinced he was correct.

The older Swift had a word with his Security chief before calling Jackson Rimmer for a definitive answer to the surveillance question.

As Tom and Bud taxied to the runway for their takeoff, the attorney was telling his boss to go ahead with the unobtrusive surveillance measures.

"I hate having to authorize this," Damon admitted, "but I'd rather we all be safe with a few people feeling like Big Brother is watching them than for us to be sorry later."

Since Bud and Red Jones had flown the new jet the day before the leak had been found, Tom left it to his copilot to get them into the air while he watched all the readouts.

He called when they were at the theoretical takeoff speed, but Bud shook his head saying he wanted five more knots before they pulled the nose up.

Exactly when the flyer indicated the nose wheels came up from the tarmac and the rest of the jet easily followed. Before they even crossed the wall boundary of the company they were at five hundred nineteen feet and starting to speed up and rise more quickly.

"She really has a great takeoff profile," Bud commented as he tilted them to the right in preparation for their westward flight.

Tom was on the radio seconds later thanking the people in the lower control tower and connecting them with the upper tower on the hill above Enterprises.

"Roger Swift Experimental. Continue to altitude three five thousand before turning to heading two-seven-three for transit to West Coast destination. Call when at three zero thousand."

"Will do, and thanks. Out." He turned to Bud. "You want this all the way out and I'll bring us home, or what works for you?"

"Tom. You do know who you're talking to, right? I'll take it out, back and all around if you let me. However, I am a reasonable man and will allow you to take some degree of control on the flight back."

Their flight path would take them over the westernmost part of New York as they continued gaining altitude. When the time came less than three minutes later, Tom made the call of their reaching thirty thousand feet and received permission to go on up to eighty thousand for their test flight.

"Thank you. We will be lighting a candle as we cross above angels fifty. Swift Experimental will call in at ten-minute intervals."

Soon, they were over Lake Ontario skirting down the middle. Buffalo passed them on their left and was behind them as they readied to start the scramjet engine. As this craft only had one, and not the two of the final aircraft, Tom was cautious of stopping the ramjets too early. Given what happened a couple months earlier to Bud and his precipitous drop while trying to get the one-man version to power up, he wanted to be assured they were starting to get the higher power plant online before flipping the switch to draw the ramjet pod up and into the fuselage.

They were required to remain in U.S. airspace so they steered slightly to the left passing over the lake's coastline as the scramjet engine began its warm-up. It caught with a noticeable roar and they surged forward as they reached Lake Erie and the jet took another steep climb until Bud leveled them off at 200,000 feet.

It was to be their cruising altitude for the thirty-seven minutes they would be under scramjet propulsion.

As Bud piloted and Tom kept track of their instruments, they passed over lower Michigan and even made it into Minnesota before either had the opportunity to take another look outside. In the permanent twilight of this altitude the land below looked almost like an illustration in some Atlas or from an online service.

"Look at those contrails," Bud exclaimed looking more than 150,000 feet below them. As far as they could see were a hundred or more crossing trails of condensation. Some were sharply defined, even at this distance and they could trace them to the head of those lines where unseen aircraft would be. Others were wide and near the point of disbursing and disappearing.

"We miss that as we zoom into space because we are through this point so fast," Tom stated as he looked at the spectacle below.

He adjusted their radio and made the third of their check-in calls before turning to a different frequency and calling ahead to their destination.

"Fairchild A.F.B., this is Swift Experimental approaching Spokane airspace in fifteen, that is *one-five* minutes, and on course for your location. Do you read?"

It required the other end a moment to respond.

"Roger, Swift Experimental. Read you perfectly. The Major wants to know if you are in the air."

"Roger that. In the air and half way there. Please advise him we will be touching down in twenty-one minutes. Unless you have conflicting traffic we would like a direct vector to your runway two-two. We can redirect slightly to our north for alignment but will need to do that in the next three minutes."

"The Major says he hopes that runway suits you as it's the only

one we have!"

He next gave them permission to vector to the north so that when they came down in altitude they could line up with the runway.

"Runway is clear of traffic. Length is thirteen thousand nine hundred feet minus about eleven feet. Conditions are..." and the man rattled off seven different items such as temperature, wind direction and the barometer reading.

In no time at all Bud had slowed them down and Tom released the ramjet pod. Their forward speed was high enough to ram the air into it and startup took fewer than three seconds.

That accomplished, the scramjet was turned off and the fuel inside the system drawn back into the holding tank.

By then they were at only 18,000 feet and their speed was nearly at subsonic.

Tom made another call to Enterprises to advise them of their eminent landing in Washington as they crossed over the panhandle of Idaho. The lower end of Lake Pend Orielle sped by as Bud made their last, minute course correction.

Three minutes later they were touching down just two hundred feet from the end of the runway and starting to slow. As soon as their speed was within reason, Bud turned them off at the third of five cross taxi lanes heading for the parking area where three groundspersons were waiting with lighted flags.

Unlike the previous iteration of this jet, this one featured indented steps down the pilot and copilot sides that opened once Tom presses a switch inside. He and Bud came down on opposite sides with the flyer closest to a small group of uniformed officers. As Tom came around the nose the man with the insignia of a Major was extending his hand toward Bud.

"Welcome to Fairchild. Great to have you here with us." He shook Bud's hand.

"Well, thank you. And, if I might present my boss, this is Tom Swift." He pointed to the inventor who stood there trying to hide an oncoming grin. This was not the first time someone had mistaken Bud or even Harlan Ames for Tom or Damon Swift.

To his credit, the Major recovered quickly. "Welcome, Tom. Uhh, your pilot friend's name escapes me for the moment." He glanced to Bud.

"Bud Barclay. Pleasure."

Together the five men from the Air Force led the duo from Shopton over to a waiting van. Unseen by Tom and Bud, a small team of enlisted men brought out a thin blue tarp on two long poles and pulled it over the jet.

They drove across the airfield and to what they assumed was the airfield's Administration building.

Parked along the way were about a dozen old B-52 aircraft, once used in great abundance but today only about fifty remained in active service. They saw several refueling tankers before they turned off the parking apron and onto a street the Major told them was West Arnold, named after famous military aviator Henry "Hap" Arnold.

They soon pulled into the parking lot of what might pass for a recreational center in some higher end housing development. It was the base Admin Headquarters as one of the three attending Captains told them.

"So, how long do we get to keep you, Tom? And, Bud."

"I'm afraid once your team gets the refueling tank hauled over there and we get back out, we will need to fill and fly. But, we can stay at least an hour if you wish."

"I'd love to have you here overnight to show you some Spokane hospitality. I've already had our people pull a nylon tarp over your jet. Security from prying overhead eyes, you understand."

Tom did. That morning he had to remove his own covering on the jet Harlan had insisted on since it was pulled from the assembly building two days earlier.

They enjoyed an early lunch before being driven back out. The Major had base business to attend and so he begged off. At the jet, a team was sitting in the shade under the left wing.

Standing up, one of the men, a senior enlisted man bearing the insignia of a Chief Aircrewman, approached. "I've got that special dual tank mix you sent ahead. We'd have put it in but can't find the fueling port. Besides, I didn't want to crawl over your aircraft and get boot prints on it." He smiled.

Tom took him to the rear of the aircraft and pointed a fob at a place barely discernible as any different from the rest of the surface. A door popped open revealing a standard refueling port.

The process for this aircraft required a slow and steady approach so it took almost a half hour to complete. Once finished, the man handed Tom a clipboard and asked for a release of his crew.

He took it back, stepped back a full pace and saluted Tom.

"Aircraft fueled and returned to your care, sir. Have a safe and pleasant flight."

He turned smartly on his heels and marched to the waiting truck. Seconds after climbing aboard, the fuel tank was towed away. The *Super Queen* would come out in a day to pick it up.

Twenty minutes later Tom had contacted Enterprises and the FAA to tell them of their impending takeoff. He received clearances and the jet was in the air nine minutes after that.

And, an hour later they were back on the ground at Enterprises.

CHAPTER 17 /
BACK HOME TO MORE TROUBLES

HARLAN HAD been having great difficulties in getting any agency in the U.S. or even Interpol to go to Honduras to intercede in the dangerous affairs down there. It frustrated and made him angry which in turn meant his people had to put up with a very grumpy boss for weeks on end.

He kept at it even to the point where, when Tom told him he was recalling the *Drug Mule,* the Security man begged him to leave it in place as long as possible, or until it became imperative to bring it back.

"Technically it can stay up there for a number of months, so I guess it's okay to let you play with it a little while longer. Just let me know when you want to get rid of it and I'll have it back here in a couple hours."

"I hope to be able to tell you to bring it back within the week, but cannot promise that, Tom. It is still collecting some incredible evidence."

"I might need to go down and do something if this keeps up. I can't stand by while we are being attacked from without... and possibly within."

He did not need to tell Harlan he meant the acts of sabotage that so far had not been stopped, nor had the culprit—or, and Tom hoped this was *not* the case, culprits—been apprehended.

"So, as for you going down, I'm certain your father would say exactly what I am about to. Don't be a knucklehead! Don't even consider that Tom Swift is going to get directly and personally involved in this mess. I realize I haven't been shining a bright light on all this and solving things, but I do know that you can't do what the rest of the world is not willing to." He considered his statement and held up a finger to forestall any comment. "Check that. I *know* you can and regularly do what the rest of the world cannot, but this isn't something you can program or design or build. So, do you and your family a favor and get the 'going down there' thing out of your mind."

Even though Tom knew the man was right, it still rankled him to think some unknown enemy or enemies were out to cause anything from trouble to harm to anyone associated with the Swifts.

The next afternoon Harlan appeared at the door of the shared office. He came in and sat down heavily.

"Well, someone has the wrong end of a stick and it is poking it in a bad place. I have been informed the North Korean Ambassador to France has officially registered a complaint with the U.S. Government over Tom's hyperplane as they considered it a prelude to a spy mission over their territory."

"Ridiculous!" Damon stated angrily. "What the heck are our politicians doing listening to those state-sponsored terrorists?"

Before Harlan could answer them, the phone rang. It was the direct number only a few people had. It turned out to be one of those five.

"Damon? If Tom is there and if you can get Harlan Ames on this call, I need to inform you of some rather disturbing goings on."

"If you mean the North Korean complaint about Tom's jet, then we know a little about that. I'm hoping you can tell us more, Peter. And, Tom and Harlan are both here. I've put you on speakerphone."

"Good," the politician stated. "So, and via their embassy in France —the one country that seems determined to welcome any and all nations with evil intentions to anyone *except* the French—the northern branch of Korea has sent the following:

"To the enemies of the glorious nation of the free people of North Korea, we state in no uncertain terms that we will do everything including the destruction of the spy aircraft currently being built by the imperialist company of Tom Swift.

Peter changed his tone, adding, "There is a lot of other rhetoric and about five more paragraphs trying to stir up the rest of the world against both you and the U.S. It is mostly saber rattling and reads like a spoiled child's tantrum. The issue is they do have the weapons and the right to shoot anything coming over their territory at up to fifty miles." He paused. "Please tell me you are not going to fly over their country?"

Tom was indignant, but his father was the one to answer that with a hearty laugh. "Peter. Tom's jet is only a prototype of a future airliner that is capable of flight up to about Mach-5. It will only fly low enough to bother them when landing or taking off. It most certainly will *not* be doing that in *their* country!"

Now, Tom spoke up. "Senator. Dad's right. The hyperjet will travel steeply up to about fifty-eight miles for cruising. And, because it will get up to hypersonic speeds even before it reaches that height, it would take quite the missile to get to it. And, with our tomasite coating it will be impossible for them to get a lock on. So, and I promise you none of our tests will be anywhere close to even the middle of the Pacific Ocean, much less over either Korea, their complaint is just the grumblings of a government trying to discredit us. Me."

There was a deep sigh on the line.

"Yeah. I know. But there are a few ultra-something politicians down here who want everyone to love us and want all things that are not sweetness and light and pretty butterflies to just go away. I've taken two calls from a couple of those people and basically told them this smells to high heaven and to stop being pawns in that dictator's games."

He told them a few other minor details and assured them he would not allow this to interfere with Tom's tests. He hung up a moment later.

"Well, that's one possible source of our attacks and sabotage heard from," Tom told his father.

"That isn't all," the Security man told them. "The nation of Costa Rica also is rather up in arms over what they believe will also be a jet capable of spy missions over their sovereign territory. Nobody is sure why they are worried, but there is another possibility for troubles."

Damon considered the problem before inquiring, "Do you believe this is coming from them being, well, incited by the Koreans?"

Harlan's jaw set in a determined manner. "Could very well be."

Nobody liked the thoughts they had next.

Hank called to ask if he might come talk to Tom about the one missing item from his pre-production list.

"Sure. I'm in the big lab. See you when you get here."

The Engineer strode in just two minutes later. He smiled. "I was in the hallway when I TeleVoc'd you. So," and he reached over to pull out a lab stool on which he quickly sat, "we are still missing the skin of the forthcoming hypersonic jet. I've had a couple ideas and I know you've been experimenting with a few things. Is this a good time to try to tack that down?"

Tom agreed it was about the best time if a little late in the game. "So, your ideas?"

"Well, do you recall a few years back when your dad was working with the Air Force on their own little Mach-7 or 8 hypersonic test aircraft?"

He had to think a moment before Tom nodded. "Yes, I do

although I was only tangentially involved. Why?"

"Do you recall a little alloy you helped develop for that?"

Now, the inventor had to really search his memories. He did recall he or at least the folks in Metallurgy had come up with some mixture of metals, but wasn't able to bring up specifics.

"Let me refresh your memory, skipper. Think about a GalioCupreTanium mixture."

Tom's face showed his recognition now that the actual name had been spoken. That experimental metal alloy consisted of nearly equal parts of Gallium, Copper and Titanium with about one-point-five percent Gold and a smidgen of Molybdenum.

It was not just heat resistant at the high-friction speeds of that now abandoned aircraft, it had a property that made it practically unique.

The more stress and pressure placed on it, the stronger it became. Because of this it was nearly unbendable in flight and certainly unbreakable. In fact, of the nine test craft flown, with eight of them exploding from internal pressures and one disintegrating from a construction fault in the scramjet engine, the only recoverable pieces had been the Swift alloy.

And, that was one other property most metals did not share; it almost floated in seawater. Not by itself, but if there was anything structurally containing some trapped air that had been enough to allow large portions of the skin to be recovered and by the United States, not any of the other nations that would have loved to gain an advantage by understanding the metal's properties.

Tom and his Metallurgy people knew the simple formula was not enough for just anybody to make it. Getting at least three of the metals to combine was nearly impossible and had only been discovered along with the means of accomplishing the process by accident. While it was a nice accident, the odds of some other facility stumbling onto the secret had once been computed at over seventy-three million to one.

"I hate to keep coming in here with bad news, but to go along with that North Korean complaint comes word from Interpol I believe you both need to know." Harlan had come into the office a day later.

"Take a seat and, I suppose, give it to us straight."

The three were soon seated and Harlan came to the point.

"Interpol has a strong reason to believe those Kranjovian rebels who disappeared never actually set down in Guatemala City. The managing official at that airport assured agents they had received a request for permissions, but then soon disappeared from their RADAR."

Tom opened his mouth to speak. "Don't I remember you saying something about them turning their IFF off part way across the ocean?"

Ames nodded. "Yes. They did turn it back of briefly while contacting the La Aurora airport tower, but when permission to land was delayed—they were told the irregularities of the non-squawking IFF boxes meant the airport needed to contact their military—and those signals went off again and the jets dropped to an altitude too low to see."

Damon asked, "So, they just disappeared? Is it likely they made a turn and set down someplace fairly close? I'm thinking about fuel reserves making alternates at any great distance unlikely."

Harlan sighed as he responded. "It is entirely likely they did a left turn and headed for Honduran soil where they paired up with the drug lord."

He reminded Tom and Damon the CIA man he'd been in brief contact with had told him his suspicions of the Gracias City connection, at least so far as the drug people.

"I just hate the idea of Kranjov rebels and drug dealers in cahoots!"

"We all do, Tom."

Trent announced a call coming in for Tom from Senator Quintana on Monday.

"Tom. I hate like the proverbial devil to ask you to do something that should not be necessary, but a small bunch of rabble-rousers in the House are calling for an investigation into your forthcoming jet. And, that is all due to the North Korean complaint. Uhhhmm, can you come down on Wednesday for possibly a three hour ordeal? I'll be there trying to keep things from getting ugly."

Tom told him he could, but would likely bring Jackson Rimmer with him.

"We generally do not like to appear with legal counsel, and mostly because it automatically makes us look guilty of something, but I had talked this possibility over with him and dad the other morning and they agree he should be there. Is that going to be okay with you?"

Peter laughed. "Your Jackson Rimmer's reputation precedes him down here. It'll put those blowhard fools on notice they can't try to threaten you. So, I say bring him. Bring two of him! The table in that room can hold up to four people. The more on your side, the merrier this could turn out to be."

When the session was called to order, Tom was sitting with Jackson and Peter Quintana.

The Chairman looked over his reading glasses. "Mr. Swift. I see you have brought a retinue so I must ask what you possibly have to hide that you need high-powered backup?"

Jackson answered that. "Mr. Swift has been open and forthcoming on what he can tell about this company secret project with certain members of Congress. Because the entire Swift organization appears to be victim of a concerted effort by one or more Federal agencies—the Federal Aviation Administration for a start—it is believed best that all questions from this body be vetted by legal counsel and by our esteemed Senator, The Honorable Peter Quintana."

The man at the high desk looked slightly angry at this response.

"Surely, even a mere lawyer can see how badly this appears." He looked as if he expected Rimmer to lower his eyes and admit something. He was in for a disappointment.

"No. And, quite the contrary. It raises the question of why this small body of State Representatives seems either nervous or hesitant about speaking with Mr. Swift unless he is all alone. Have any of your members an ulterior motive? Are any of you prepared to attempt to grill Mr. Swift over something none of you had the decency to let us know about prior to coming here?"

Several rather nervous, or at least uncertain, glances were shared between the five people at the desk. Finally, a woman Tom knew to be from Hawaii, and who had been elected on the platform she was going to Washington to clear up all the boondoggle contracts being issued for things she didn't believe were necessary, c;eared her throat getting Tom's attention.

"This body of senior Governmental officials with great standing in this Government hold no fear for the son of an industrialist. What we have are questions and a set of intractable demands. Ready to go?"

Peter stood up. "Well, for starters you do not have the charter to hold any sort of inquisition of any private citizen. Secondly, Mr. Damon and Mr. Tom Swift are not accountable to any body in this *Government* for anything they are totally funding within their organization. And, let me assure you if you believe anything to the contrary, this is not being requested by or funded by the *Government*. It is not taxpayer funded and is, unless I have misunderstood things, simply an effort to design and construct a potential civilian aircraft."

He folded his arms over his chest and stood there scanning from person to person. At least three of them dropped their gazed and seemed to be studying something on the desk.

He continued his attack. "If this has anything to do with the recent and inflaming complaint from the northern half of the Korean Peninsula, then I have to tell you seven words. Stick. Got. Wrong. End. Of. You've. The. And, finally, another The. I will leave it up to you to figure out to appropriate order of those. I will add," he said before any of the Representative could utter a rebuttal, "that giving in to any complaints made by a government, or worse yet, a moderately minor official in that nation we do not fully recognize, is one of the worst messages you can send to your constituents.

"'Let's roll over and make them like us!' I mean, seriously! Once I leave this chamber I am calling a press conference to name each of you and tell the public what sort of shenanigans you are up to."

Now, he sat down.

When the first, rather tentative, question came to Tom, it was from the Chairman. "Uhh, is it true you are building something that can be used as a high-flying spy plane? And, if so, why are you not doing this for your Government?"

Jackson nodded and Tom saw this. "Mr. Chairman and the rest of the panel. What I have been trying to design is, yes, a very fast civilian airliner. It is not a spy plane. It cannot be reconfigured to be one as the materials we will use, once set and in place, cannot be altered without destroying the aircraft. The details of what we are attempting have been a company secret and so they shall remain until we have proven the concept and made enough test flights—over no territory claimed by the North Korean government—and at a time when we try for FAA certification.

"What I need to ask each of you is do you know about what the FAA, or at least several individuals below the agency Director's level, have been doing or allowing to be done to my company?"

He looked at them all seeing no signs of any recognition. He tapped the desk and Jackson rose with a half-dozen folders. These he handed to the Master at Arms who took them to the front desk.

"If I might suggest something," Tom said, "can we have a recess until you all have the chance to look over those pages? I believe there is a lot of misunderstanding, or complete lack of knowledge, on the part of this panel."

The Chairman held up one finger and began looking through his folder. Two minutes later he looked to his left and his right and brought his gavel down.

"We will recess for about one hour for study. Do not leave the building."

Fifty-three minutes later the Master at Arms came out to the hallway where they sat on a somewhat uncomfortable bench and told them they could leave.

"So, nothing more?" Jackson asked.

The man shook his head and left them.

Peter let out a sigh through puffed cheeks. "And, that is why we have one of the most inefficient democratic governments in the world. Come on, let's go get a drink!"

CHAPTER 18 /
PLANNING THE DANGEROUS JOURNEY

PLANS BEGAN the next day for a possible flight down to the Central American country of Honduras. If for no other reason, Tom wanted to bring back absolute proof that the Kranjovian rebels were there, or had been there. He wasn't certain what he might do had they departed. Tracking them down was likely to not be an easy task.

Damon only supported his son's adventures to a point, and this was beyond that in his mind.

"Son, I have to tell you this is not a good idea. Your probe overflight showed there are nasty things going on down there like those surface-to-air missile launchers. That tells me they are deadly serious about keeping people away. Snooping people who do not have the wherewithal to land and fight and capture them. So, until we can get assistance by one or more military organizations—and frankly it doesn't look hopeful that the Hondurans want to get involved—I have to say this does not have my vote."

"The big problem is the *Drug Mule* we recently recalled was not a smart probe so I am of the belief it could have been looking at something else when interesting things were happening. I want to perform an intelligent reconnaissance of the area and that means someone human needs to be there. Since neither you nor I ever expect other people to do what we are not willing ourselves, I can't shove this off on anybody."

Damon could not articulate a rebuttal to that. He realized Tom was right.

"My issue with that logic, if there can be one," his father stated, "is that what great video evidence it did collect has fallen on deaf ears and blind eyes in the international community. Harlan is about to start tearing his hair out over this. Even Pete Quintana is incredibly frustrated that nobody wants to take responsibility for digging into this and going down there." He stopped a moment before reaching back and extracting his wallet.

As Tom watched, saying and asking nothing, the older Swift pulled out the four photographs he kept with him at all times. The first, which he turned around to show his son, was of his wife, Anne. The second one was Tom himself at the age of about six. Photo three was of Sandy when she was four and had begun to change from a little girl into an attractive preschooler. Finally there was a more recent picture of Tom, Bashalli and their three children.

"These are the reasons I want all the bad things stopped, and also the people I most treasure and never want put in harm's way. A decade ago I would never have expected you to understand that, but now that you are a father, I think you can see all that."

Tom could only nod. He'd felt a sudden lump come to his throat over his family photo.

"Yeah. But," and he pulled himself up even taller than he normally stood, "it is all that telling me I have to put a stop to it. Somehow... non-violently... and without endangering anybody from our end. I've actually been contemplating just going down myself, but I will guess nobody around here is likely to allow that to happen."

"Not even your old dad, Tom. But, let's not be too hasty for you to fly away from here. Let's give Pete and our State Department one more week to see if they can come to some plan of action."

Tom looked sadly at his father. "And, if the bad guys disappear before anything can be done?"

Now, Damon's face mirrored his son's.

"Then, I suppose it begins all over again. But," and the younger man got a small glimmer of something in his eyes, "just possibly before that the bad guys might lose the will to attack us. Not certain how to do that, but wouldn't it be nice if they disappeared into the woodwork and stopped being a danger?"

Nothing of any consequence happened on the political front for two more days.

Tom and Bud were siting in the conference chairs of the big office when the door opened slowly. Sandy's face came in followed by the rest of her and she stood there as the door slip past her, bumping into her left hip as it did.

Neither of the men could tell what her face was saying, but she did not look as if immediate questions would go over well. Tom sat and waited as Bud got up and gently took her into his arms. If he expected a flood of tears, he was going to be disappointed.

Sandy Swift-Barclay took a very deep breath and held it several seconds before she pushed herself away.

"He's ours," she stated almost too softly for them to hear and in a little girl's voice. It was then the tears came and she nearly shouted those same two words. "He's ours! Oh, Bud, the adoption folks called about ten minutes ago and told me that if we want to keep Samuel for the rest of our lives, we can!"

She started to dance around a little at that point grabbing her brother's hands, pulling him up and kissing him right on the lips.

Now both of them understood and were immediately as happy as Sandy was.

The door opened again and Damon walked in. "Umm, a celebration?" he inquired as his daughter rushed over to him, embracing him and also giving him a kiss. "Perhaps I'd better sit down. Not quite prepared for that kissing."

They all sat down and Sandy repeated her good news.

"The state adoption agency called me and said that, well, what she said was, 'You have now had Samuel in your house for sixty days and that trial period is coming to an end.'" Sandy looked stricken, "Oh, Daddy, I just about barfed right then and there. But, she went on to tell me that they had nothing but great reports from the visiting inspectors and that if we loved Samuel and want to keep him, *adopt him*, then we can sign the papers tomorrow!"

She jumped to her feet, grabbed Bud and hauled him up dancing around in a circle and laughing. In seconds they were all laughing. So much so that Trent opened the door to see what was going on. Much to his surprise Sandy released Bud and grabbed the secretary's hands and danced around with him a few seconds before giving him a warm hug and a kiss on his right cheek.

When she finally told him why she was almost giddy with joy, tears formed in the man's eyes and he stepped forward to give her a hug.

"My deepest congratulations, Sandy. And," he turned to look over his right shoulder, "also to you, Bud." They stopped and he had a questioning look on his face. "So, I will need to check, but *do* you give an adopting mother a baby shower?"

Sandy laughed. "Not a shower, Trent. Samuel is nearly a year old. But, we can have a big party and people can bring him toys and things. Or, nothing. I just want to share our joy with the people we know and love."

When the control tower called to inform Damon an aircraft carrying the Honorable Peter Quintana, Senator from New Mexico, was approaching on official business, the older inventor smiled. He knew a number of people would have listened in on that radio call and somebody out to annoy or harm the Swifts might be one of them. Put those miserable curs on their toes, he thought before telling the woman who called to give full permission.

"And, please call Harlan or Phil in Security and ask them to get out to the civilian terminal in our shiniest limo-like vehicle to bring him and whatever retinue back to my office. Thanks."

He immediately TeleVoc'd Tom telling him of the impending visitor.

"Pete's making it sound like a visiting head of State is coming so let's roll out the metaphorical red carpet and make a very public showing of his being here."

Easily catching on with his father's meaning, Tom added, "Then, we disappear where nobody can see or hear us and give someone something to worry about?"

"My exact thoughts. I need to call Security and have this office swept of any bugs that may have been added to he furniture in the past two weeks since their last walk through."

Gary Bradley arrived nine minutes later complete with the two different detecting boxes and a third one into which anything located would go.

Damon knew to say nothing in case they were being spied on, so he allowed Gary to do his job. The first box indicated nothing.

The second box showed there was a small listening bug planted under the front edge of the visitor's chair in front of Damon's desk. It went into the transport box and that went into Gary's pocket.

"Now, you are clean. I do have to ask who all sat in that chair in the past, oh, thirteen days. Do you recall?"

Damon said that his memory included Harlan, Hank, Dianne Duquesne, Tom (of course), Munford Trent, and the intern, Valerie, from Propulsion Engineering.

"She and the other one, Becky, came in here last Tuesday for a meeting. She sat in that seat, Becky in Tom's visitor's chair, and Artie Johnson perched on the closest of the conference area seats." He looked Gary in the eyes. "Doesn't look all that good for our second intern, does it?"

With a shake of his head, the Security man said it most certainly did not.

"You do know she is on Harlan's keep a close eye on list?"

"I do. I came darned close to dismissing her when she was in here but not for suspected spying or the sabotage incidents. The fact is she isn't very knowledgeable in the field she is supposed to not only be studying, but excelling at as measure by her grades. You folks do what you have to, and if possible I'd like daily sweeps in here for the next few weeks."

"Even if Harlan decides she has to go?"

"Yes. Even then. If more bugs show up then we might have the wrong individual."

The special jet assigned to their visitor, similar to the one Damon and Pete had flown in to New Mexico years earlier, landed and taxied to the small terminal building the FAA had insisted on being built when Enterprises was getting her certification for the airfield.

At the time, Damon saw it as an unnecessary waste of his money, but soon found out that not only was it a deductible expense—since it was a Government mandate—it had proven its value time and time again when important visitors arrived.

Right now, Peter Quintana fell firmly into that "important" category.

On being ushered into the large office, he was still chuckling.

"The only thing missing in that was a red carpet. I suppose there is a good reason for making a public spectacle of my arrival?"

"Our carpet is dirty and we can't have a personage of your stature walking across our nice, clean tarmac on a dirty carpet."

They shared a smile before Peter asked, "May I inquire as to why the pomp and circumstance?"

Damon filled him in on the possibility of a saboteur on the grounds and how that individual might also be keeping an eye on what was going on, reporting things to an unknown person or persons.

"Plus, we found a small listening bug right where she had been sitting a week earlier."

The Senator looked crestfallen. "I hate the thought of anybody spying on anyone on American soil, but I have a special affinity for you and Tom and everyone here, so this angers me a little. Uhh," he glanced at a paper he'd just retrieved from his briefcase, "could whomever she is reporting to be located in a Central American nation beginning with the letter 'H' and ending in 'onduras'?"

Damon had to admit that was the current thought.

"Ahh. I see. And, all of the pushing and secretive supplying of visual evidence of goings on down there in, I believe the place is called Gracias..." he arched an eyebrow to which Damon nodded, "Yes, in Gracias, Honduras, where someone believes a set of rebels that escaped, or left in a hurry, from Kranjovia a few months ago might have ended up setting down some sort of roots?"

"I have to answer in the affirmative, Pete. Even though they seemed to be heading for Guatemala, nobody there says they ever landed. Requested permission to do it, but never arrived. Harlan and

I believe it was a little ruse to cover for a low altitude and no IFF signal change of course taking them into Honduras and probably that once deserted airport that has been fixed up and armed with at least three and possibly four ground-to-air missile launchers of the variety once called the Katyusha, vehicle mounted by the way, but recently has been upgraded to a ground-mountable unit containing up to a dozen missiles capable of altitudes of over forty thousand feet."

"Word is within the halls of Government, that range has been extended to over seventy thousand feet." Peter was at a loss for words for a full minute. Finally, he asked, "Is there any way to verify all that?"

"Capabilities, actual location, or all of that?"

Peter shook his head. "No. I believe the capability stuff, but the actual appearance of such launchers. And, how the hell did they get those? It is illegal as anything for the Russians to have exported them."

Damon offered a guess. "I think the Kranjovs took them as a spoil of some attack and the rebels took them off the hands of the legal government and brought them down in those jets that have gone missing."

There was another moment of silence between the two men.

"Okay. Let's say they have those and possibly a full load of missiles inside them. That would be up to forty-eight. Since you have more info at your fingertips than I do, what is the destructive power of those missiles?"

Damon referred to something he had on his monitor.

"If they are similar to the long-range ones I've looked at, they used carry about a dozen pounds of explosives, but it was recently replaced—and, yes, before you ask, prior to these having likely been taken—by a highly compressed explosive with about the same destructive power as twenty pounds of plastic explosives. And, they appear to be sheathed in a girdle of steel spikes that fly out to about fifty feet and can tear a fighter jet into pieces."

They had been brainstorming for nearly an hour when Tom entered the office.

"Have I missed anything interesting or important?" he asked sitting down in the chair adjacent to Peter.

"Your dad and I were talking about those horrible people down in Honduras, the horrible weapons they seem to have and that we know about them having thanks to, well, an anonymous source of crystal clear video evidence. We were also getting into the meat of this visit trying to come up with a way to make things go away down there. Any thoughts, and no penalties for covering the same ground we already have. We shall both sit and listen."

Tom started to recap everything he knew but could quickly see both men had covered those things. He stopped, looked at them, and asked, "Has dad told you I want to mount a mission down there, at very high altitude, and get even more evidence? Stuff I do not believe the sweeps of our video source was able to detect? Things that ought to convince someone this needs some priority in the getting it taken care of department?"

The Senator looked at the younger Swift. "Those are things he did not need to tell me, Tom. I have known you since you were in your early teens and have come to believe I can second guess what you consider to be fair game. And so, I am here to tell you that I will do everything I am able to ensure nobody from our side either know about what you intend to do, nor will they be privy to anything more by way of information or evidence until I am assured our Government is going to intercede and make things right!"

Tom could not stop himself from asking, "Is that a guarantee?" He slapped his right hand over his mouth realizing what he'd just uttered.

Peter Quintana laughed. He just didn't let out a little chuckle; he let out a roaring laugh that caught both Tom and Damon by surprise.

"It might interest you both to know that I have some influence in D.C. and I also have some connections in other nation's governments. In fact, I believe the Honduran President is fairly strongly on our side. Even he knows the dangers of both the drug kingpins as well as unintentionally hosting rebel military men from a formerly very unfriendly country."

Tom asked again about the implied immunity, and about the possibility of him going to Honduras to see what could be done.

Senator Peter Quintana, friend to the Swifts for more than a decade, nodded.

"Yes, Tom. And, unless Damon here says an emphatic 'No,' I say 'Go!'"

Damon gave his son a somewhat reluctant nod.

All Tom could do was smile and wonder if he was planning on something that could get him and his team into serious trouble.

CHAPTER 19 /

BAD PEOPLE FERRETED OUT, or
"IT AIN'T A BOMB IF'N IT DON'T EXPLODE!"

PREPARATIONS TOOK more than a week before Tom was almost satisfied with what he intended to do, and how he wanted it to happen.

During this period he took great pains to keep from alarming Bashalli over what was going to happen. Bud had agreed to keep quiet to Sandy, even if she threatened truth drugs, bamboo under the fingernails, or tickling anything out of him.

"She can be determined if she believes something is up. I am hoping that having Sammy in the house is taking up a lot of her time. Oh, and thanks, by the way, for having a talk with your mom," Bud told Tom at lunch. "Sandy was sweating bullets over imposing on her after all the time she spent with Bart before Amanda came into your lives. Remind me to talk to the two of you about nannies once we get this little excursion over and done with."

"Of course, you do know Harlan and his people were deeply involved in vetting Amanda and the other three women we interviewed. Those got through from an initial list of about ten. He, dad and I will all insist you and Sandy do nothing rash that could endanger any of you. Just make sure she understands that!"

* * * * *

As Tom and his team were readying the *Sky Queen* for her trip to Central America, Chow ambled over to see if the inventor had any special food requests.

"Now, I can pack us all some great fresh foods if'n I'm gonna have enough time ta build breakfasts, lunches and dinners. But, I heard Buddy say this little excursion is gonna take all your attention and then some. So, I have a bunch o' my ready-to-heat meals in the freezer. What's yer choice?"

Tom stated he always loved the cook's lasagna and also his spaghetti and meatballs.

"You sure you weren't born an Italian, Chow?" he asked kiddingly.

"Naw. Just found that sort o' food is pretty easy to make and generally tastes better a day or so after ya make it. Freezes real good ta boot! I'll just fill the fridge with some fresh-made things."

Chow appeared to be considering something important, by the

his face, so Tom gave him a minute to form what he wanted
/.

Umm, Tom. I gotta question fer you an' I don't want ya ta get all upset and such, and I do know your daddy and you don't like any sort o' weapons, but I had a thought last night. If we do find them hombres sittin' on the ground, how're ya gonna make sure they don't come on up and try to do us a mischief?"

"That's a legitimate question, Chow. I guess we can't do anything but leave the area faster than they can fly toward us."

"Hmmm? Okay... say they got some o' them ground-ta-air missiles. What then?"

Tom reminded the westerner that nothing could lock onto the tomasite coating on the *Queen's* hull. "That, plus our speed and ability to go straight up very quickly will protect us."

Rather than being assured, Chow's face scrunched up in deep thought. He reached up to take off his Stetson and found only his baseball cap. He took it off anyway and fanned his face a moment with the bill.

"Okay. And, while I do know all that, my thought was, last night at least, we put some heavy things in the hangar back here," and he swept his right hand around indicating the aircraft's hanger above where they were standing, "and just shove 'em out straight down on their missile launchers and them jets I hear say they got." He smacked one fist into the palm of the other hand. "Bang! Instant no working bad guy stuff."

It took Tom a moment to form a reply. On the one hand Chow was correct. He and his father hated weapons. On the other hand...

"You were right about no weapons, oldtimer. We do carry the e-guns for personal protection and not for attack, but that's about the extent of anything smacking of a weapon."

"Shucks, Tom. Ain't a weapon if'n it don't go boom or explode. Right?"

Now, the inventor had to really consider his friend's statement. Basically, Chow was correct. But, only if they could be assured nobody was inside one of the jets or sitting at the missile launchers when something—and he was trying now to think what they could carry that could be dropped with precision—landed on them.

An hour later he was sitting across the desk from Harlan. After explaining the cook's idea he looked at the Security man and asked a simple question.

"Can we do that?"

After seeing the nod he received he asked his follow-on question.

"What?"

Ames sat forward steepling his fingertips in front of him, elbows on the desk. After a moment he replied, "How about water?" He had a slightly wicked grin on his face silently telling Tom his suggestion was likely to be a bit more than dropping water balloons from a great height.

Tom asked for some amplification.

"Okay. I will assume you are more than familiar with the episode of battling the Electricity Vampires." Tom nodded and his brow creased. "Fine. I recall you dropped some sticky, iron-enhanced gunk on their ship from moderately high above that short circuited their entire ship. And, I see in your eyes some sign you may know where this is heading."

Tom did.

"If you mean the sticky bombs we dropped that exploded a little above and spread out the black slurry, then I do remember those very well. That *is* what you meant, right?"

"Yes, it is. But for this go-around I am not suggesting that they carry anything other than innocuous H_2O and that you do not arm them with any sort of pressure or explosive capability. Just the outer case and the couple gallons I recall they held all nice and neat in a semi-guided and finned case. You go down there, fly over them and if—and only if—they get set to fire on you or try to take off in any aircraft, you let fly. Hit their jets in the wings if possible or their anti-aircraft batteries straight down the middle."

Tom decided to put off the flight for two days in order to construct about twenty of the droppable containers and their associated electronics. He opted to make them all human-guided rather than trying to come up with any sort of lock-on and self-guidance. Simpler and faster by a factor of many times.

The inventor was a man in his own right and had—when Damon was incapacitated by a brain tumor—taken command of Enterprises and all the other Swift companies, and could make his own decisions. Tom also believed his father's opinion on anything he did was important and so, with a few hours to go before the water "bombs" would be loaded, finally told the older man of his intentions.

As the words, "drop something on them," had come out, Damon had tensed and started to look bothered, but the more he listened the more his features relaxed.

"So, no dropping on buildings or the middle of the jets?"

Tom shook his head. "No. Just dropping from about forty thousand feet to incapacitate their ability to respond with any violence. Plus, I believe we owe them a bit of damage for what they did here on Enterprises' grounds when they crashed that old 727 jet."

If nothing else, Damon's attitude about weapons, even defensive ones, had mellowed over the years. These were more dangerous days and definitely a more ruthless enemy than he had faced when he was younger and more of an adventurer, like his son.

Certainly his own grandfather, the first Tom Swift, had created weapons but had also been a humanitarian and a good man.

With a small sigh, he agreed to Tom's plans. "But, you were going to take them anyway, weren't you?"

Tom's brow furled as he answered, "Take them but using them only as a last resort if you had major reservations. Thank you for trusting my judgement on this, Dad."

Hank stood waiting for Tom by the rear of the *Sky Queen* with a trailer that was covered by a light blue tarp.

"Got you a load of guided water buckets, skipper. We had a little extra time what with you not taking off for another hour, so I made an even thirty of them. All filled with highly salt-saturated water so they will not freeze on the way down from high altitude, and the salt will make them a bit rougher on any equipment they hit. Each one is about four pounds heavier as well. They are in a self-dispensing rack..." and he pulled off the tarp, "that'll be poked out the back of the hangar when we're ready to let them go. Remote control from up in the SuperSight room behind the cockpit will release as many as five at a time, or singly if desired."

The six rows of five each, with some sort of electrical lead going into a box he was certain contained a computer, attested to this capability.

Tom helped a team of three people as they moved a forklift under the rack and started to hoist it into the back of the hangar where it would be quickly strapped down by a technician.

"Uh, you do know we have a better aircraft for this, right?" Hank asked. "Better aiming and control equipment? Launching tubes?"

Tom stopped and looked at the man. "Well... I suppose... and then again I am not exactly sure what you mean."

The engineer patted the closest of the water bombs. "Remember that small cargo jet you reconfigured for the Electricity Vampire bombing run?"

A light came on in the inventor's mind.

"Sure. As you mentioned. The one with the built-in tubes pointing down and with all the aiming and tracking gear. Now, I feel foolish. So, let me call for it to be brought over and we'll load these into it."

When the totally sealed and insulated jet—capable of heading into space for a few hours at a time—arrived, they worked with the technician to get the individual water bombs out of the drop rack and into the jet.

While Tom and Hank put the first set of twenty-four in their now heated tubes and stored the others in a built-in rack, the tech took the control cable to the side and plugged it into a multifunction data port before turning to nod at Tom.

Hank and Tom met up with Bud and Red Jones at the side hatch and entered the special purpose jet.

"I see the *Little Queen* is getting another shot at fame, skipper," Bud commented. Tom nodded and agreed it was about time to give the aircraft some work to do.

A minute later and all were in their seats, ready to fly.

Eighteen minutes after taking off, the radio came to life. It was Harlan.

"Tom? I just received word from a, shall we say a *confidential* source, that the local Army troops in Honduras are preparing to invade that airport, but they are waiting to do a mop up rather than an all out attack. So, you are on for this very unofficial incursion. Uhh, I maybe ought not tell you this, but they are stating they would prefer our visit end in the termination of anyone at the airport."

"You know that isn't going to happen, Harlan. We are just going in to disarm, as it were."

The Security man chuckled mirthlessly. "Yeah. I let that be known. Not certain how big and brave and strong those troops are, but as long as you get those jets and perhaps the missile emplacements, you may demoralize the bad guys enough. Good Luck!"

"Please get word to them we plan on taking action just before dawn tomorrow. Thanks!"

Two minutes later the *Little Queen* was still rising and passed forty thousand feet; its nose swung to the south and it began picking up speed as well as additional altitude.

Tom's plan, and to keep prying eyes and tracking of the jet from occurring was to head to Fearing Island where they would appear to be landing. At that time the IFF transmitter would be turned off and the jet would zoom up to one hundred twenty thousand feet. It would traverse on a mostly direct course for Honduras and should be arriving there at about 10:00 pm.

The altitude and darkness would hide them from even very good binoculars and telescopes, neither of which Tom believed the drug runners would have.

Fifteen minutes before the sun would rise enough to shine on the high, hovering jet—possibly giving some indication of their position via a reflection of the light—Tom depressurized the tubes and opened the outside tube doors. The drop-ready lights all came on and with a flick of a single switch, the safety interconnect was unlocked.

"If you have any reservations, skipper, I can do the releases and guidance," Hank offered.

The inventor looked at the image on the large Super Sight monitor and shook his head. There was no indication of anyone outside all around the airport property. He could vaguely see the aiming RADAR dishes attached to each of the four missile launchers and they were rotating and moving up and down searching for any incoming targets.

With the tomasite coating, *Little Queen* would be invisible to them.

"I'm making the first drop on the jet parked farthest from that central building," he told Hank and Bud who was also standing behind him.

"What about the other two jets?" Bud asked.

"I'm dropping four on the first jet then twenty seconds later four on the second old regional jet and finally a spread of three on that rather ancient French fighter. One on each wing and one in the cockpit. It looks to be empty so I have no issues with that shot."

He sounded so determined that nobody said anything more until the first of the water bombs was away.

With the heated tubes they would not have a repeat of the nearly disastrous freeze up that happened with the Electricity Vampire drops.

"Straight and true, Tom," Hank reported. He had slid into the seat next to his young boss and was using a joystick and a series of buttons—one to activate the steering on each bomb and for switching between them as necessary—and had the first four right on target.

"Second set away... now!"

Again, Hank took control of them and gave two a slight correction putting them on their intended paths.

"Three more now heading down for target three," Tom told them.

From their height it would take a little over twelve minutes to hit. Hank would be concentrating on all eleven water bombs so neither of the other men spoke.

However, Tom was not idle. He had already targeted the missile emplacements and would be dropping four bombs in a fairly tight cluster onto each one beginning once Hank reported his first bombs were just half way to the ground.

The already used tubes had been closed and reloaded in the meantime.

Tom used the override control at his station to move the jet two hundred yards to the west to better target the first of the missile launchers.

"Coming up on second set of drops, skipper," Hank reported. "Any time you are ready, so am I."

Each of the bomb sets dropped away. Hank had already told Tom he would only need to take control of them as they reached about 10,000 feet or forty-five seconds before impact.

"For those I only have to send commands to one of each set," he explained when Bud questioned that delay. "They have proximity sensors and stay in a cluster just six feet from each other. Control one and it steers the others to match and keep their pattern."

Tom let out a gasp. "Look! They're launching missiles straight up!"

Hank and Bud were stunned. It should not be possible, but Red called back to them giving them an idea why it was happening.

"The sun came up high enough to reflect off of us. Looks like we picked up enough glare for someone down there to see. Want me to scram?"

Tom looked at Hank who answered the silent question. "I can keep control out to about five miles either side before the angle makes it difficult to line things up. I say let's skedaddle a bit."

"Red? Drop us back into the darkness and move us to the side about two miles. I'll try to give you any other maneuvering orders quickly."

They all felt the jet as it side-slipped to its new position and dropped fast enough to give them a plunging elevator sensation in their stomachs.

Tom checked the progress of the missiles. In all, three had launched with one he could see faltering as if its solid propellant had failed. It was dropping almost straight back down to the airport grounds and when it impacted near the western end of the runway, it exploded. The bright flash made it impossible to see what damage it had done. Besides, there were two more coming up and did not appear to be slowing down.

"Get ready, Red," Tom called out through the door. "We need to go back up... no... wait! Down. I think those missiles are being controlled from the ground and if we stay dark and move forward a half mile or so they should not see enough to make corrections. Plus, those things can't have much more time under power. Go."

The jet moved again and reached its new position about the time everyone standing by the SuperSight station saw the bright rocket exhaust on first one and then the other extinguish. The missiles arced up and tipped over another thousand feet higher but had barely reached the *Little Queen's* new, lower altitude.

"That says they can't hit us if we stay up above ninety thousand, I'd say," Hank stated. "Where are they going to impact, and I need to give those last three groupings a little nudge."

Thirty seconds after he adjusted the trajectories for the emplacement-bound bombs the first set hit the first of the old regional jets.

"Jetz!" Bud exclaimed and then whooped in excitement. "Direct hits and big holes in the wings that'll keep them out of action for a very long time."

The performance was repeated with the second passenger jet with three of the bombs hitting as intended and one must have picked up a slight gust of wind as it veered slightly to one side and back hitting the jet in the tail. It crumpled to the ground.

"The last set ought to hit that fighter in eight... seven..."

"What about the missile stations?" Tom inquired.

"Well, they are all going to hit, but I think I see enough activity in placement two to say they are going to fire at us again. "Yep! Here come two more... oh and two... one... et cetera."

The fighter jet took all three direct hits with the one in the cockpit hitting some weak point and the aircraft sagged in the middle. It would never fly again.

"Skipper?" called back Slim Davis who was sitting in the copilot's seat. "We have a radio transmission from the Honduran Army telling us that, whoever we are, we are not supposed to be up here and to set down and prepare to be impounded. Evidently they didn't get the word we're the good guys. What should I do?"

Tom had to think and during that time Red made two maneuvers to avoid the new missile threat. By this time the two of the first batch had hit the ground and likely enough to the southwest of the airfield to not hit any housing areas.

"Tell them we are leaving the area and trust their troops will follow up and take the bad guys into custody."

"Emplacements one, three and four appear to be totally out of commission, Tom, with number two taking a couple hits but their RADAR is still in motion."

"Thanks, Hank. So, while I would like to find out what those troops do, I believe our work is finished here. Let's drop the remaining water bombs on the missiles and go home."

He gave the order to Red thirty seconds later and they turned back to the north and picked up speed soon surpassing Mach-1.85 on the way home.

Word came to Tom and Damon via Harlan Ames the following morning that the Honduran troops, who had the airport grounds *almost* surrounded, had swooped in and captured about fifteen of the suspected nineteen people there.

But, not until more than twenty minutes after the *Little Queen* left the area!

"Unfortunately, and as happens at these times, the leader, his wife and one of their children escaped. The other two kids are in custody and apparently had—" and he made finger quotes, " 'no idea their papa was doing anything wrong.' Nobody believes them as they both told the same story, word-for-word, as if it had been well rehearsed in case of their capture."

"Did they get any contraband?" Damon asked.

Harlan nodded. "Yes, but only about fifteen million dollars worth of cocaine and heroin packed in one of the regional jets. That's the good news. The bad news is they believe there is easily twenty times that amount hidden elsewhere just waiting to be distributed." He sighed. "Oh, well. Even a partial win is a win."

Of sorts, he thought to himself. *At least we know of three jets that won't take part in that!*

"Did they find evidence of the Kranjov rebels?" Tom asked. "Did they capture any of them?"

"No. They were long gone... if they ever were there. We might never know."

After Harlan left the office Damon turned to his son. "How close are you to flying the full hyperjet?"

Tom smiled. "Well, if I put my mind to the task, shoulder to the wheel and nose to the grindstone, two weeks. And, all sorts of other clichés. Actually, most things are in the hands of the finishing team in hangar ten and Dianne and her folks who are putting together the fuel load. Once that is finished it's down to just flipping a few switches and pulling back on the joystick!"

CHAPTER 20 /
TOM SWIFT AND HIS HYPERSONIC SPACEPLANE

BECAUSE IT had been communicated to Swift Enterprises it would be impossible to receive permissions from the FAA for flights over the majority of the Eastern Seaboard at anything over Mach-1, Tom had to head back out over the Atlantic Ocean before lighting off the hypersonic scramjet engines.

He wasn't certain just why permissions were not forthcoming as he and Swift Enterprises had proven time and again their ability to break the sound barrier without causing anything close to a sonic boom. For some unknown reason it had even taken three days longer than normal for the agency to respond.

If it were not for a secrecy agreement he might have mentioned to the authorities there were at least two Swift-built military aircraft in U.S. skies that exceed twice the speed of sound and could fly at moderately low altitudes—under three thousand feet at those speeds —and go undetected by anyone on the ground at night when they were not immediately visible.

But, he did not say anything about that and now had to content himself with his first full-sized spaceplane lumbering across the east of New York state, over Vermont, New Hampshire and the southern tip of Maine before he could "light the fuse," so to speak.

After reaching an altitude of fifty thousand feet and crossing south of Portland, Maine by nearly sixty miles, he knew the time had arrived. He made a fast call back to the tower at Enterprises and they advised him they'd already handed off control to the combination Enterprises and FAA tower up the hill above the complex.

"*We just called up to them and they said to tell you to head over the ocean and go for your test*," the tower controller told them.

"Start main engines sequencer, Bud," he directed as he disconnected the contact. Moments later the status lights on his part of the wraparound panel all showed green.

"Fuel pre-heat on and we're about fifty degrees from ignition," the pilot reported. "The turbo pumps are coming on line and are at forty percent of full power. Now, forty-six and still rising normally."

Things went smoothly for another minute before Tom received a radio call.

"*Unidentified aircraft. You are under RADAR contact by the United States Air Force. You must immediately turn around and put down at an airfield we will escort you to. I repeat...*" and the voice did just that.

Bud rolled his eyes told Tom, "Just get us ready to zoom the heck out of here. Let me handle this." He keyed his headset microphone.

"U.S.A.F. flight whatever-you-are. This is a Swift Enterprises aircraft on a registered and announced test flight with, I will add and then say word again, *with* full permissions from the Federal Aviation Administration. We are squawking full and known IFF and are now traveling outside of U.S. territorial airspace. Why don't you tell old Bud why you guys are up here and what's this bologna about having us on RADAR. We both know you do not. We do not reflect RADAR. We don't even reflect a LASER paint. So, what's the story?"

There was silence on the frequency. It lasted two minutes during which time Tom readied the hypersonic engines for firing. They were fast approaching the point where the Aerospike engines would be started.

"We have just achieved all ready status. Give them a heads up, flyboy. They seem reluctant to talk. If they get uppity about our flight plans, refer them to this FAA number," and Tom handed Bud a piece of paper from his flight suit breast pocket.

Bud nodded and grinned. "Hey there, U.S.A.F. folks. I can see you are still pursing us, and falling a bit behind. I hate to tell you but we are about to leave you in the dust. Be reasonable and talk to me before we file a complaint with the FAA and a couple Senators and Congresspersons the Swifts know. Huh?" He referenced the FAA number. When asked again, he repeated it.

A reluctant voice came back. "*Umm, are you really a Swift aircraft? We've, uhh, we were told to look out for a North Korean spy plane coming down over the pole.*"

"Do we *look* like a spy plane? Do I *sound* vaguely like I am from North Korea? Do we look like we are coming south from over the North Pole? And, just who was it that told you all this malarkey?"

"*Sorry. All I have is orders from our brass. No idea where it originated. Can you slow down and come back to forty-five thousand for visual I.D.?*"

Bud looked at Tom who shook his head.

"Negative. We are committed to hypersonic flight mode. I'm guessing you have a rank of Captain or above; you must be smart enough to know something is goofy with your info, so watch us disappear into the distance and then go back and tell your brass the Swifts want to know who called and said we are the bad guys. In fact we will insist on it even if it needs to go up to the President of the

United States. Even he knows about this flight for crying out loud. Adios, amigos!"

Tom pressed the final firing button and the Aerospike engines began to purr and then to roar behind them. Five seconds later they had picked up speed and were passing fifteen hundred miles per hour. The engine noise faded into nothingness. Ten seconds after that they crossed Mach-2 and were approaching Mach-3 within another thirty seconds.

Tom had already completed the pre-firing sequence for the scramjet engines and they were showing readiness. He pressed the button to shut down the Aerospike and retract it after a ten-second cooling period and to start circulating the fuel around and into the scramjet.

Eleven seconds later he and Bud were gently pressed into their seats and the jet shot forward.

As their speed increased, pressing them both back further against their acceleration seats, Tom made an input on his arm-mounted control panel and pulled the nose up a few degrees and they crossed both Mach-4 as well as one hundred thousand feet at the same time, both increasing.

"Want to qualify as an astronaut?" Tom asked teasingly.

"Always wanted to do it!" Bud responded with a grin.

Another six minutes passed and the spaceplane poked above the Kármán line, that point some three hundred thirty thousand feet above the Earth's surface... about sixty-two miles up. By now they were nearly at the one-quarter point across the Atlantic.

Tom now throttled the engines back to maintain a Mach-5 speed, the setting he knew would allow them to cruise over to Europe, make their intended wide swing around and cross back to the United States with their current fuel load. And they had to maintain enough of a reserve for their turbines in case they had to make up to three passes at the Enterprises landing strip. Or, divert down to Kennedy International or even back to Boston.

"How are environmentals doing?" Tom asked.

"I show greens across the board with O2 levels within a quarter percent of sea level. Pressure is set at five hundred feet and we have temperature of sixty-eight with humidity at seventeen percent. In other words, just the way that feels comfortable at home. If we had passengers they would be getting ready for a lightning fast beverage service. How about you?"

Tom had to agree things felt just fine, but he knew that many people, including a majority of women, might like it more if the temperature were one to three degrees higher.

"Make a note that I need to look into either individual seat heat settings, or ventilation that can be set to gently increase or decrease each seat area by as many as four… no, make that five degrees. Unless we get someone with a really strange metabolism that should cover just about everyone."

They flew for another minute before Bud had a question.

"Just how high will this eventually fly? I mean, isn't there a point of diminishing returns what with climbing and heading back down where a trip actually becomes longer?"

Tom told him the latest computations showed that a maximum altitude of fifty-eight miles would likely be the norm and perhaps even lower for shorter runs like New York to London.

"I really do not want the average customer flying in one of these to be thinking they'll be classified as an astronaut. I'd like to reserve that for the people who have earned it and not just bought a ticket."

Bud had to agree. He and Tom and people like the men and women at the old Outpost in Space and the new *Space Queen*, plus the few hundred men and women who'd traveled up atop rockets over the decades, should not have their accomplishments so easily beaten or minimized.

In the inventor's mind he was making a mental note to set limitations to the altitude and a top speed of Mach-5 that could not be overridden by any pilot wanting to fly up a little bit higher or faster.

They were now at an altitude where Greenland and Iceland were plainly visible to the left and most of upper Eastern Canada behind them. Soon the tallest mountains in Europe started to poke up into view.

Over the following nine minutes they veered eighteen degrees to their right so they could line up for the proper swing back to the United States.

At the computed moment Tom turned them to the left with nearly a twenty degree bank and the jet started its lengthy swing around, one that would take them from their current course heading for the central coast of Morocco and would see them as far to the north as being even with about Aberdeen, Scotland, before they were heading back home.

To aid in the brevity of the turn—and lessen the G-forces they were going to experience—he also lowered their speed to Mach-3.25.

He made another mental note that he would need to advise any future pilots of the handling characteristics that would not allow late or rash maneuvering decisions.

"Take the stick, Bud," he requested even though there was no "stick" at this speed. Everything on the spaceplane was 100% computerized above Mach-3.25 requiring minimal pilot intervention. "I need to talk to dad."

It took three minutes but his father's voice came over the radio.

"Yes, son? I hear you made some people rather upset in the Air Force. What's going on?"

Tom told him of the radio accusations and his decision to not turn back but to carry on with the approved flight. "I'd love to find out who told anyone we were a North Korean spy plane and that it made it out to the military without being challenged."

"I'll get to Peter and ask him to set them straight," he promised before asking about the aircraft. "And, I'll see if he can find out who was responsible for that... umm, erroneous information. So, your impressions of the Hyperplane?"

"Well, Bud just told me he thinks it needs a bit more of a name so I think this is going to be the HyperSonic Spaceplane even though I don't want it traveling into actual space." He quickly told his father his reasons for that. "But, you wanted to know about how it is flying. Smooth as silk and a lot faster acceleration than I believed possible. It still skids around corners like a cow on ice skates, as Bud once said," and he looked over at his grinning friend, "but good altitude and speed. I may even key things down to no greater than Mach-5 for the sake of a number of things."

He told Damon he believed trips between New York and London would be accomplished in about an hour with Paris twelve minutes father on and Berlin just another eight past that. They spoke about theoretical range with the younger Swift saying he believed Los Angeles to northwestern Australia was possible.

After suggesting Tom and Bud slow down a little on the return flight, Damon promised to get back as soon as he had heard from the senator. The call was disconnected after that.

"If we start to run low on fuel, do we put down in Gander again?" Bud inquired seeing the fuel state sitting at fifty-six percent.

"I'd rather not. We'd be stuck there for a couple days getting permissions to fly in a tanker of our fuel. It might be clean burning, but some of the ingredients are still on hazardous materials lists in Canada, even though they have been totally denatured and changed in the process of combination."

They flew along in silence both still marveling at how incredibly quiet the spaceplane was at such a high speed. Of course they each understood the physics of it, but the fact that no vibrations or sounds were transmitted through the hull still amazed.

Soon, Iceland appeared again, this time to their right, and in the distance was Greenland.

Four minutes later Tom decided to slow them to just Mach-2.3 so their flight time back into U.S. airspace could be delayed by twenty-six minutes. It was about the slowest the hypersonic engines could go without cutting out, and for now, Tom wanted to remain as high as they were and as fast as was reasonable.

It was getting fairly close to the time he needed to make a decision about performing a 360° turn off the east coast of the coming land to stall for time when the radio came back to life.

"Swift jet. This is Major Artemus Drake, U.S.A.F. Uhh, we have been informed of your clearances for the flight you are undertaking and I have come up to personally ask you to accept an apology from this wing of the armed forces, and to suggest we can escort you to any field of your choosing. All I ask is that you drop to subsonic as soon as you cross over land. Please respond."

Tom keyed his mic. "U.S.A.F., this is Tom Swift. We understand and accept. I have to say we were still confused over what would seem to be a SNAFU, but there has obviously been an effort to make us look bad by someone with a lot of money and some connections. We are currently squawking IFF one-seven-seven alpha-charlie-whiskey. Do you have us?"

"Affirmative. We cannot see you but know about where you are. Can you slow down?"

"Roger that, sir. We need to transition from one form of propulsion to the other and that will take us two minutes. We wish to head for Shopton, New York to coordinates 43.8384° N, 73.7618° West. Do you copy?"

"Affirmative to that. Interrogative, distance to home before you wish us to release you."

Tom suggested about the time they crossed over the Vermont and New York state line.

It was about at that point the *Super Queen* appeared in the sky in front of and slightly below them.

"Air Force? Our own escort is waiting. Thank you for your time, Major and that of your team."

"Roger. Leaving area now. By the way, hell of an aircraft, Mr. Swift!"

The grin on Tom's face didn't disappear until it was time to set down on Enterprises longest runway.

Right there to meet them were Bashalli and the three Swift children, plus Amanda, and Sandy carrying a slightly surprised-looking dark haired boy.

Bud set his flight helmet on the asphalt and rushed to his wife and son.

He kissed Sandy first before taking the boy in his arms.

"Hey, Samster! How's my boy?"

Sandy looked at the man she had known she would marry since she was a young teen and frowned. "I suppose the whole *Samster* thing is going to stick? Not Sammy?" Inwardly she sighed.

Bud nodded and gave her another kiss around the boy's head. Then, he planted another kiss on his son's cheek making Sammy grin... and making Sandy's heart melt a little.

It might have been the lunch hour when they got back to the Administration building, but Harlan Ames was waiting for them as was Damon.

The Security man looked a little grim.

"We have news, Tom and I do not like it one bit. I will assume the day that old airliner crashed here is etched in your mind." Seeing the younger man nod, he continued. "Okay. Peter Quintana got to the bottom of who that was. He had to threaten to expose the head of the FAA, and I believe to bring into question whether that agency was a money waste or a godsend to this nation, but in the end he prevailed."

"Did he tell us who?"

"And, can I get my hands around the son of a— that fellow's neck?" Bud asked angrily.

"Yes to Tom and no to you, Bud. The man was a former industrialist from Saudi Arabia. One of their minor Princes... and they have about a thousand of them. He made fortunes in oil, as did many, and then he made more money providing aircraft and weapons to many different sides of the various wars and skirmishes over there. The reason for the secrecy is this was a CIA operation to get him and they could not jeopardize that. They felt strongly enough about your ability to not get injured they sort of left us all dangling!"

"But, how did he manage to influence people over here?"

Harlan looked at Damon who spoke. "Money."

"Right. Money spread liberally among a few politicians and people in organizations like the FAA, the NTSB and even the Federal Bureau of Transportation. People with known problems be those money, drugs, alcohol or something else. And, enough greedy people took bribes and were or have been on his payroll for a few years, enough to make a list that will keep the FBI busy for a year or more bringing them to justice."

"Cancel their passports," Bud suggested, still angry and brooding. He thought what Chow might say and came up with, "Hangin's too good fer em!" It made him grin.

"That is an excellent idea and I think I will leave it to you to call the senator and suggest that. As for me, I have a young intern to talk to and to dismiss."

Tom had a sudden dread that it might be Becky Carter. Seeing this, Harlan hastened to tell him it was not her; it was the other female intern in Propulsion Engineering.

"She is someone who took money from this Saudi prince. Not bright enough to not just put it into her checking account where anyone could find it, so once the FBI got the warrant, they found it in about an hour. My guess is the few small sabotages she was able to introduce were all ones meant to keep you from succeeding for the past several months. Wish me luck and tell me to not strangle the little... *dear* as I go pack her up for the Feds," he said through clenched teeth as he left the office. He could tell them later that prince had been arrested and was under a charge of treason in his native country.

He called them ten minutes later to say the girl had been caught trying to drive out of Enterprises in one of the electric runabouts.

"She got too close to the gate and the computer disabled the car. Only executives and previously cleared people can take one off premises as you intended. Our very own Davey at the front gate took her into custody. Uhh, you do know he is leaving that post, don't you?"

Tom smiled. "Yep. He has his Electrical Engineering degree courtesy of evening classes and is taking a position in that department as of Monday. I hear we have a good person coming to replace him."

"We certainly do. Oh, and that nasty North Korean complaint? Retracted as of eleven-fifteen this morning our time. Seems someone there was speaking out of turn, at least according to their official news agency."

When Tom got home that afternoon, Bashalli was anxious to hear everything about how the flight had gone. He decided to not mention much about the Air Force or about the accusations, but concentrated on the positives.

"Then, it sounds as if your supersonic plane—"

"—HyperSonic Spaceplane," he gently corrected her with the new formal name.

"So, the hyper fast flying thing is going to be a success?" She smiled at her husband and he smiled right back.

"I hope so."

"Okay, then we will go on a vacation, just the family and Amanda and not with Sandy and Bud this time, and we will have a wonderful time for at least two weeks before you come back and get into more mischief. I mean, another project." She smiled innocently at him.

"You already have the tickets?" he guessed.

"I do!"

It was Jake Aturian at the Construction Company who fielded the first sales inquiries over the HyperSonic Spaceplane. He had been provided with as much promotional material as George Dilling and his people could put together on one day's notice, which would be enhanced in the coming days, but the first call came in the morning after the successful flight.

"Jake, it's Paul Williamson at National Aerodynamics in St. Paul. How are you today?"

Never having met the man, but knowing his no-nonsense approach to manufacturing aircraft and in making deals for subassemblies, Jake believed this was an important call to turn into a success.

"I'm quite fine, Paul. Yourself?"

The man laughed. "I'm good. Well, enough polite chitchat. I would believe you know the reason for this call. To put it bluntly, we want to manufacture that hypersonic plane of your owners and to sell it directly to the airlines. I've had two calls this morning from a couple of the very big players in worldwide transportation that I'd like to turn into satisfactory contracts for the two of our companies."

They discussed potential sales figures and Jake had to admit to himself such a contract would do two important things. First, it would bring in a lot of money from both licensing of the design as well as giving Enterprises the contract to supply the outer skin components, and second, it would take the bother of building the spaceplanes off of Enterprises' shoulders. With his numbers for possible in-house construction putting output at just a spaceplane a month, he knew they needed National or some company just like them to fill forthcoming orders.

An agreement was made for the two companies to begin negotiations the following week.

Thirteen days into the fifteen days Bashalli had booked in a beach home on the island of Maui, she rolled over on her towel and placed a hand on her napping husband's chest. The sunshine was still beating down on the large umbrella sunshade they were reclining under, and the temperature was the fairly standard 82° on the islands.

"Hmmm?" he muttered just slightly on the other side of awake known as "slumbering off in the direction of Dreamland."

"Thomas?"

"Hmmm? Yeah?"

"We are going home the morning after tomorrow and I want you to know this has been a most wonderful vacation. Amanda has kept the children occupied and I believe even she has enjoyed this. I only have one question for you... well, two."

His eyes opened behind his sunglasses and he rolled toward her. "Okay. I'll even allow you three." He smiled at her and she rewarded him with a tender kiss.

"Fine. And, here they are. First, have you enjoyed this time away from everything?"

"Sure have. What's the next one?"

"Do you love me as much as or even more than ever?"

He could see her biting her lower lip. It made her look both beautiful as well as vulnerable. He didn't keep her suspense.

"I absolutely do!"

She took a deep breath. "Do you have any idea what sort of thing you are going to let yourself get into once we get home?"

Now, the inventor raised himself up on his left elbow. He shook his head. "Nope!"

Little could he know that there would only be a three week reprieve before something old was repeated and something he could have never expected, happens.

<•>—< End of Story >—<•>

This has been book 29 in the **New TOM SWIFT Invention Series**. Read them all, and look forward to the next books, also listed here:

{1}   TOM SWIFT and His EvirOzone Revivicator
{2}   TOM SWIFT and His QuieTurbine SkyLiner
{3}   TOM SWIFT and the Transcontinental BulleTrain
{4}   TOM SWIFT and His Oceanic SubLiminator
{5}   TOM SWIFT and His Cyclonic Eradicator
{6}   TOM SWIFT: Galactic Ambassador
{7}   TOM SWIFT and the Paradox Planet
{8}   TOM SWIFT and the Galaxy Ghosts
{9}   TOM SWIFT and His Martian TerraVironment
{10} TOM SWIFT and His Tectonic Interrupter
{11} TOM SWIFT and the AntiInferno Suppressor
{12} TOM SWIFT and the High Space L-Evator
{13} TOM SWIFT and the IntraEarth Invaders
{14} TOM SWIFT and the Coupe of Invisibility
{15} TOM SWIFT and the Yesterday Machine
{16} TOM SWIFT and the Reconstructed Planet
{17} TOM SWIFT and His NanoSurgery Brigade
{18} TOM SWIFT and His ThermoIon Jetpack
{19} TOM SWIFT and the Atlantean HydroWay
{20} TOM SWIFT and the Electricity Vampires
{21} TOM SWIFT and the Solar Chaser
{22} TOM SWIFT and His SeaSpace HydroFarm
{23} TOM SWIFT and the Martian Moon Re-placement
{24} TOM SWIFT and the Venusian InvulnoSuit
{25} TOM SWIFT and the HoverCity
{26} TOM SWIFT and the SubNeptunian Circumnavigation
{27} TOM SWIFT and the Marianas AquaNoids
{28} TOM SWIFT and the Starless Planet (2019)
{29} TOM SWIFT and His HyperSonic SpacePlane
{30} TOM SWIFT and the Space Friends Return (early-to-mid 2020)
{31} TOM SWIFT and His Antimatter PowerGrid (late 2020?)
{32} TOM SWIFT and His Inter-Dimensional Pepperoni Slicer (huh??) *

* Yes, I *am* running out of good title ideas… but there will be more books coming!

And, he has co-written—with author Leo L. Levesque—a quartet of novels staring Tom Swift as he takes on the rescue of a secret slave colony on the Moon. Called the **Tom Swift Lunar Saga**, it includes:

- Tom Swift and His Space Battering Ram
- Tom Swift and the Cometary Reclamation
- Tom Swift and the Lunar Volcano
- Tom Swift and the Killing Moon

Collections of novellas, many dealing with some of the individual characters in the novels and/or the lesser known inventions coming from the mind of Tom Swift may be found in:

- Enterprising Characters
- Swift-ly With Style
- The Spirit of Enterprises
- Enterprises Extras
- Tom Swift's Pocket Book of Inventions
- Tom Swift's Another Pocket—More Inventions
- A Newer Pocketbook of Swift Inventions
- Tom Swift's A Fourth Pocket of Inventions
- Tom's 5th Symphony of Swift Inventions
- Ten Tom's: A Collection of Invention Shorts
- The Operator's Guide to the Fat Man Diving Suit

In addition to the teen/adult Tom Swift stories he also has a book of stories about young pre-teen Tomas he starts to find his way into the world of inventions:

- The Young Tom Swift Stories

Tom's father, Damon, stars in his own series of novellas and several novels. The collections include:

- The Wonderful Damon in Oz
- Damon Swift Invents…
- The Duly Deputized Rhino and Other Stories
- Yes… It's Another Damon Book!
- A Pair of Rather Long Short Stories
- Damon Swift in Flight

And, the Damon novels that tell the early tales of Damon Swift and his rather impressive business empire:
- Damon Swift and the CosmoSoar
- Damon Swift and the Citadel
- Damon Swift's Greatest Enterprises

then, a long-*ish* novella of how Tom Swift met Bud Barclay and Chow:
- Damon Swift and the Citadel 2: A Bud and Chow Story

Tom's mother, Anne Swift starts in her own series of medical mysteries, The *Anne Swift: Microbial Detective* series contain novellas about her secret FBI work. There are three collections in this series plus a biographical novel about how it all began:
- Anne Swift: Making the Molecular Biological Detective

…Check out and download this little freebie, a short story—600 words—written for a contest back in 2011:
- *Tom Swift and the Frictionless Elf*

Find it at:
http://tomswiftfanfiction.thehudsons.com/TS-Yahoo/TS-Elf.pdf

Mr. Hudson has also written a couple of strange novellas that are available as Kindle ebooks. None are serious and were only written to amuse the author. Even so, he decided to share them. **Do not** expect life-changing literature for $.99 (US) each:

- *The Fiendish Bucket List of Dr. Fu Manchu*
- *Drew Nance: Up On The Housetop, Click, Click, Bang!*
- *Drew Nance: The Massive Mart Murder Mystery*

Fu Manchu's story is included in a trio of short stories staring Fu, Sandy Swift, and Tom and Bud (and Sandy and Bashalli and a bad guy named Mousie):
- *A Trio of Shorts: Three Short Stories in One Medium-Length Book*

And a collection of odds and ends (also a 99¢ Kindle book):
- *Don't Write Fan Fiction Until You Grow Up, and other short stories too short to sell individually*

Along with Chow Winkler, Mr. Hudson has written several cookbooks. The first and second shorter ones are part of two of the short character collections. Numbers three and four are standalone books:

- Chow Winkler's Three-Wheel Chuck Wagon
- Chow Winkler's Wide Open Range

You might enjoy Thomas Hudson's first foray into the world of Romance novels. He wrote this as part of a bet with a fellow author that they both could not complete a romance story even if given ninety days. He did it in nineteen: *

- The Love of Skunk

Finally (for now) on a dare, he wrote a strange story about a young girl with both a physical and emotional difference to 99.99999% of people out there. It is an <u>adult</u> autobiography/biography and features her life story starting when she was a young teen.

This is NOT a Tom Swift story in any way, shape or form!

- *The Life of BI: Complete*

---

* Which is about fifteen days more than Barbara Cartland, Queen of Romance Novels, spent on any one book!

Everything above may be found on Amazon.com in paperbound as well as Kindle editions, and many of this author's works can be purchased as Nook books from BarnesAndNoble.com and from:

www.lulu.com/spotlight/tedwardfoxatyahoocotcom

<•>—< End of Book >—<•>

Manufactured by Amazon.ca
Bolton, ON